First Gray,
Then White,
Then Blue

First Gray,
Then White,
Then Blue

Margriet de Moor

Translated from the Dutch by
Paul Vincent

THE OVERLOOK PRESS
WOODSTOCK & NEW YORK

First published in the United States in 2001 by
The Overlook Press, Peter Mayer Publishers, Inc.
Woodstock & New York

WOODSTOCK:
One Overlook Drive
Woodstock, NY 12498
www.overlookpress.com
[for individual orders, bulk and special sales, contact our Woodstock office]

NEW YORK:
386 West Broadway
New York, NY 10012

Library of Congress Cataloging-in-Publication Data

Moor, Margriet de.
[Eerst grijs dan wit dan blauw. English]
First gray, then white, then blue / Margriet de Moor.
p.   cm.
I. Title
PT5881.23.O578 E3713 2001   839.3'1364—dc21   2001021938

Manufactured in the United States of America
FIRST EDITION
1 3 5 7 9 8 6 4 2
ISBN 1-58567-137-1

Ich fühle Luft von anderem Planeten

Arnold Schönberg,
String Quartet No. 2
in F sharp minor, Op.10
Sehr langsam

PART ONE

Chapter One

He gets up at six-thirty every day. A few minutes earlier, un-prompted by any mechanical violence, he opens his eyes and comes to his senses. Without moving a muscle he recognizes the smell, the gentle warmth and especially the position of the bed he is lying in relative to the windows, the door and the walls of the bedroom. Next he recalls a detail, recalls the two beautiful Irokezu erotic prints, on the left above his head.

Once he remembers where he is, a familiar vague restlessness overcomes him, forcing him to use his brain. He rejects the notion of asking himself what he is doing with his life. Once there were my childhood dreams. I want to know what has become of them. Nonsense. His hopes had never been that high. He was a lad who got excellent marks and every winter had three weeks off school with severe bouts of angina. So it is another question that is weighing on him.

Above the curtains there is a strip of light. It is still quiet outside. What will the day be like? It slowly comes back to him: not unpleasant: two routine operations are scheduled for this morning, starting at eight o'clock. Straightforward cases of catar-acts in octogenarians, perfectly healthy people who have decided to have their eyes fixed. When I enter the operating theatre in a little while one of them will be lying ready on the table.

While my assistant inserts the drip into the arm, I am helped into my apron and gloves. Then I sit at the head of the operating table and pass two strong needles through the upper and lower eyelids. I position a clamp to keep the eye wide open and then run a thread through the top of the conjunctiva so that the eye, now staring at me like that of a great dead fish, can still be manipulated a little by tugging gently on the cord. I slide the stand with its two microscopes – one for me and one for the theatre sister on my

1

right – over the patient's head. I am handed a pair of scissors. I begin. Completely cut off from my hands by the technology, I steal a look at my work, and see that I make a perfect incision. I immediately cauterize the tiny blood vessels that start bleeding . . .

He has had an aversion to blood ever since childhood. On Easter Saturday morning his mother holds the largest and plumpest Leghorn chicken firmly between her knees. She is swift and decisive and has sharpened the knife in advance on the brick ledge of the kitchen window. One of his little sisters picks up the head from the tiled floor out of curiosity and he, walking off with a proud expression, sees, with the greatest possible clarity, that the stream of blood spurting into the bucket dries up only when the creature's futile struggles subside. 'Do you want some more?' asks his father the next day. He nods, and dips his young fingers into lukewarm water with flower petals floating in it. For as long as he can remember he has wanted to be a doctor.

Night fades. Beside him Nellie is asleep with her fist against her cheek. Not only now in the dim light of the summer morning, but also in the pitch dark of December, he knows there is a contented expression playing around her mouth. Her dreams are still in full flow. She claims that she never dreams of anything but the previous day's chores.

'I was on my knees unpacking an order in the shop,' she says. 'I carefully unwrapped the tissue paper and found myself holding an expensive Delftware plate. It was cracked.'

She suspects she is one of the least enigmatic creatures on earth. He resurfaces with a yawn. That's enough for one night, you've had your fun, the dream is over, it's time you rejoined your real self. This house: they managed to get the quaint little villa very cheaply at the time, with coat collars turned up they strode round the place. A sea breeze was blowing. They looked proprietorially at the bedroom windows nestling in the dun-coloured thatch. A house for the family you are going to start. Old cupboards. A cellar. A hearth that draws beautifully. You won't be alone.

2

Now that their son is approaching twenty, Nellie has started a job. Four days a week she sells jewellery and porcelain and in the summer season especially money pours into her nonchalant hands. On his way back from his surgery he drives slowly down the Duinweg. The illuminated shop window is at the foot of the slope, and just as he has to stop for the junction she opens the back panel. She does not see him of course. She leans forward and picks up a crystal bowl.

'Are you sure it's not too much trouble?' the customer asks.

'Not at all.'

'Is it really the only one you have?'

'Definitely. This firm takes ages to deliver. I was surprised to find the bowl in with the last consignment.'

Still talking, she comes from behind the counter. As she opens the dark red partition daylight pours into the shop from the street. She bends forward.

She rolls over against him in her sleep, makes funny snoring sounds and wraps an arm round his shoulder. He knows that despite her dreaming she is acutely aware of the time. She quite likes him having to free himself from her embrace in the mornings. What is the built-in mechanism that controls me? From the very first I tended to follow her imperturbable lead. Now she is in charge, furnishes the house, does her own painting and paperhanging. 'How does a holiday in the Dordogne strike you?' she asks by candlelight. He presses his unshaven cheeks against her face and gives way indolently to her self-assurance. For years they have been on the most intimate terms. He does not know his sock size. Whenever he leaves the house, he clearly enjoys telling her, his first love, what time he expects to be home without her asking.

This house. This son. His wife has been trying for twenty years to turn this dune top into a garden. She levels the earth and covers it with dark manure, and with a grim expression plants hedges and double roses, but nothing survives longer than a season here. How come she of all people is able to persuade him that their son is doing fine? If you want to see flowers on these windswept

3

heights, Nellie, you must bend very low, believe me, I've always lived in the village, once your nose is virtually touching the ground, there they are, the pitiful little star-shaped flowers of the celandine.

Six-thirty. He must get out of this bed at once.

Chapter Two

He takes a shower. Puts coffee on. Eats a slice or two of bread. When he opens the doors to the terrace, drops of water fall onto his hands and he remembers the short, violent thunderstorm late at night. This clearing of the air was long overdue. The village could scarcely take the heat of the last few weeks any longer. He leans against the wet wall of the balustrade and looks out over one part of the place he lives in: the church, the town hall, the hotels, the blue signpost *To the Beach*. Everything has changed. Everything is lying there cool and neutral under an overcast sky. The playthings discarded by a child that has finally calmed down and gone to sleep. Although he shivers, he is in an excellent mood. The heat has gone, and with it something else, something extraordinarily malicious, which he now remembers has been hanging around the village for much longer than this summer.

Yesterday it was at its worst.

Towards dusk, after sitting inside all day with doors and windows closed, Nellie came out of the house. It must have been about nine-thirty. Startled by her faded, aged face, he let the magazine he had been reading slip from his fingers.

She looked at him. 'For God's sake let's go out for a bit, Erik.'

He had got up obligingly and walked with her down the path through the prickly vegetation. At the top of the steps with which they had made their dune accessible, she turned and raised her head. The attic windows were wide open.

'We're just going for a walk!' she called out in a motherly tone.

There was no reaction at all. He knew that Nellie did not expect one. Their son rarely replies. All she wanted was for the two of them to acknowledge his existence, the telescope set up in the open window and perhaps the calm young man himself pointing the lens. Or else his brilliant white shirt. Gaby is mentally

5

retarded. He is obsessed with the moon and the stars. Other people have only the vaguest notions of his interior monologue. Erik and Nellie are used to his face, to his eyes set in his head like stones. 'It's your birthday tomorrow. You'll be eighteen, nineteen. What shall I cook?' Nellie keeps on saying to him. 'You look pale today. If you've been up all night, at least lie in till midday. What are you laughing about? Don't be so silly, tell me. When you laugh like that, it sets me off too.'

They had trudged down the pine-log steps.

Erik really can't remember how they suddenly found themselves outside Robert Noort's house. They must have walked in a daze down Astridboulevard and along the Duinweg and then turned into the Oude Zeestraat – only now does he find it odd that they should have avoided the beach: was it because of the jellyfish that had been lying there for days with their blue and green slime evaporating in the boiling heat?

He hesitated at the gate, looked awkwardly at Nellie, not feeling at all like dropping in this evening on the friend he had grown up with. His aversion to Robert is a passing phase, or at least so he imagines, so why not give into it? Robert – for quite some time – has been someone who sits smoking in silence with a bleak look in his blue eyes. Erik has known him for decades. He knows his family, the formidable father, now dead, his mother and younger sister who told tales on them and was the favourite. They had once stood dancing with glee when the girl dropped an ornamental silver fish. The angel. Suddenly their living room floor is strewn with hundreds of scales, glittering in the afternoon sun. She'll get what's coming to her now!

They were classmates. Every year Robert managed to secure the desk right next to the door, and the boy who never took off his coat, only unbuttoned it, was invariably the first one back in the playground when the bell rang, standing with legs wide apart in the drizzle, the wind, the sunshine, waiting for him, Erik. Around 1952, when they were about sixteen, his friend's features suddenly became sharper. The cheekbones and forehead became prominent, his eyes sank, he began to look incredibly like Vincent van Gogh and, sure enough, years later he gave up his law studies overnight to become an artist. Coming home on the tram one weekend Erik saw an idiot in the distance sitting painting the frozen bulb fields! With a hat on, in an enormous overcoat, gulls wheeling round his head. Then, in the winter of 1964 – it was hard to comprehend at the time – he showed up with his wife. With Magda. A girl who might just as well have been anyone else had brought Robert to the point of holding forth proudly about love, in complete seriousness. Something strange has happened to me. This year, this summer, like everyone in the village he has been brooding about her disappearance. The disappearance and Magda's shameless return have aroused universal and malicious interest.

He was just about say to Nellie, 'Shall we head back?', when Magda came along with her Bouvier dog, the old black creature panting hard.

'Come in for a drink,' she said. 'It's a hopeless evening. Hellish.'

But she laughed softly and as she opened the gate for them it struck him how cool and vital she looked. Following her he caught a whiff of her scent. He looked at the woman's full, slightly tanned back moving about under a pattern of cross-straps.

Robert was sitting in his usual spot. The house has a nice terrace at the front – paving slabs, flowerpots full of roses, a view of a section of meadow with cows grazing – but he, Magda and the dogs prefer the yard next to the kitchen. When Erik saw him slumped in a lopsided armchair by the light of a neon strip, haggard and sweating, with Magda's two panting lapdogs between his legs, he again had the impulse to turn round and leave.

Robert looked up, but scarcely acknowledged his friends. When Magda came out with a tray of drinks, he immediately stuck out an arm. She gave him a whisky on the rocks.

'How are things at the works?' asked Erik after a while.

He knew he could equally well have asked how things were with the sales of prefabricated panels, aluminium frames and dyes. Robert is managing director of a steelworks. Without ever succeeding he has tried often enough to explain his struggles over cost price, his disputes with the authorities, his feats on the transport front: the whole fluctuating battle which results in wealth.

A dutiful smile. He only seemed to be answering because Erik kept looking at him.

'We're starting work on a new rolling mill. If I'm lucky I can get my hands on a nice piece of local authority land.'

His voice sounded bored. He stared into the semi-darkness with the eyes of a drowsy animal. Depressed, Erik brushed the gnats out of his face and fell silent. He could vaguely hear the two women talking in the doorway. He did his best to imagine that the taciturn person next to him was the same person who for as long as he could remember was never at a loss for words on any subject under the sun, be it God, death or love.

They had sat their high school entrance exams with the Franciscans in Leiden and were travelling back home on the tram. As the tram entered its narrow lane, it slowed sharply, and they could easily see right through the houses to the back yards where the washing was hanging out to dry. Robert raised his head, sniffed and said, 'Fire.' Shortly afterwards they saw the dirty yellow column of smoke. The sky clouded after. They stopped near a courtyard between the houses.

It was Gerardus's house. A maze of boxrooms and corridors, with its front door on the tram square, and its back door in the alleyway next to the fish curer's. Gerardus lived there with his two daughters, Paula and Agnes, girls with black eyes and bushy, red hair – very unnatural, people said, about the living together and the hair – and a mongrel Alsatian which it was rumoured they ill-treated. Gerardus himself was almost blind, which served him right, as he was a meths drinker.

Quite a crowd had gathered. Some people stood there in

silence, but others were dashing in and out of the house's entrances, which had smoke pouring from them. Robert and Erik looked on in astonishment as these people put their backs into it and toiled to save the chairs and tables of someone they only ever referred to as a gypsy, a scavenger, a bloody fool.

Then they saw Gerardus and his daughters. They were sitting a little to one side, on chairs with the springs sticking out staring straight ahead as if the whole affair had nothing to do with them. At their feet, paws extended, lay the dog. 'Dead,' said Robert.

There was something terrifying about the group. They looked so calm, so indifferent. A blind king, two princesses and a dead dog. One of the girls, the youngest, Agnes, was rocking her foot. Only the week before Robert swore he had seen her coming out of the sea without a swimsuit. Erik had not believed him, as he was always telling tall tales, but now he had a feeling that the encounter was not a figment of Robert's imagination. She emerged from the water like a white, dripping fish and then trudged coolly past him up the dune. There is a large copper-coloured mark on her lower belly. The tram started moving again.

That evening he ate at Robert's house. They had strawberries and Russian salad and large jug of cold chocolate. 'I don't eat strawberries any more,' said Robert to his mother. After supper Erik reminded him angrily that if he did not eat he would get ill. In three days' time there was a football match against the Protestants coming up. Robert looked at him with a determined expression. 'I'm not playing.'

And a week later he announced in the same tone that he had lost his faith. 'I'm not bothering with it any more.' They were getting changed in the sacristy. There was a Mass of the Angels for the hairdresser's little daughter, only four years old, who had died. Everything was white, the robes, the clothes, the flowers. The chaplain looked at his watch and gave a signal. They got in line, Robert rang the altar bell and marched straight off.

*

'What is the meaning of life?' asks Robert one evening.

He is a pain in the neck. He sits in the corner of the half-darkened room. On the table there is a circle of letters and in the middle a cross-shaped piece of wood that has to be lifted with the fingertips, he will not join in. He scoffs at Erik, Nellie and Magda. To demonstrate that he does not believe in such nonsense, he asks a silly question. Cheeky too. However, the ghost answers promptly. Curtly and precisely the letters are indicated one by one.

'Emptiness is fullness for those who can feel it.'

They all burst out laughing.

Heat, no sign of it cooling off, he wondered where the thunder-storm had got to. Anyway, it's fine by him if Robert does not feel like talking!

Glass in hand, he looks unobtrusively at Magda. Platinum blond, almost green in the artificial light, rounded ankles and wrists, until recently he saw her as very ordinary. Now he is interested in every movement she makes. While she sits talking to Nellie, she rocks her foot. She is wearing flip-flops, and the toenails of her sturdy feet are painted bright red. Magda is the only woman with whom I have been unfaithful to Nellie.

Of course they are only moments, smouldering, scarcely conscious, when her tenderness appals me. How on earth did I come to give her this monopoly? I take advantage of her love as much as I can and she, with her generous nature, does not make it too difficult for me. But how am I to protect myself against her kimono on a hook in the bathroom! From the smell of sunflowers in the wardrobe! From her nylons, her sweater over the back of a chair, the teacup with the dark red lipstick marks in the middle of the table and my furious flash of realization: she's not home! Why does it never occur to her to thumb through my diary, or search my inside pockets? After a party she persuades me to give a lift home to a girlfriend of hers who is all alone. How can I pay her back for what she does: as I hold open the street door for the lady,

I see her out of the corner of my eye bending down to clear the fridge, her tight dress is starting to inch upwards in a familiar way, she knows damned well that I'll be back in no time . . .

In the distance a church clock chimed. Then there was a moment's deathly hush. He looked at Magda, who was staring innocently at the tops of the trees along the Oude Zeestraat. Since the day when she had found an original way of lifting the dead weight of silence between them, he has had a different view of himself.

She bent down and took the bottle out of the cooler at her feet.

'Yesterday we wrote to Pittsburgh Observatory,' she said to Nellie.

'Oh. That will keep him busy. A whole batch of stuff arrived yesterday, from Texas I think.'

He realized that the two women were talking about Gaby. Magda is the one who has opened up the world and, in a way, the heavens to their son. She is good at languages and gave the boy the idea of writing to the great observatories. She helps him. Books, brochures and even invitations to conferences regularly arrive at their home. Gaby sits at the table opening the mail with an earnest expression on his face. He studies the photos and tables – often he has Magda read the text aloud in translation – and then goes upstairs to store the documentation in a heavy iron filing cabinet with numbered drawers. 'Fog and gas in Monoceros,' he comes out with unexpectedly at table. Or: 'The forty-eight-inch reflector on Mount Palomar.' He raises his dark, troubled eyes and briefly scans the face opposite, his mother's face.

Erik started. Suddenly he saw Nellie shoot a look full of suspicion at her friend from her hunched position. No, it was not the look of a woman who suddenly, unerringly senses the erotic power of a rival. He recognized the look in her eyes. That was how the faces in the post office had looked, that time that Magda walked past with her dogs. People gave each other – him included – knowing looks. There she goes. A furious whispering started up.

Disappeared off the face of the earth for two years. No trace of her. And then when she comes back, she just carries on as before and does not give us the slightest explanation . . . It was raining hard. There were dark puddles on the pavement. Can't someone trip her up?

The atmosphere was stifling. Now the sun had gone down the smell of oil, fish and rancid salt seemed to rise from the ground with full intensity. Next to him sat Robert, glum, unapproachable, a cigarette in his fingers. Why doesn't Nellie get up? I am used to her common sense. She is the kind of person who senses well in advance that the bar is about to close, that the host is getting drunk, that the wind at the end of the day is bringing that certain touch of damp, grubby twilight and despair. He swallowed.

'Let's be going, Nellie.'

She rose, exhausted.

Chapter Three

The pavement is still wet, the sand in the verge a shade darker. He savours the grey morning, which gives him the feeling that it is September and school has restarted. The courage of the first day back. The neatly ironed clothes and a new leather satchel which, as he now knows, smells of formalin. He can easily make the hospital in twenty minutes.

Turning into the Oude Zeestraat, he is surprised to see Magda's dog standing at the gate. The animal, which is put to bed every evening by his mistress on a child's mattress in the kitchen – in bad weather tucked up in the fur coat she no longer dares wear – is soaked to the skin. He pulls over and brakes.

He should recognize me. I am a friend of the family who should be greeted with a wagging tail. Come on, old boy, tell me about it. Why have you been outside all night? Why has the fire in your eyes gone out? But the animal only reacts when he stops stroking its head and starts looking around. Then it lets out a howl, very short, like the cry of a sick person. His blood runs cold. God help me. He goes to the kitchen door, which turns out not to be locked.

The smell of dried home-grown plums, cake, ironed linen, trimmed and shampooed Pekinese. Magda is a translator. Disliking the sedentary nature of her work, she is in the habit of suddenly jumping up and exercising her muscles in lightning tempo. He goes into the hall. Through the open door of the living room he sees in passing the rows of art books, higgledy-piggledy, some of them open on the floor, indicating intensive use. Robert is an industrialist. He knows all about French painting, up to Cézanne, that is; after Cézanne, he believes, everything went downhill. There have been evenings when Erik has discreetly avoided looking

13

at him when his voice has become too slurred. He has not often been up these stairs.

A bedroom door is open. He walks slowly towards it. He walks, purely instinctively, on tiptoe. And yet he has known all along that this furtive entry is inevitable, has been imposed on him against his will. He hears a familiar panting sound: the Pekinese are getting old. Strange that when he enters the room he keeps his eyes focused on the two small animals, which are shivering and panting beneath a chair over which a silk dress is draped, a flimsy thing with cross-straps. He looks at them for as long as he can, stares very strangely, lingeringly, time stands still. Then he has to redirect his gaze.

Magda is lying on the floor. A lace blouse, or maybe a shift, covered in a wet, dark red stain is bunched up around her waist and hips. As she received the sharp stabs she must have slid off the bed, the movement of her body can be traced on the sheet. He suspects that she tried to turn onto her stomach. Her hair fell over her eyes. As he kneels down beside her he sees that in her last moments she remembered to close her eyes. He is a doctor. Despite the terrible state of her chest, he feels the pulse. The body is already cold.

You are on your way to work. You imagined yourself racing through the fields around Rijnsburg at a hundred and forty kilometres an hour, along the course of the disused tramline, past the former coffeehouse, you are used to getting to town by about seven-thirty.

A young secretary hands you the list. Operating theatre eight. You are impressed by the soft arm, the tapering fingers, the perfume which announces that someone has showered and washed with exquisite care. The eyelashes cast a shadow over a pair of softly coloured cheeks, there is a line next to the mouth, a brief indication of a number of very deep and very confused emotions. You have not the slightest desire to make love to this woman.

14

It is fairly simple handiwork. People are usually satisfied with the repairs you carry out for a handsome fee. Occasionally there are moments of drama. At New Year you are always on duty. A seventeen-year-old jailbird is brought in, he has already lost an eye and part of one hand, but he'll be in the fray again next year. The nose and cheekbones are not your concern, but his one eye is saved, you expertly remove splinters and grit, disinfect the vitreous humour and insert stitches which in three weeks' time will disintegrate into tiny fragments.

He glances up from the turmoil of the moment. Robert. He has known all along that he was sitting there, on the floor next to the open door.

Robert is sitting in his underpants, one leg bent and one extended, against the wall. Erik has the feeling that he is wounded. He goes over to him, squats down and examines the arm. The tissue of the left wrist has a couple of shallow cuts, there has been some blood loss, far from fatal, but enough to keep the man from the chaos of actual facts for the time being.

He looks up in a daze and calls Erik by name.

'Erik.'

By his foot is a thin-bladed knife. Erik studies it for a moment, intently, in total incomprehension.

'What happened?' he asks.

A weary gesture.

'Nothing . . . Nothing at all.'

It is a silver dagger. An unfathomable object that Erik has never seen in this house before. The blade looks rather dirty.

'Odd,' says Robert.

'What's odd?'

'The letter-opener.'

'What about it?'

But instead of answering he grins in surprise, extends his other leg and ducks back into the alcove of his madness. Erik understands him perfectly. He is playing for time. Passing time. There really is no reason to hurry. Why shouldn't I come to terms with it? In the street below he hears a car start up and drive off with a growl. Take it easy. I really will make those phone calls in a bit. Their doctor and the police. Something terrible has happened, come at once. The address, Oude Zeestraat, Oude Zeestraat, I've forgotten the number, eight or ten, there's a dog at the gate, standing dead still . . .

The room is cold and bright. There is a window open. This damp grey weather will drag on for days. Although he gave up smoking ages ago, he is now dying for a cigarette to help him sit with the friend of his youth, the murderous lunatic on the floor next to him. Soon he will go to the telephone and sound the alarm. Robert could not care less. For the next few hours he doubtless intends to stick to his view: the death of Magda Rezková, born 20 November 1938 near Brno, Czechoslovakia, emigrated in 1947 with her mother to Quebec, Canada, where in December 1963 she married a serious Dutchman who painted landscapes, leaves him utterly cold.

Erik has stood up. He rests his head against the wall.

Chapter Four

If he closes his eyes he can see Magda appearing behind the snow-covered figure of her husband.

On the evening of 22 January 1964, Robert came round to introduce her to Nellie and him, he remembers the date so precisely because their son Gabriel was born that same night. He stands in the doorway. It is a bitter night. Sheets of snow are swirling over the dunes. They have climbed the steps, with Robert leading the way. His face is chalky white in the light of the porch lamp, steam is coming from his mouth. As he stamps his heels his laughter sounds absurdly cheerful. Then he steps aside and pushes his lawful wedded wife into the hallway.

Erik is immediately reminded of a maid. She is short. Wears a green woollen hat. Her smile is open and appealing. He shakes her hand with a sense of disappointment.

He had run into Robert by chance that afternoon in the village. Not having seen him for over a year, he wasn't sure at first. As far as he knew he was building a terrific career for himself as an artist in New York with the help of the money inherited from his father.

'Erik!'

The figure in the purple overcoat strode across the street, steered him into the bar and ordered fried fish and wine.

'What a bloody hole this is,' he said and began filling Erik in on his bride of a month.

Magda did not die in the coldest winter of her childhood. She may have been an anxious little waif of about six or seven and the airfield she lived close to may have been half-destroyed by bombing, but she survived. In August 1947 she and her mother embarked on the Swedish troopship *Goya* and after a voyage of just over three weeks across a calm, dark green ocean arrived at the

17

east pier of the port of Halifax, a part of the world that in her mother's view was far enough away from Europe.

She grew up in the French-speaking town of Gaspé. A girl with narrow green eyes. There were some photos, not many, of her and her mother. Magda could be seen at a school desk, on skates, with a donkey on the beach on the Gulf of St Lawrence. Sometimes she is wearing knee-length stockings, sometimes socks, and finally, one summer, there is an eighteen-year-old with shiny legs and a mass of platinum blond hair.

But she was absent-minded. Twice she was involved in traffic accidents. She was picked up off the road and woke up in a bed with bars. Once she did not wake up completely. She stared at the wall which had a poster of a herd of elephants bathing pinned to it and for days was inclined to leave it at that. The creatures with their trunks and huge tusks and their friendly smiles represented enough of the tangible world as far as she was concerned and one evening it looked as though dawn would not find her alive.

They stood in a corner of the bar with their overcoats on. Erik knew that he did not have the time to listen so attentively to a stranger's life history. But the comfort of the bar – the round stove, the cigarette smoke, the bottles in front of the mirror with its yellow lights – had immediately stupefied him. Those with a religious upbringing remain attracted to the glow of sanctity all their lives. And anyway it turned out that both he and Robert were starving hungry and dying of thirst. They ordered another round. After a few glasses Erik started looking his old friend in the face with a carefree expression again, his ugly mug was as congenial as ever. His tales, his confidences. The past and the personality of his wife appealed to him.

'It's the strangest thing,' said Robert. 'I never wanted to get married, never wanted a family, the idea of having to come with the same woman at all costs has always struck me as ridiculous. Most of my girlfriends were dark-haired, that was coincidence, I didn't pick them specially because of that. Mainly I liked them for what they did not do. They did not nag me about what I got up

18

to, they did not believe my passionate lies – I have never experienced that with anyone else – at night after a fight they did not run out into the street in bare feet and with their hair loose, they did not whine while we screwed and did not claw my back with their nails. There are enough guys who light up a cigarette afterwards and manage to get away as soon as possible. That causes resentment. I used to stay the night, with their heads on my shoulder, their glowing warm legs over mine, I put up with their snoring, their lip-smacking, their anxious nightmares. But I never stayed for breakfast. The moment there were signs of daylight behind the curtains, I just had to escape. The delicious smell of coffee could no longer keep me. Walking down the street, with the rising sun in my face, I felt better and lighter at every step. The indispensable chore had been done and there I was, alone again. Why people needed the constant presence of another person, was a total mystery to me.'

His cheerful face clouded a little.

'In June I took a trip up north. I wanted to see the Great Lakes, the Appalachians, the Canadian coast. How do you come face to face with true love? In the most idiotic way. Having a beer on a seaside jetty. It was the first time I had a lover with blond hair bleached by the sun. I was jealous for the first time. Her silence made me angry. I couldn't sleep. How could we join our lives if she kept things to herself? What does the love of a Romeo Montecchi or an Alexei Vronsky mean without the background of their mistresses? I would not leave her alone. In the middle of the night I rang her and forced her to tell me her private thoughts. One day she said, "I knew at once that this would be for keeps." Her words did not even shock me. I had already noticed that I could only live with myself when she was there.'

Nellie and he take the overcoats and gulp when they hear Magda's French lisp. A pale blond head of hair has emerged from under the green hat. Nellie motions them towards the living room.

Huge in a dark red and yellow striped dress, she waddles after her guests.

It is a quiet evening. They drink and listen to the wind. Erik speaks scarcely any French and Nellie none at all. Out of loyalty to her future friend, she smiles and says nothing. She also gets up a lot to fetch things from the kitchen. Robert sets out his plans to them. He says, 'When it comes down to it, you can only paint in Western Europe.' They have bought an old farmhouse in the Cévennes. There is a spring, a slope with room for a vegetable garden, after dark the owls start hooting over the valley.

'A wild, unspoiled place,' says Robert. 'Just what we were looking for.'

Erik nods. All evening he was to forget the imminent arrival of his child. Only when they were alone again at about midnight did Nellie show him her contorted face. She had broken out in a cold sweat.

Chapter Five

When he goes downstairs to make the necessary phone calls, the Pekinese follow hard on his heels. He sees how nimbly they manage to get downstairs despite their short paws by letting themselves drop from one step to the next. What is wrong with first giving these creatures the breakfast they want so badly?

He hunts through the kitchen cupboard, finds the tins and opens one. As he distributes the disgusting contents over the three food bowls, the smell of an army camp in winter penetrates his nostrils and without the slightest effort he remembers the huts, the guardhouse and the parade ground. He was a serious married medical NCO on national service who tended to his fellow conscripts' piles and runny noses. Nevertheless, six weeks' basic training had taught him the right angle at which to drive the bayonet into the body, using all your strength, giving it several twists and roaring your head off.

He calls, makes coaxing sounds: the big dog does not react at all when he puts the food outside. The animal remains standing at the gate just as Erik had found it earlier that morning. An hour ago! Five minutes! He calls again. The dog's name escapes him. He is well aware that he cannot put off phoning any longer.

'We'll be right there, sir!'

The routine voice has listened to his story and taken it seriously. Next a few questions are asked which he answers sitting in Robert's comfortable reading chair. He gives his name. He gives the names of the occupants of the house where he is. At his feet, lying open on the soft carpet, are books containing reproductions of paintings. Ponds full of water lilies. Fruit trees. Whirling suns over the sea.

He looks at Bonnard's *Woman in the Bath*.

'The address, sir!'

She is lying chaste and flat in the water, her ankles crossed. With one hand she is shading her eyes, the other hand is fractured by the waterline. This female mollusc is protected by light and colour. Light and colour, he thinks, all that the human eye can take in, everything else is delusion. The white rim of the bathtub. The sunshine. The blue tiles. A put-up job. Signs from a past which is growing heavier and heavier.

'Can I ask you again for the address!'

'Oude Zeestraat . . . Oude Zeestraat . . .' he mumbles.

'Number?'

There is a moment's silence.

He cannot remember what he finally answers, it does not matter anyway. As the other party hangs up he leans forward, closes his eyes and presses both fists to his mouth to stifle the scream which cannot deflect the vision that pierces his brain like a cannon shot.

Breathing in the morning air. Breathing in the night air. A blind person experiences total reality, as his profession has taught him. Indeed, in some respects the world of darkness is richer than the visible one. Slowly and ponderously, but free of the illusion of a horizon, the blind person navigates his way through limitless space. He understands the landmarks – shapes and volumes – better than the sighted person. No one is capable of seeing a shape. Only someone who has explored the curves and hollows with his fingers can subsequently accept them as true. Greek sculpture, says Robert, only became plastic when it was made with the hand instead of the eye. The blind person's hands remain forever the inquisitive, sensual hands of the child.

Once one of his eye operations went disastrously wrong.

I can see him standing in front of the washbasin mirror with his mouth and eyes wide open. I can see his frozen gesture of horror:

the tapering fingers, extended, scarcely spread, close to his face. This patient, Maurits, aged thirty-four, had been blind from infancy. I can see the hospital ward around him – three patients with bandaged eyes in beds, one abandoned bed, a table with brightly coloured flowers on it – and remember the uproar I had just heard while doing my rounds in the department. I remember that two nurses ran into ward 407 from the kitchen. However, the uniformed girls are not doing much to calm the patient. They are standing in the middle of the light, spacious room and letting the patient stare at them. Like me. The patient has turned round and is peering at our faces. All three of us keep perfectly still. The fear of making our features even more repulsive by a movement, paralyses us. He turns back towards the mirror. I can see that his eyes refuse to accept the optical illusion: he casts a glance over his shoulder to see who is standing behind him. No one. Then he strokes his eyes, mouth and nose with his fingers. When the howling starts again, I hear him say, 'Holes . . . dreadful holes . . .!'

Erik had had high hopes of this operation. It was one of those cases where a normal transplant is impossible, because the cornea has been damaged not only by scars, but also, and most importantly, by blood. Blood causes foreign tissue to be immediately rejected. What solution have we eye specialists come up with? We make a window of bone, taken for example from the patient's hip, and position this mini-frame in the hardened and clouded cornea, exactly above the lens. After that, because the surgical aid comes from the patient's own body, we can do what we like, and we insert a plastic lens. However, among Dutch eye specialists there are quite a few misgivings about this spectacular *tour de force*, concerning its usefulness. These lesions of the cornea generally occur at such an early age that the optic nerves do not develop. In a nutshell, the eye may be technically capable of sight but the brain will not cooperate.

For this reason Erik had studied the patient's case history. He had fallen ill in a camp during the Japanese occupation of

Indonesia. Malnutrition, measles and that was that. Blind at the age of six. He had slept on it for a couple of nights. Six was a borderline case. His hunch that the optic nerves were intact was confirmed when the bandages were removed. Sure enough, the patient could see.

The two nurses put him to bed and rebandaged his eyes. The patient calmed down. After that he must have spent a week coming to terms with the memory of the horrible vision before daring to face it again. Even then it took days before he could accept that those dreadful holes had anything to do with the information – deep, soft, slimy-warm – that his hands were used to.

'His hands have lost out to his eyes,' said Robert when Erik told him about the case.

The incredible actually happened: he seduced his friend's wife. He bumped into her one sunny February afternoon. The weather was chilly, she was wearing a short brown imitation-fur jacket and brown boots, the skirt had three buttons at the side which she was to undo shortly afterwards before the garment slid to the ground while he watched. How could he become caught up so effortlessly in this erotic adventure?

'Where did you get to for those two years?' he had asked her.

He already knew at that moment that she would not give a straight answer. No facts, no dates, no coherent narrative of events. Pathetic categories which we are used to asking for explanations in. He was leaning against Magda's roll-top desk.

Magda. Disconcertingly pale and soft in her silk shift. Disconcertingly warm in the glow of the restless fire in the stove behind her. The cast-iron doors were open. The smell in her room had struck him the moment they had come in. The smell of allotments in autumn. What are you doing? Burning old papers. Old cashbooks, old insurance policies, old diaries. And maple leaves to counter the stink that dusty old junk always makes. Just a moment. Still with her coat on she emptied the contents of a wastepaper basket onto the ashes which started smoking profusely before finally bursting into flame.

He had only asked his question because he had solemnly resolved to do so on the way to her house. She was going to reveal her secret to him. His friendship for her husband had been the trigger. She would finally unburden herself and once started the process would continue. Robert, on a business trip to Algiers, would be given the facts straight from the horse's mouth when he got back.

They had gone down the hallway. The door of her study was open. The smell, the light, the sick dog which lay down under the desk: the day's centre of gravity shifted. How can you know the ploys you have to use to get what you are after? One thing he would always be convinced of was that he seduced Magda at the moment his dutiful brain prompted him to ask the question he had rehearsed.

There was a silence.

'Look at me,' she said, and began taking off her coat.

He leant against the desk and did as he was told. He watched her unzip her boots, let the skirt slip over her hips, pull the sweater over her head and then shake loose her blond hair, and take off her knee-length stockings by crossing one leg over the other in the classic fashion. A fool asks more than a wise man can answer. What does this mean? Even though you are curious, be a little patient, you can only falsify history in retrospect. Where is your intelligence? Nowhere. Magda began her discreet answer to his impudent question. She took a step forward, stretched out her arm and pulled him to her with the assurance of a lover. He smelled the bitter scent of her armpit.

He had spotted her while waiting in his car at the traffic lights. It was getting on for four o'clock. The winter sun shed a deceptive light over the junction: it would be dark within the hour. He was on his way to a meeting at the hospital.

He thought she was coming out of the Hillegom coffeehouse with her dog. The building has become a rather sorry sight since the widening of the exit road. The trees in the middle of the carriageway had to be felled. The privet along the cycle path disappeared. The dead straight road gave the sea breeze ample opportunity to destroy the creeper against the back of the building.

What is Magda doing here? This is a coffeehouse for old men. He found her touchingly pale. Her eyes were screwed up against the low sunlight as she came round the corner. She appeared to see nothing and no one, and since her body was bent back slightly, perhaps because of the dog, her gait reminded him of a blind person's.

Suddenly, at the moment the lights changed to green, he had the strange feeling of really being close to her, he was her father or her elder brother, her music teacher or her hairdresser. Overcome by a sense of affinity with her imperturbable solitude he pulled away from the lights. Without asking himself why he parked across the street and got out.

Magda was lost in thought. She only noticed him when they had got to within a few metres of each other. She beamed.

'Hey, Erik!'

For some reason he was scarcely able to raise a smile in response.

'You're a bit out of your way,' he said.

Her look was non-committal.

'How was it with the old men?'

His words seemed to mean nothing to her. She raised her eyebrows. To hide his embarrassment he bent down to stroke the dog's nose. The animal stared listlessly ahead.

'I've been to the vet's with him,' she said.

Still bending down he looked up to see the backward motion of her head: the vet lived close by.

'What's wrong with him?'

'Nothing. He's old.'

While his fingers stroked the greasy coat, he suddenly thought:

one day she'll pour out her story to the first person who comes along. One day this dungeon-like silence will be too much for her.

'He's old,' she repeated absent-mindedly.

He stood up. The keys in his coat pocket jingled. For a few seconds they stood facing each other without a word. Lost in thought, she stared at the bottom half of his face.

Then he said, 'I'll run you and the dog home.'

Her eyes lit up.

'No. He's had an injection and has to keep moving for a bit.' She frowned. Her expression was suddenly peevish as she said, 'But if you want to come home with me, walk along with us.'

Leaving the junction behind them, they turned left and walked into the centre.

A tourist village in winter. No more flags, no more hanging signs with their bilingual slogans, the shiny white seats are gone from the front gardens. Customers have to adjust once again to the standard fare. Ribs, mincemeat, a joint on Saturdays. They are one big happy family again. So let's swap the latest gossip over the counter.

'Erik, I need to get some bread.' She motioned the dog to sit and pushed open the shop door.

He would have had to be deaf and blind not to notice that her greeting was returned without the slightest warmth by the girl in the shop. And that two people, with their arms full of bread, left the shop after giving her absurdly icy looks.

'Half a sliced white loaf,' said Magda. And, a moment later, 'A packet of rusks and a dark rye loaf.'

It was as if her order had filled the air with a string of oaths. The slicing machine broke a very charged silence. He stepped back and positioned himself among the customers who had come in after him and it was not too difficult for him to pick up the frequencies of their indignant silence. Magda should be a bit more polite and friendlier.

You're really no different to us, we have our dramas of loving and being misunderstood just the same as you. But for God's sake, if you want to keep in touch with other people, you'll have to talk. We are used to telling each other everything. This is an age of candour. This is the age of autobiography. After a day during which we have opened our heart to at least one stranger, we switch on the television in the evening, have a cup of coffee and let some total stranger tell us about how they have been raped, have murdered someone, have had to let go of the hand of the child they were trying to rescue from a burning department store . . . Magda is neglecting her friends by imposing a rule of silence on herself.

'She's back,' Robert had dropped in to tell Erik and Nellie one afternoon.

Of course they already knew. The village had been buzzing with sympathy for a week and the women particularly felt a lot of respect. Let's be honest, we should all have liked to do it. Magda, up until a short while ago a little too naive and hard of hearing, has run off, had a couple of years' fun and now she comes back as unconcerned as a young girl. We want to know the details of her story.

Robert sat at their kitchen table staring out of the window. Erik and Nellie were in celebratory mood. Their faces glowed. They had opened champagne, got out beautiful glasses, they were too exhilarated to sit down and busily rearranged the flowers, the ashtrays and the savoury biscuits. Finally they stopped dashing about and raised their glasses. Their eyes sought Robert's. So, what's the story?

He drank quickly, shoulders hunched, elbows on the table. When his glass was empty, he pushed it away as though frightened of hurting himself.

'Where has she been?' cried Nellie.

Silence. Fingertips together. A deliberate smile.

'Well,' he said. 'That's a good question. I haven't the slightest idea.'

Erik changed the subject to football, and then politics.

. . . I know that I'm not a particularly remarkable man. I live with the people that fate has dealt me. Perhaps I love them out of laziness, even as a child I was obedient. Walks through the dunes with my silent father. Fetching in the sheets for my mother. I admired the way my sisters giggled all the time and their dresses smelled of sunflowers. Quite possibly I could have seen a bit more of the world. Whoever is stupid enough to make do with one woman? In company she notices I am looking at her legs and parts her knees a little. Sometimes she tells me her silly dreams. Not even when she is old, at death's door, will there be an end product to her existence. One rainy day I think of my son, the worrying offshoot of Nellie and myself. My heart contracts. I know precious little about the people I live with.

They left the baker's shop. The harsh yellow sunlight had given way to mist and wind, he was reminded of the chilly expression that Robert was assuming more and more since the afternoon he came to tell them of his wife's return. It was a shame that they had to walk so slowly because of the sick dog. He was in a hurry to fire the questions haunting his thoughts at Magda. Let's talk about your childhood. Do you still remember the language? The house where you lived? The garden? You were only six . . . Does Robert still wake you up in the middle of the night? He's jealous of your thoughts. Come on, tell me a few of them. What did you see on your travels, who did you meet? Surely you know we'll all soon be dead, gone, forgotten. Why make things so complicated? . . . If you don't tell someone your dream quickly when you wake up, it's gone in a few seconds. What is not told to anyone doesn't exist . . .

She bent down to open the garden gate.

'Wait a moment. The lock's rusty.'

Only after a couple of tugs did the iron bolt shift. She smiled up at him. Her eyes and mouth could not have been more forthcoming.

'All right, all right. You go on ahead.'

The dog pushed past her.

*

29

A sofa in a lumber room. Brightly glowing embers but no more flames. Outside the windows the cries of the seagulls have died down; now the moon is rising the creatures make for their sleeping quarters God knows where.

He looks at the tiny beads of sweat on her breast. At the face which at this moment she is keeping as expressionless as a mask. He rests on one elbow. His hand feels the arch of an eyebrow, strands of hair, the graceful edge of an ear. There is still enough light coming in through the window to mark the shadowy spots on the woman's body. Her expression reminds him of a stone idol. This reawakens his intense curiosity. They have not done with each other yet. As long as his hips are lying against hers, as long as his sex is still enclosed by her alert warmth, their conversation has not finished.

He makes an almost imperceptible movement. She immediately responds. An amused, mocking smile plays around her mouth. A conversation in primeval sign language.

'Do you know something?' he has just said in complete sincerity, 'I can't live without this.'

'Without what?' she murmured from far away.

'This new smell, this new hair, these new hands.'

For a second she was quiet as a mouse.

'Neither can I,' she said.

Of course he is no stranger to this mirror system of rising and falling, this finger-stopping, this drawing of a bow across a string taut with supreme expectation. But this time it is no longer a sexual embrace, not even lust, it is the compelling call of adventure, limitlessness, frenzy, phantoms, deep-sea diving expeditions. He has the strange feeling of having travelled to the other side of the world in pursuit of this woman.

A glass of Bordeaux? A brandy? She gets up, having offered him a drink. Yes, he says, accepting the offer timidly, a glass of brandy would be nice. The moment she has gone he begins moving about, half groping. A cloud must have obscured the moon, but the dark room is as familiar to him as his boyhood den once was: the smell of scorching, silence, dreams. His hands will always remember the structure of that fiery, gently moving woman's body.

'Where are you?'

He takes the glass from her hand. The taste of her lips is suddenly hot and sharp.

Chapter Six

There are three figures standing in the doorway. He starts. Two young uniformed policemen and a man of about fifty in plain clothes are looking at him. They do not approach him, but their expressions beckon him. He pushes the art books a little to one side and gets up out of the armchair.

They stand surveying each other.

'It's upstairs,' he says.

He leads the way like a host. The three men follow him in such ghostly silence that he turns round halfway. They focus their calm gaze on him but still say nothing. There is no need of course. Our respective roles are quite clearly defined. It is my task to show them the spot where the events which life imposes have become intertwined, and then they, on the basis of laws and ordinances will endeavour to disentangle things. He catches the scent of blood. Fully aware of the sight that will meet his eyes, he pushes open the bedroom door.

He does not move. Does not breathe. His nails squeeze rhythmically into his palms.

'Could you please move aside.'

Someone pushes him out of the way, someone rescues him, it is the plain-clothes man who now turns to the two policemen, their eyes are stinging with alarm and disbelief – they are only boys. 'Investigation support team,' he hears. One of the boys leaves. The plain-clothes man goes up to Robert, who scrambles to his feet with a polite expression on his face.

'He's confused,' mutters Erik, coming closer.

The man in plain clothes smiles faintly. 'Help him get dressed.'

Shortly afterwards the room is occupied by a number of experts. Photos and notes are taken. Erik looks on with shocked revulsion. This businesslike approach is undermining the question to which his consciousness is clinging with iron tentacles. Why did she have to die? She was his lover. Who is to remember that secret afternoon? The warmth? The darkness? The smell of burning? Moonlight must have fallen on my face too. Did it reveal an expression of curiosity, of pleasure, or of the deep, mindless love that a woman may laugh at in her heart? My memory can tell me so many things.

She is dead. Numbered cards are placed next to different objects, including the letter-opener which he had gaped at just now. Meanwhile Robert has put on a pair of grey trousers and a white shirt. Erik kneels on the floor and slides a pair of canvas shoes on his feet. 'Can I have a cigarette too?' he asks as he gets up again. Robert and he are given a Bastos and a light, they grin at each other and for a moment Erik imagines he sees an impersonal kind of irritation in the other man's eyes. Christ, what a mess. Now the doctor leaves the corpse for a moment in order to put a bandage round the suspect's wrist with great dexterity, shaking his head at one of the young policemen. Handcuffs cannot be used, the wound is superficial; but no handcuffs. Then Robert is taken by the arm by the man in plain clothes. Erik opens his eyes wide: meekly his old friend allows himself to be steered out of the door without even looking round for a moment. Flashlights go off round the room. Blinded, he goes over to the window.

An ambulance. Police cars. Heavy, grey sky. An autumn breeze playing in the poplars. He waits till he sees them come out.

I don't know what happened last night. Magda has been murdered. Probably Robert doesn't know either. Probably he murdered her. One is what one does. One is not what one does. Robert does business, looks at paintings, weighs his wife's birthday present in his fingers: a double string of garnets. In a little while a fragment of his life will be put under the microscope. Time, weapon, motive: meaning. The longer one pores over it, the more blurred the case becomes.

Last night. An instant of horror, a densely compacted present, full of heat and love, weariness, stories within stories, past moments, including the time when a skinny lad solemnly resolved to find a wife who was different to his mother and sister. There he is.

The three of them are walking down the path. Robert seems to be in a hurry. His hair and shirt are waving in the wind. When a couple of men carrying a stretcher approach from the opposite direction, the trio steps aside into the flowerbed. Flaming red dahlias and pink-and-white phlox reach well above their knees. Robert pulls back his shoulders and straightens his back like a soldier, the expression on his face is no doubt cooperative.

'Would you mind coming down to the station to answer a few questions?' Erik stiffens. Someone has tapped him on the arm.

'Why not?' he says without averting his gaze.

He sees them get in the car. The Mercedes makes a sharp turn.

Were they happy in France? He was a painter. What did he paint? Landscapes? I wonder what they lived on. And his wife, Magda, what did she do all day? Did she work? Of course they had a vegetable garden, animals perhaps. Wasn't she bored?

He looks into the good-natured eyes of the police inspector. A man of his age who is simply doing his job. They are sitting at a low table in an office, with two upholstered chairs and an ashtray. Behind him is a clerk, no doubt with a shorthand pad at the ready; they use psychology here and work without a tape recorder. The man waits patiently for an answer. He has been asking stupid questions, which does not matter at all, since he knows very well that stupid questions can often elicit very useful summaries.

'I didn't have much contact with him at that time.'

'Didn't you visit them then?'

'Oh yes. A couple of times.'

As though I had nothing better to worry about except the ideals of a boyhood friend, a Romantic who had set up house on a mountainside in France. When I went to see him for the first time, in the summer of 1967, he had been living there for three and a half years. In those days I thought of him as a man alone, and simply could not call his wife to mind.

It was August. A scorching hot mountain road with Nellie map-reading. 'Saint-Paul-le-Jeune. Les Rosiers. Turn left towards Alès,' she says, always right on cue. She sits at an angle so as to be able to smile occasionally at Gaby, who is strapped in a linen hammock on the back seat and of course does not smile back. When the road climbs, he starts hissing, and keeps it up for a good fifteen minutes, sometimes even half an hour. On straight stretches he looks out of the window. Can you really see those gigantic granite ridges, the yellow, scorched fields, the herds of sheep under the chestnut trees? He waves his hand in front of his eyes non-stop. That summer was the first time they had been on holiday together as a family. Nellie had decided. We can do it, she had said, everything will be all right, you'll see. By everything she meant their astonishing child.

'There it is.'

She pushes up her sunglasses, peers past him and points. Just in time he sees the narrow opening in the cliff. He turns and accelerates, the path is very steep and bumpy, an intense hissing starts up behind him, yes, son, we are climbing like goats, we are slithering upward like snakes, a green creature darts away just in front of the wheels, he is worried about the brake pipes. Then there is an area with a hardened surface, and he parks next to an ancient Renault. The heat drives them out of the car. He puts Gaby down and forces the child's hand into his. They walk upwards in the still air. Crickets, summer flowers, a rock overhanging the path and a strange noise, possibly of metal against metal, growing louder all the time: creak! creak!

There was the farmhouse. Magda was sitting under a canopy of leaves rocking on a rusty swing. Absorbed in her thoughts she looked up.

'You didn't get a very warm welcome?'

We got a very warm welcome. Magda turned out to speak a little Dutch. Robert had grown into a lean, tanned, proud man. In no time we were in a fortress-like kitchen sitting down to a meal of white goat's cheeses, salad with garlic dressing, wild mushroom pâté, ham, black and green olives, chestnut cake, bread, clover honey and a jug of chilled rosé. I, at least, immediately got most pleasantly drunk.

Benevolently I survey the company, formidable, forceful personalities, including Gaby, who sits staring ahead and rhythmically shaking his head. Oh, I know him: sure enough, on the chest of drawers there is a small clock with a brass pendulum. Then Robert pushes his chair back. He picks up two glasses and a half-full bottle containing a clear liquid which he holds to my nose for a moment. There is a dead mouse in the bottom.

'Eau de vie de Saint-Josèph,' he says. 'Come with me. I'll show you my work.'

In Robert's wake he stumbled into an unexpectedly dark and cool room. He could smell damp and paint and could see walls, outlines, black beams, the studio was a former barn partly carved out of the rock. Then light flooded in, Robert had pushed open the shutters, and immediately the canvases against the wall and on two easels acquired warmth and colour. Confused, he looked around him. Landscapes, still-lifes, nudes, portraits. For a while all his eyes could do was to pick out the blue, grey, yellow and white brushstrokes. He knew he was supposed to make certain remarks – Robert handed him a glass with a tense look on his face – but he had not the faintest idea what.

I shall not forget the taste of that mouse liqueur in a hurry: grain, sun, a small wild animal. He took a couple of sips and then – probably already utterly drunk – came out with the following observations.

'Isn't it extraordinary that the smudges of colour on those canvases should evoke the notion of a mountain, a woman or apples in anyone's head. Just think about it. Do those daubs of colour bear even the slightest resemblance to the substance, form and dimensions of the actual mountain or the actual woman?'

His words seemed to please Robert. He turned round, strode about with the bottle and glass and then looked up energetically. Erik knew that a pseudo-profound theory was about to follow.

'All you can do is to counter that inaccessible authenticity of things – these apples, that mountain, this woman – with another authenticity. That of a logical system of colour, for example.'

Befuddled, Erik glanced outside. Outside the windows was a panorama of mountain ridges, undulations dissolving into ever paler blues. He suspected that behind them lay the real region, invisible to him, the region of owls and golden eagles, scorpions, lynxes and shepherds.

He mumbled something like 'Intellect versus savagery,' to which Robert replied that intellect itself was savage too.

'More savage than the claws of an animal.'

Only now does he remember that that triumphant voice provoked a vague feeling of revulsion in him. Did he perhaps begrudge Robert his exalted ideas? Robert told him that he forced things to have an affair with him.

'A love affair, don't laugh. If I had to I would use force to make them communicate, yield up their confidences. What do you think of this stuff? Has quite a kick, hasn't it? Here they see the mouse as the symbol of the loyal Joseph.'

Erik did not reply. He looked at the canvas right in front of him on an easel, a life-sized woman's portrait. Although it was not apparently like her, Magda had undoubtedly sat for it. The portrait was painted in crude areas of paint, not with a brush but with the palette knife, and it seemed to him, much more than the landscapes and the still-lifes, first and foremost an account of work in progress, a fever, a battle with light and colour.

He asked, 'Can't you love the landscape, objects, a woman,

without wanting to turn everything into something that belongs to you?'

Robert motioned towards the window with his arm. His self-defence was passionate. That was impossible. He could not and would not do it. Everyone tries to make the things they see and admire their own. Human beings are jealous creatures. I love this landscape. I regard it as mine. My eyes take it in, my brain makes sense of it and my hands subject it to a calculated system.

Almost resentfully he examined the canvases.

'Cobalt, cobalt emerald, grey, grey-white, umber, Venetian red. My strictly personal translations of roundness, softness and depth.'

They drank in silence for a while. Erik had sat on a stool against the wall, he still remembers the friendly coolness at his back. Robert leaned comfortably against the window ledge.

'Now that you ask me, Inspector. Yes, in my opinion he was very happy that summer.'

Suddenly Robert burst into excited laughter. When he had calmed down, he looked at Erik. 'Sometimes I think that life consists of nothing but the confusion you are born with.'

He poured the last dregs into the glasses.

Erik saw the mouse sliding up and down in the bottle and then left at the bottom like a bundle of rags.

That evening Gaby sits under the starry sky, in the summer evening air, on the swing with Magda, on her lap, with his hands clutching her knuckles. He does not know if she is a woman or a human being, that does not interest him. He is interested in the space above his head which cannot be grasped but can be absorbed via the eyes in more or less the same way as eating and drinking through his mouth. Daytime smells – sun on blooming marjoram – rise up from the valley. There is not a breath of wind. Scarcely any sound. An occasional dog barking down below, an occasional remark by people sitting out in their courtyards after dinner, the creaking of the swing. Magda pushes off with one foot and looks at the constellations, she feels like listing the stars that she knows by name. Great Bear . . . Ursa Minor . . . Cassiopeia . . . the psychotic child repeats them after her without much trouble. This kind of child is interested in heavenly bodies, in clouds, in high towers, it likes peering through narrow openings, through glass, through a drop of spit, it takes a thread, pulls it taut and moves it slowly backwards and forwards in front of its eyes, enabling it to look both above and below it. It does not like mirrors, photos, and if you look at it, it immediately averts its gaze . . .

The confusion you are born with.

The second time everything was different. Without really thinking about it he assumed at the time that the cooler atmosphere was a product of the time of year, spring was late in Holland too. There was a mist which cut the farmhouse off from the valley. The vegetable garden was covered in black plastic. Light blue rabbit hutches stood open lopsidedly on the grass.

'The winter has had these heights in its grip for too long,' explained Robert while he put a grill in the kitchen hearth. The fire of smoking, spitting pinewood gave out little heat.

Looking back he realized that Robert and Magda were already saying farewell to their ideal spot.

After dinner Gaby had managed to get Magda to come outside. Erik had not been paying attention, but could imagine how the child had grabbed her fist and dragged her to the door like an object. His gaze shifted to the bay window and there he saw them, grey and shapeless against the darkening sky, on the swing. Why does Magda still not have a child? He looked at her legs in wellingtons.

Their son was now nine. An inflexible boy who had managed

to carry his mental illness through into his fingertips, his toes, his strange hair that sprouted in all directions.

He saw Nellie glance at the pair and then hurriedly look away. She accepted the coffee that Robert offered her and moved closer to the fire, shivering. She was in a bad way. The therapy that she and Gaby had been through that winter had exhausted her. Eye contact had to be restored. Physical maternal nurturing must be imposed on the child by force. The American method had an amazing record of success. But Gaby was already fat and strong. They lay on the floor on mattresses. Nellie needed all her strength to hold both his wrists behind his back with one hand and with the other to press him firmly against her soft breast, her soft belly, producing loving words, baby words, and tried to push her cheek against his. Once she had realized that she was trying to push her knee into his groin. I'm capable of anything, she wept at night under the sheets. I'm capable of abuse, of rape. What do you think, Erik, is that acceptable, salvation through crime? Her son finally resolved the dilemma: during the final sessions he fell asleep within fifteen minutes.

'Can I see your work?' he asked Robert the next day.

The path to the barn was muddy. A chicken which scuttled away in front of their feet slipped over, but neither of them laughed. The cross-bar of the door stuck. Robert pushed his cigarette into a corner of his mouth, pulled hard and gave a muffled curse when he cut his hands. The door slid open with a fantastic creaking sound.

What a change! He looked in astonishment from the paintings to Robert. He would have liked some explanation, for these bleak, monochrome expanses of paint. This painting represents red. This one blue. This is the depiction of white. What do you think of yellow? But Robert, with his back to his visitor, was sweeping a couple of empty tins into a corner with his foot.

Erik finally made an observation.

'Not at all,' said the other man gruffly. He did not turn round. Nor did he take his hands out of the sleeves of his sweater. 'Cool.

Go and stand right up close. These are very sensitive pictures and react to life itself. To light, to shadow, to you.'

Erik did as he was told and stared at the red. Red. The red was covered with a damp layer of dust.

In the summer of 1974 they came back. They moved into the house on the Oude Zeestraat, where the Bouvier was joined by two Pekinese which Magda acquired from the dogs' home. These temperamental creatures got into the habit of hopping upstairs to the bedroom a step at a time on the dot of eleven each evening.

Magda started taking language courses. She had a perfect command of Dutch, English and French. She soon secured a translation commission: the municipality of Noordwijk had official relations with Upper Volta. In the spare room, at the roll-top desk which had been set at right-angles to the window, she toiled over elegant, simple formulations.

Robert went into business. His first deal involved the absurd batch of picture frames which a local joinery business had been left with, he told Erik the story – childishly simple and moreover highly amusing. In the course of the year he became in succession managing director of a brickworks, the agent for a carpet sales firm and a partner in an ornamental aviary business.

'That's the beauty of this work,' he said to Erik. 'The objects are completely arbitrary, completely abstract, they are just the raw material. The real stakes are elsewhere. No, not in money. In profit. The player with the most passion gets the profit. It is not about greed, it's about talent.'

Then he became what he had imagined all his life he would refuse to be: his father's successor. The Noort metalworks, on the point of collapse, was rescued by Robert, restructured and tastefully renovated. Abstract silkscreen prints from an art lending scheme appeared on the walls. Robert had them changed before he could get tired of them.

Occasionally Erik would bump into him by the canals. What could be more logical than an invitation to visit one of their regular bars? However, sometimes he avoided him. Sometimes that seemed far wiser. How was he supposed to react to the woman with whom his friend was strolling ahead of him arm in arm. Let everyone do as they please. She was wearing a shiny black coat, a belt, high-heeled boots. Her profile was shabby and very attractive. It was spring. Sunlight fell on the bushy red hair that looked even thicker and redder than twenty or so years ago.

It is nearly noon. He is walking home along the Oude Zeestraat. They offered to drive him home in a police car, and it really is quite a long way, but he refused. Having told them so little, having provided them, between discouraging silences, with such a scant amount of information, most of which they already had, it seemed the decent thing to do not to inflict his presence on them for a moment longer.

'Was the marriage so unhappy?'

'I don't think so.'

'But one day she vanished, just like that, without a word.'

'Er, yes, that's right.'

This afternoon Robert is to appear before an examining magistrate. I suspect that he will not have much to say either.

PART TWO

Chapter One

He has slept deeply. Arms and legs outstretched, mouth open, in complete abandonment. A pale red sun climbs over the bulb fields, it is still early, it is an early morning in May 1980, the night before he has found out that his wife has disappeared. Now he is trying desperately, half awake, head buried in the pillow, to hang on to the comfortable world of his dream. No doubt, no misunderstanding, no betrayal. Knowledge keeps pace with perception. There is not the slightest need to worry unduly about animate and inanimate things: you are a part of them and that's that. Suddenly his face clouds over. The muscles in his chest contract. With full force the information from his memory has struck home, when he got back at about ten yesterday he had to retrace his steps along the garden path and open the front door with his key; he stepped over piles of newspapers and mail; the dark rooms were filled with a smell of absence; there was no sign of the dogs.

He stood at the bottom of the stairs and called her.

'Magda!'

And again, in his raincoat, chin raised, 'Magda!'

Silence.

Then he put down his suitcase, turned the light on and began inspecting the house. This many coats on the hallstand is overdoing it. As soon as the dogs are gone the carpets start smelling. The French Impressionists are at head height in the bookcase. He slid his hand under the foliage of a fern; this plant has not had any water for days. On the draining board in the kitchen he discovered half a brown loaf, a dirty knife and a cup. Not really alarmed, he lit up a cigarette and stared at the woman's shoes on the mat. She has not bothered to pick up the brush and a tin of shoe polish. The door of her study was open. By the light of the centre lamp the room seemed entirely strange to him. He glanced out of the window at the garden

– it was raining – then his eyes caught the roll-top desk. He stiffened. His suspicions aroused, he stared at the empty spot on the writing pad. She has taken the portrait of the two lovers with her.

. . . The woman is delicate. With her oval face and shoulder-length hair she seems younger than she is. Her dress too, one of the girlish models that were being worn that year – 1936 – strengthens the impression that life in all its richness has yet to begin for her. As though it were not already there! As though her husband were not standing right next to her in his riding breeches and boots! He is tall, earnest, a lock of dark hair falls across his forehead. This moment is not something imagined, it is real. Against the background of a summer garden Magda's mother-to-be has put her arm through that of her husband, is smiling bravely and disbelievingly into the lens of the camera and seems to be thinking: this is the man I shall stay with for the rest of my life. 1936. Their daughter has not yet been born.

He felt a draught behind him. A squall of rain lashed the window. Without taking his eyes off the desk he reached for an ashtray. The excessive tidiness with which she arranges her work things. Now that it had gone he could observe the silver-framed photograph better than in the years when it had stood between the paper clips and the postal scales. He smoked with hunched shoulders. What theatrical whim had got into her?

A bronze chime resounded through the house. Disconcerted, he began pacing about the room from one corner to the other, this had once been his father's study. A floor which creaks in all the familiar places, a matt-black stove with its doors open, the smell of ash, paper, of panelling which radiates a deep orange glow on summer afternoons. In her pining widowhood his mother had hit upon the idea of putting a sofa under the windows. He stood still. While the clock continued to reverberate – Magda had wanted to keep the thing as an heirloom – he realized that the faded snap was the only thing in the house which had alluded to the strictly private background of his wife.

*

In the summer they had moved into the house where he had been born. His parents' furniture was still intact.

'It's only temporary,' he said to Magda after they had clambered up the two flights of stairs to the attic.

Their paradise in the French mountains had been sold off, he was full of business plans, and how convenient it was that his mother had chosen to move into a splendid, white building where she would be looked after and, if necessary, helped in an emergency. She had wanted to take only a few old woman's household effects with her.

Magda said little. She did not react to his words, but stared at a colourless item of furniture under the attic roof.

'How lovely . . .'

He followed her pointing hand, looked in vain among the junk and said, 'As soon as my business gets going, we'll convert the house. Modern bathroom, modern kitchen, you name it. We'll renew the whole of the inside.'

The flush in her cheeks, her contented silence, the willingness with which she descended the stairs ahead of him; didn't she realize that she was wandering through his deeply despised childhood memories?

'Or else we'll buy a seaside flat,' he said to the back of her blond head.

In the front bedroom she went over to his mother's mirrored wardrobe – a prematurely grey woman who usually looked up ill-temperedly when a brat interrupted her trying on a dress, a brooch, a hat – she opened her eyes wide, raised her chin and stroked her neck with her fingertips. Turning round she said, 'What do you think, will the white wine have chilled a bit by now?' She made no objection to replacing the ghastly twin beds.

While he busied himself with cynical amusement in the next few weeks clinching a deal which coincidentally involved a batch of picture frames, Magda took possession of every inch of the house. She aired the rooms, washed the curtains, counted and sorted the sheets embroidered with the family monogram. In addition she painted and emulsioned the woodwork and walls white and frowned long and hard before daring to knock a nail through the wallpaper or reposition the odd picture.

One evening in autumn, he came home. Magda was in bed with a textbook – she was studying Dutch – her hair was loose and she was wearing a beautiful satin bed jacket with rolled up sleeves. He turned on the bath taps, listened to the moaning of the wind in a drain pipe, stepped on the scales in his birthday suit – still seventy-seven kilos – and a little while later saw that Magda had fallen asleep with her book beside her. While he looked at the questioningly becalmed expression on her face he thought – and there was something unbearable in the thought: She is my wife . . . From under a chair came the rasping breath of her two Pekinese.

Still in his raincoat he was standing in front of the mirrored wardrobe when the phone started ringing downstairs.

Don't answer, he said to himself soothingly. As long as you hear nothing and see nothing, everything will stay bascially as it was. She hasn't bothered to leave a note, either on the bed or in the bathroom. There is no message anywhere, and although her toothbrush has gone and as far as one can see half of her perfume bottles and tubes, she is not going to disturb your well-organized life; so take that bewildered expression off your face, it looks like fear.

Did someone tell her something? Write her an anonymous letter? There is a particular pleasure in committing an act of cruelty the source of which can never be traced.

As though he had not got into this situation, which brought him some relief, by pure chance. These things happen to men. One fine day a red-haired saleswoman with firm hands opens up a shoe for you, she has dropped onto one knee in front of a footrest with a sloping front and helps you slide your foot in, on her advice you move your toes about. When she looks up to see your reaction you recognize her. She immediately bursts out laughing too, and there in the middle of the shop unpins her hair. Agnes Rombouts's bushy red hair falls right down her back. Twenty years on, she allows herself to be hugged and kisses with her mouth open. You admire her build and the way she can move her ears, but you do not want to hear a word of her wearisome life story. After a business trip of four or five days you stare at her messy profile in a hotel room and there is fire in your belly.

The phone kept ringing. He adjusted his expression, went downstairs into the living room and picked up the phone. It was Nellie.

His eyebrows shot up.

'Nellie!'

He moved a couple of books from the armchair and sat down.

'So the dogs are with you?'

A roundabout story began at the other end of the line. He took rapid drags on his cigarette and now and again let out an affirmative grunt.

'All right. Early tomorrow evening. Yes, I'll come and get them. What?'

He listened with his lips first.

'Er, no, not really. In fact, I don't know much about it. A family visit, you say. Well, it looks like it. First to my mother's and then to my sister's . . .'

There was a look of astonishment on his face.

'Well no, I am not saying that. Of course it isn't odd. It's just that . . .'

' . . .'

'Yes, probably. In passing, I imagine. It must have gone in one ear, and out . . .'

He laughed, mumbled a goodbye and listened for a moment

to the silence, to the crackling and the buzzing. Then he hung up. He hoisted himself to his feet and yawned. Nellie's woman's logic had brought him wisdom and comfort. Now he was going to bed.

He had no sooner stretched out than a familiar weight began pulling his arms and legs downwards. He lay on his back like a ship and listened to the wind. The wind over the fields rose, dispelled the rain, cleared the sky of clouds and finally subsided. The morning would be blue and transparent.

Chapter Two

He is at the works at the usual time. Noort & Co. Ltd opens at seven every morning. When Robert Noort arrives an hour later the central shed is an inferno of noise, fire and indescribable brute force. With their backs to the soft grey morning light filtering in through the side windows, sixty employees tend the rolling presses, the drop hammers, the hydraulic presses and the spouts of molten fire.

Robert Noort feels that a certain detached respect for the heavy work strengthens his position as Managing Director, he uses the office entrance. In his summer suit, clean-shaven and despite his private worries well rested, he walks through the quiet part of the building where the porter is sitting reading the newspaper and greets him with a wave of the hand, where the director's secretary looks up earnestly from her crimson nails, where there is not a soul to be seen at the drawing boards, the engineers are still stuck in traffic. He passes a wall hung with contemporary graphics, takes the lift, closes the door of the boardroom behind him and is alone with his thoughts.

These tall windows are definitely ideal. They look out onto the River Zijl with its broad green banks, a windmill and a distant farmhouse. On the other side is the town. A perfectly chosen spot! Through these tall windows I can effortlessly survey all I have achieved. The works are accessible by road and by water. On the quay boats are tying up or are on the point of leaving, and with nonchalant ease, heavy materials, heavy structures glide through the landscape. I always refused to become my father's successor. He died and I stuck to my principles. Only when the whole business was on its last legs did the thought of the worthless portfolio of shares begin to attract me. The road is a lot wider today. In order to expand the car park I had to have the elms removed. Containers can be unloaded direct at the sheds. I am loath to give up what I have once made mine.

He turns round, there was a knock on the door. A small man with a round head and, behind spectacles, a pair of eyes of a most velvety, trustworthy brown, has entered the office. This is engineer Zijderveldt, his second-in-command. He has the documents he needs for today's tough talking session with the Investment Bank.

Robert abandons the view and bends over the graphs. 'Nice,' he says. 'Very nice. Forty per cent of the Dutch market should be feasible.' But the emptiness in his emotions, the lucid absent-mindedness in which he was enveloped just now, has not entirely vanished. He looks up inquiringly.

With modest indifference Zijderveldt puts a list of figures on the table. 'The cost projections for the first three months.'

Hiding his satisfaction, Robert rubs his jaw with his thumb and outstretched fingers. He casts a completely vacant look at Zijderveldt. This beautiful plan, he thinks. This beautiful plan originates from the same distant prospect that I have been staring at constantly since my earliest childhood. An empty spot beyond the horizon, where everything that occurs to you is acceptable and real.

'And the annual financial review?' he asks softly.

His idea is to buy the Alcom Metal Company from its ailing mother company, to transfer the pressing and plating operations to Noort & Co. and then – and this is the finesse – to gear the strong, viable subsidiary to the European market for precision-made components. This afternoon the bank will have to be persuaded to make an investment of seven million. Robert intends to rely completely on Zijderveldt, whose forecasts are seldom if ever off the mark.

A chubby hand passes over not only the papers he has asked for, but another document also. 'Here is the five-year plan. As you can see I have allowed for a possible turnaround in Eastern Europe. The meeting starts at two o'clock. Perhaps we should be prepared for the accountants to point out that there are customers unwilling to take a risk on a new business.'

'It's a company with an established reputation.'

Zijderveldt nods. 'That's true. That's true,' he says slowly, as though seriously considering his superior's remark. 'They won't be able to needle us. The profitability forecast . . . the available long-term securities . . .'

The words hang in the air like parts of a poem. The two men look past each other reflectively. How often we have performed this play, thinks Robert. The reflections, reasonings, the half-baked ideas, originating from completely separate worlds, combine like chemical elements. Mutual pleasure, mutual respect and the outcome is a policy decision taken by Noort & Co.: in the circumstances the only correct one.

'Have a good morning.' Zijderveldt takes his leave. His hand is on the doorknob, neck and shoulders thrust forwards, feet together.

'Yes,' says Robert. 'See you this afternoon.'

He is alone in the room again. Silence and morning greyness. A moment like all the others. His thoughts, which as soon as they can disperse like ants, find it as useful to be idle as to be working. He sits down at his desk and lights up his first cigarette with a mounting feeling of apathy, rage and isolation.

. . . For as long as I can remember I have been seized by absurd waves of sorrow and pleasure. When I think about it, I can remember the pleasure of one event and the pain of another, but I have forgotten the why. From my west-facing office I look out at a glorious day. What is being communicated to me? An animal understands its perceptions better than I do. My moods are more deceptive than the sea. I cannot uncover the motives that underlie my actions. Even after the event I cannot make head or tail of what I have been up to.

*

On the path through the Katwijk dunes. Summer, August probably. A red kite keeps appearing above the slopes. Down there, on the beach, there is a stiff west wind, but we are nice and warm. Our bikes are hanging in the blackberry bushes. She is eleven, you are nearly twelve, this girl is beauty personified. Skinny legs, bruised ankles, large brown shoes. On her arm a man's watch. Her watery grey eyes are beautiful too. When you talk, she talks back. When you laugh she laughs with you at the top of her voice. On this afternoon you believe in the notion that beauty is not separate from things. Then, just as you turn round and press your hollow fist over your mouth to release a blood-curdling cry into the summer air, she looks at the heavy watch. She wrinkles her nose and upper lip and you see the little bubbles of spit between her clenched teeth. You can feel yourself getting a little sick.

She says, 'Christ, I've got to go home.'

In your parents' garden. It is summer again. Under the shade of a parasol your mother is drinking tea with the lame lady from next door, who is not naive enough not to realize that a grammar school boy at the bottom of the sloping lawn is lying reading a wonderful book from which he glances up every now and then. It is the last day of his holidays. Her lameness may make the hips of the dentist's wife rather ungainly and lopsided, but her shoulders and the beginning of a pair of ample breasts are glowing with the warmth of the sun. The eyes of a schoolboy focus on a dark spot on her body. 'Have him come by and say hello, tomorrow before his first lesson,' she suggests to his mother. An early hour. A house with its doors open. You take no responsibility at all for this trudging through empty rooms, a conscript does not know the rules. She is lying in wait on a sofa in the conservatory and beckons you closer. Her ironic eyes are fixed on you, she fiddles deftly with the flies of your trousers. Then in a flash you have a view of the area. An astonishing body, large and flat. A mouth that is suddenly contorted with pain. Despite a sense of great danger you plunge forward.

'Off you go. Otherwise you'll be late.' She gives you a packet of cigarettes and pushes you in the direction of the garden gates.

In the village. The Rombouts sisters with their bad reputation, their copper-coloured plaits, their vulgar ways. It is Agnes that you keep bumping into by accident: as soon as she catches sight of you her face tenses. There is a Saturday dance in the Tuinbouw café. 'Another pils, my good man,' you say to the barman, lighting up your umpteenth Gitane. You do not look at Agnes, who is dancing in a shiny dress, your sideways look is directed at the bulb farmer who is twirling her around under the lights. His eyes, without lashes, are blank, he refuses to let anything distract him. His steps are heavy and deliberate, it reminds you of a carthorse, a pig or a bear, his ability to express himself is minimal. The way this clodhopper keeps his pleasure to himself, makes you stiff with anger and excitement. Back home you lie down on your bed, after locking the door.

In cars. On beaches. On the grubby bedclothes in student rooms. Slowly but surely they come within reach, the strange bodies drifting past. There are no longer any objections when your hand goes exploring. What was all the mysterious fuss about? The ritual requires certain tactical manoeuvres – the right look, the right smile and the determination to get what you want, and there you are, the woman's body, the mysterious thing that men ogle at, rolls on its back, belly, turns ninety degrees, kneels, pushes itself up, arches its back, twists and turns, throws both arms around you, crawls on top of you, drops like a fish gasping for breath but still brimming with life, throws its head rhythmically left and right, although you stay as still as a beast of prey, close to you there are sighs, groans, and some scream for all they are worth.

Afterwards she looks away from you with a strange expression. You are alone again and you feel good, sometimes even proud, you appear to have done a splendid job: some of them keep ringing you. But never, never once, does it bring you a moment of that new, still undiscovered happiness which could make you explode with laughter, sing songs, develop a deep-breathing technique, increase the length of your stride, sleep less, love children, animals, believe in God.

And as for women's tears, you want nothing, nothing at all, to do with them.

Incoherent fragments. Nothing but fragments. There is no through line in my life's composition. This musical idiom is strange, stranger to me than ancient Chinese court music, or the Indonesian gamelan – I might still be able to master the stamping of a Guinean fertility dance, with some effort – but I can't really appreciate this unfinished symphony. One thing should follow from another, you may be surprised, shocked, but during the musical performance your memory feels the inexorable, elegant, totally random logic of the form. Then your shoulders relax, you are swept along, enraptured.

If I want, I can picture my studio in the Cévennes. A stable half hewn out of the rock with big – enlarged – north-facing windows. I stare at the landscape, at the empty canvas: the most important thing in painting is to see the details within the whole as it takes shape.

If I want, I can remember the time – the time, not the feeling – when I believed that I could cope with the absurd challenge of things, the planes and slopes of the fields, the weight and outlines of objects, the scent of apples, the movements of the clouds, the surf and the light: everything advanced on me, in blurred particles, and occupied the vast spaces behind my eyes. It was at that time that I met Magda.

I can recall the night – the night, not the feeling, not the real event – when I stood panting for breath under a glittering starry sky. I had run and run through the darkness like a madman along the edge of the ocean, over the sand, obsessed by a joy which up to then I had, systematically, avoided. I probably laughed out loud. Rolled on the ground. Magda. I intended to enchant her with everything that I had discovered.

At that time there was a constant honey-like scent in the air.

*

54

But one afternoon she said, 'That blue shirt suits you.'

She had laid the table at the extreme edge of their property. A rocky outcrop covered with grass, which protruded over the valley behind the farmhouse. Here they would construct a terrace in due course.

He had sat down grim-faced. After he had worked from early morning, his eyes were dead tired.

He peered at the ambiguous expression around her mouth.

'Why do you say that?'

Without looking up she reached for an earthenware jug. She raised her arm and poured light white wine into their glasses.

'No special reason. The shirt is the same colour as your eyes.'

Now she rested her gaze on him for a moment. He caught his breath. At the hottest time of day, under a suffocating, blue, monstrously huge sky, he looked into the face of a woman who had not the faintest idea of the kind of love that was being offered her.

'What really turns you on,' he asked softly, 'my shirt or my eyes?'

'Your eyes, darling, your eyes.'

The laughter in her voice was intolerable. 'My eyes. And is that all? The rest is worthless?'

'Don't be so stupid!'

'I'm not being stupid. I'm asking you something.'

'Come on . . . Robert . . . stop it.'

An insect buzzed past him. A gold-green projectile zigzags around his ears, robbing him of his hearing, flies away and returns, then hurtles into the void. Gone.

With something like astonishment in his voice he repeated, 'I'm asking you something.'

But instead of answering she closed her lips tightly. She crumbled her bread and after a while, when the smoke of their cigarettes had made everything enjoyable and inevitable again, she started talking about killing one of their chickens. The creature, already a year and a half old, still refused to lay.

At night she lay asleep on her right side. The shutters were closed, it was pitch-black, warm, she was talking in her sleep. Although he listened intently, he could make no sense of her babbling. Just you go on talking! he thought bitterly. I don't understand a thing of what goes on in your head. A moment later he saw with perfect clarity – he did not know how – himself and Magda strolling into the village café that afternoon. They had deposited their shopping on the floor and ordered a Brizard. When the landlord put down the glasses, Magda spread her hands very obviously – ostentatiously, on the bar. Sure enough, the man observed, 'You have beautiful, sensual, snow-white hands.' She said, 'Oh yes? Well, rub them a bit because I've had no feeling in them for the past year.' The man took hold of one, closed his hairy fist respectfully over it and with the fingertips of his other hand began stroking the white skin, the way one lulls to sleep a newly born kitten which has been given a lethal injection. Magda's shoulders heaved. 'I can feel the life flowing back into them.' She was wearing white silk shorts, a white hat and flowery red leather shoes. Then she threw back her head, turned to look at him, Robert, and said, 'It's fine now. Once my hands are back in action, you can be sure the rest will follow.' Then she burst out laughing, loud and coarse. He wanted to calm her down and tried to shush her, but he could not get his lips to move.

Only then did her remember that he was lying asleep in a darkened room.

At the end of the winter he realized that something had changed. A revolution had taken place; when, there was no way of knowing. Probably it had been a slow, secret process in which what mattered was not what was in his blood – that would remain – but a very unpleasant unresponsiveness in the world around him.

What it boiled down to was that he began avoiding his studio with its north-facing windows. That he was gradually seized by the thought that he could just as well change the key signature of his life – not the passion, not the resentment. For the farm-ouse, the vegetable garden, the faded light blue rabbit hutches, the July nights with their hooting owls – appendages once intended to clarify and adorn the man he was – equivalents could be found. (Instead of *farmhouse* he could just as well insert *sea*, *shop*, *order book*, *fully automatic American limousine*.) The time came when he began to enjoy the following thought: my aim is to breathe new life into my father's works, the collapsing firm of Noort & Co.

In mid-September he enters his sister's house by the back door. At that moment the major shareholder is sitting at table with her children: a heavily built brunette with a restless look in her eyes. Out of habit he remembers that she used to be their father's favourite.

'I'll buy you out,' is the first thing he says to her.

Hélène pushes her baby into his arms and pulls up a chair. Amid smells of fruit, snot and porridge the matter is discussed.

'You know,' he argues effortlessly, 'if there is no solution within three weeks, the business will fold.'

He looks at his sister. As a child she was the kind of person who drilled a hole in a nice wasps' nest on the balcony railings with a pencil, who lifted up a heavy school atlas and let his two white mice escape from a box, who wore pale socks and pink nightdresses, who prayed aloud and cried in the cinema . . . Don't tell anyone, he begs and the next day his racing bike is locked up for three weeks. At the age of about sixteen she suddenly began to show warm affection for him.

She grabs a napkin and bends forward to wipe a pair of babbling lips.

'One million is needed immediately to replace the two mechan-ical presses,' he continues. His hand strokes the baby's warm skull. 'There will have to be redundancies among the older staff.'

'Some of them have been there since Daddy's time.'

He turns his attention elsewhere for a moment, a child offers him an apple, and he makes an offer. Hélène looks up in alarm.

He does not even have to point out that if they go into receivership, the value will, of course, be low.

Shortly afterwards a new boardroom was fitted out on the first floor of the offices of Noort & Co. Seated at a rectangular desk, his back to the windows, Robert Noort haggled with the bank, the board and the trade union.

This life, which should have been unfamiliar, turns out to be second nature to him. He manages to persuade one of the bigger banks of the firm's viability, he is given a loan of four million. He calls a board meeting, listens with polite indifference to the long-winded talk and has already made his calculations for himself: the core operation is to be transferred to the market for steel skeletons in prefabricated house construction. One winter evening he comes home from a dinner with his wife. He makes a fire in the hearth, in the middle of a dreamy conversation he raises his head, looks at Magda, asks her permission and drives back to the works along an icy road. In the office he takes out ledgers and files. He makes two decisions: this ludicrous administration is going to be automated within the year and the very small customers with their complicated mini-orders are going to go.

Then there was the question of the redundancies. Without scruples, he dismisses twenty per cent of the workforce. Still he was seen at the time – in the sheds on the quays, in the canteen – as his father's son, because he had been careful to keep on, and even promote, a few old employees, men who had proved their loyalty and as it were belonged to the culture of the company.

At the end of the financial year losses were no more than two hundred thousand.

Some time later – Noort & Co. was already operating with sales profits of eight million – Zijderveldt appeared on the scene. A young man with a broad bald head and the look of a tame horse handed over his card early one afternoon: K. B. M. Zijderveldt MSc (Eng.).

'Er ... where did you pick up all that know-how?' asked Robert, who had listened entranced for a quarter of an hour.

'Studied at Harvard. MBA. Placement with the American aluminum company Canal.'

'All right, give me one of those European weaknesses.'

'The production of aluminium profiles.'

'What's the supply like here at the moment?'

'Imported. Best prices from West Germany. Always long delivery times, though.'

'Estimated Dutch market?'

'Twenty to twenty-five million.'

They had not noticed the knock on the door. Suddenly a couple of thick white coffee cups were set down in front of them. The two men said no more and started stirring. With eyes lowered Robert registered the puffy little hand holding the spoon, the white cuff around the wrist, the brown sports jacket and a whiff of sweet tobacco. Someone had offered him his brain power.

Looking up, he met the other man's wandering gaze. He reached out, pressed the intercom button and cancelled his appointments for that afternoon.

Chapter Three

About six o'clock he walks across the sunny car park to his car. It is still warm, a little misty, when he feels the soft car seat at his back he imagines things are quite normal.

He drives beside the river. Along the bank people are lighting bonfires. A couple of half naked children are diving from a jetty. He turns left and – passing over the bridge, over a fast moving white canoe – reaches the Singel canal which takes him out of town in a loop. His hand gropes among the cassettes, guitar music, no, piano music, yes: his favourite sonata. Why shouldn't he allow himself that pleasure? At this moment, after one day, he is still not at all distraught about his wife's leaving him.

His smile broadens.

'Profits one point six million,' said Zijderveldt – a model of patience – that afternoon at exactly the right moment. His extremely soft voice broke a silence which had lasted a second or so too long and, sure enough, the two bank officials brightened up.

He will become managing director of the new company, with a majority holding of sixty per cent I shall retain control, decides Robert smoking, humming, vaguely aware of the rows of flowers, the fruit trees, the young Rijnsburg lettuce which will be ready for auction in two weeks.

As he drives into the Oude Zeestraat, he remembers that he has to collect the three dogs from Erik and Nellie. He turns the wheel sharply. Good God, whatever got into her?

Only the son of the house is at home.

'What time are your parents coming home?' asks Robert after he has climbed up the dune.

The sixteen-year-old boy is sitting on the floor in the living room. Robert knows that Gaby won't look up. A hand is poised above the Scrabble board in front of him, out of the corner of his eye he is watching the three dogs which have woken with a start under the table, this kind of adolescent does not like being talked to, they turn their backs to the light. Robert looks at the fingers which, at the moment the black dog gets up, carefully put down the letter block, the tips are pointed, they are slightly turned up, he takes a pace forward and reads: *canis maior*. For that matter, Gaby does not seem at all bothered by the visit, he continues what he has been doing in silence, rocking his upper body rhythmically to and fro, stroking a spot on his neck with one finger, softly, very gently, just below the ear, this kind of adolescent does not like being touched by strangers, they prefer playing with the surface of their skin themselves. Robert stops in the middle of the room, hands in pockets, and cannot take his eyes off the movements, the obsession, he would prefer to leave but he is forced, as if in a trance, to follow the rocking, the rhythm, the hypnotic rhythm that suddenly reminds him of the padding of a tiger behind the bars, of the thrashing of a stranded fish – mechanical, unplanned, frantically the animal demands the water back – of the stubborn willpower with which a bluebottle attacks a window pane . . .

The boy gets up, shoves the little rack containing the letters into Robert's hands: *here they are*, it says – and leaves the room.

At that moment Erik and Nellie come in noisily, saying hello, carrying flowers, boxes of shopping which they drop onto the table.

'God, she's simply gone off for a week or two,' says Nellie a little while later crossing her legs. And to Erik, 'Why don't you pour us a red wine.'

From their armchairs they are both staring at him, a little pityingly, a little giggly. He realizes that, for their own pleasure, they are acting out an elegant little comedy. They are in on the secret. Magda has hidden in the wardrobe.

Erik produces a smile.

'I expect she'll ring this evening.'

61

NELLIE: Oh, I'm sure she will.
ERIK: You're not getting worried, are you?
NELLIE: I think you look a bit worn out.
ERIK: Robert, you can't be serious. Come on, sit down. This is a very good year. Why are you being so anti-social?

He opens the French windows, leaves off all the lights, slips off his shoes, his tie, finds a box of black cigarillos – lights one, pours himself a whisky – which he has not drunk for years – lies full length on the sofa and puts the bottle within reach. Her absence annoys him beyond words.

Evening sounds penetrate from the street. Footsteps of people out walking, a stifled laugh, a cry of surprise and then suddenly a passing bus: how dare you disappear just like that, tell me at once where you've got to and what time you are coming home. He shivers. This cold draught has nothing to do with you and me, with our life, with our evenings by the fire. But when he gets up he leaves the French windows as they are, open, he simply fetches a heavy overcoat which he puts over his legs when he lies down again. There is no love at all in you!

Now he could make a couple of simple calls. He could phone his mother or his sister Hélène. Is Magda still there? Would you put her on? He wouldn't dream of it. He would not have this humiliating conversation with either of his two blood relations. Good God, you are treacherous!

For that matter, he cannot really understand the affection she feels for his mother, his sister and her family. The dates in her diary – hey, Robert, tomorrow is the second Sunday in May – the visits, the phone calls. When his mother is on the line, her voice is softer than usual, with his sister she is in fits of laughter.

'What was the big joke?' he asked in surprise.

Nothing.

At Christmas she insists on having the whole family, including Hélène's two or three brats, over for a meal. For several days she is busy preparing a mushroom consommé, a salmon mousse and a sucking pig with an apple in its mouth. Why go to all that trouble, he wants to know.

'I think it's nice,' she says, producing her smile.

Has she ever responded properly to his questioning?

The cigar has gone out before he has finished. He looks for a lighter, plays with the flame for a moment, staring at the circle of light; then pouts: if he gets it right a smoke ring will float up through the darkness, for a moment he thinks of his childhood, then he sees Magda's face in front of him. It strikes him as very withdrawn. You are deceiving me with your absence, your calm, your unspoken and completely private preferences for animals, hairless babies, shoes with ankle straps, aquamarine jewellery. When you get out of the bath, you rub yourself all over with oil you got from a weird Surinamese shop. I peep at you through half-closed lids: you are giving free rein to your thoughts. You are deceiving me!

You are deceiving me!

For years we used to fish in the river. Magda likes sleeping late but I was sufficiently determined and prodded her awake. To make up for it I thrust a cup of piping hot tea into her hands as soon as she tottered into the kitchen. Her mood brightened. I liked watching her standing on the stones in bare feet and deftly manoeuvring the fish out of the water, the river was very fast-flowing at this point. You are exactly right, I thought. You are exactly as I want you to be, in this grey, neutral light, by this ice cold water, in this valley in the mountains where you don't know a soul except me.

God, I was really high! Art is not life, it is another form of life. It is not about making, but about attempting, not about being awake, but about sleeping and dreaming, not about walking, but about dancing on a tightrope. There is a restlessness in you that has nothing to do with breaking bounds.

What bounds? I can't see any bounds. Play-acting, violence, detachment. I read quite a bit. You appreciate theories for their playfulness and charm and that's that.

What interested you in those years was not life, but paint. Paint, touch, tone: dimensions of things which hide from you. What curiosity! But what you were trying to find does not reveal itself openly. A painting is an analogy.

Art is not life, life is its raw material. I used every circumstance that I have ever been in – my father and mother, my sunrises and sunsets, my ideas and delusions – and, in those days especially, I used Magda.

Magda was the thread that linked me to the world. God, I was high! I worked in my north-facing studio, knowing she was asleep in the sun. You are a mythical creature, I thought, a blue flower, a mystery to everyone except me.

Chapter Four

64

At the end of a winter day she comes in. She is wearing a woollen coat. Without budging I continue working at my drawing board as I start turning the pages of my sketch-book, I feel her closeness just behind me, neither of us says a word but we look at what I have been trying out that day. Shapes, lines, dots in all kinds of colours.

'Now I am looking into your head,' she says after a while. 'I can see the movement of your thoughts.'

That evening I take her badly grazed hands in mine. 'Damn, damn, damn,' she stammered when she came into the house. She slipped in the dark. I look at the grazes, the blood, the white edges of skin sticking up and the clear liquid, the same that wells up from freshly cut wood. 'You should be careful,' I scold her gently, because I feel the pain. I feel the pain in the hands that are mine, I see the irritation in the eyes that I possess completely, the green eyes which are already beginning to brighten again. I hug her: my breasts, my intestines, my womb, my thigh muscles . . . isn't it insane? Almost enough to make you die with laughter? This soft creature is not a stranger, she is not even – in the strict sense – another person. I have imposed the system of my love on her. She is part of me now.

But one night I could not get to sleep because I thought I would choke in the darkness. A few hours before she had said, 'I want a child.'

The hospital is in the centre of Le Vigan. When he took her there for the first time, it was autumn. They chose the route over the Col de la Triballe because it was the shortest and still quite passable. At the highest point Robert slowed down as usual, they liked looking out at the mountain ridges undulating southwards, row upon row, in ever vaguer blues. They knew that on the plateau beteween them a bloody religious conflict had once been fought out to the last man.

Today a strong wind was blowing. Magda, muffled up to the

chin in an old fur coat gave a short laugh when the car lurched to and fro and at the same time a handful of chestnuts rattled onto the roof. Robert was nervous. Just before the bridge over the Hérault he changed gear so abruptly that they both shot forward.

'Are you OK?' he asked in alarm.

She sat looking at the gleaming black water far below.

The sun dipped below the horizon. It was getting dark. The villages clung to the mountainside like cobwebs. A dog loomed out of a barn door, barking at the car furiously, and pursued it for quite a way. At the moment they entered the town the street lights came on but it was not busy yet and they easily found a parking space. Magda needed no help getting out, she was only bleeding slightly. She was not even three months pregnant yet.

For the first time in their marriage they were separated. A determined world snatched Magda away. Blood samples, forms, a stretcher on wheels. After she had been laid on her back in a high narrow bed, Robert was allowed to say goodbye. In blinding light, discreetly peered at by a dozen women patients who were just lifting the lids off their evening meal, sniffing intently and then tucking in, Robert brushed his wife's lips. He saw and felt nothing.

'How are you?' he asked the following day and laid a couple of sprays of heather across her legs. His hands were very dirty. Just beyond Saint-André the air filter had come loose and crashed against the bonnet, which was no problem, apart from half an hour's fiddling about at the edge of the ravine. When he finally entered the ward, Magda was asleep, and when she opened her eyes she seemed surprised to see him.

She reassured him with a faint smile. For a moment he glimpsed something in her face, something small, shadow-like. She was fine.

'What did the doctor say?'

He was to come early that evening.

'Are you in pain?' he asked before he left.

She took his hand. Of course not.

He drove back in the drizzle.

66

She was not kept in for long. When Robert sat down by the bed for the fifth time, Magda, deathly pale and propped up on a pile of pillows, tried to convince him that no permanent damage had been done. While he looked at her startled eyes and thought: It is still October, the sun is shining on the golden leaves of the chestnut tree, and in the cellar there is a shipment of Lubéron, very tasty, he heard her say, 'Medically there is no reason why it should not be OK next time.'

She began to keep a calendar. On her desk next to the portrait of her parents, next to the writing pad on which she wrote her weekly letter to her mother in Canada, Robert found a list of dates crossed off in red. On these days she served dinner later than usual, banked up the fire higher than ever, looked at him with eyes beautifully lined in black and blue, bent over his shoulder to refill his glass to communicate her warmth, her rainforest smell to him. Oh God, yes, she knew him. She knew the pressure with which her hand must look for him and find him – calculatingly, she watches his desire mount and meanwhile gives free rein to her own feelings – till he followed her to bed in the darkness, where dull, deaf, without the slightest expression of love, he was forced to take the initiative. But on one occasion he struggles free of her embrace. He puts a coat round him, opens the door and stands in the bitter night. Leaning against the wall of the farmhouse, he looks at the trees and the covered vegetable garden in the moonlight, the bright blue sheds and hutches in which animals are sleeping, the moon glides between the wispy clouds, disappears and re-emerges over the studio, glowing white against the rocky wall against which rests a large unfinished abandoned canvas. You are deceiving me!

It was high summer when they made the journey for the second time. At high speed they drove over the pass, ignoring the vistas, the scorched slopes, the flocks of sheep under the chestnut trees, and descended into the valley of Le Rey, where the river was no more than a thread of clay among the boulders. After a journey of three-quarters of an hour, they reached the town dozing in the afternoon heat.

No space was made for Magda in the white ward. Without further ado she was taken to operating theatre two. Suction curettage is a simple business. The woman is given a light anaesthetic – she entrusted herself to the care of an anaesthetist with deep black eyes and eyebrows, hurtled backwards and was suddenly overwhelmed by colourful but not unpleasant dreams – she is opened up with the help of practical machinery, and the defective embryo is removed. The job takes scarcely twenty minutes, as a rule the woman can go home with her husband the same day.

They sat outside in the indescribably mild evening. Magda has put on a bright green silk pyjama suit, she has accepted a glass of cognac and has not even refused the stool under her feet. Robert glanced sideways, she was smoking with serene eagerness. What bunglers we are, he thought with satisfaction.

Winter set in. One Monday Magda went to the village on foot through the woods. When she came back she went to the bedroom without a word to pack a bag. The test had been positive again, her breasts were already filling with milk, this time she was to be put on a drip immediately. Three times, no less, Robert was able to visit her without problems. He waited on the sofa in the hosptial lobby, endured his feeling of desperation and behaved as normally as possible: when the doors to the corridor swung open at the appointed time he joined a small grey band, brought flowers and presents with him and took up his post by the bed.

Then came the snow. The snow appeared like an icy white animal, like an adversary in a dream. When Robert came out in the morning he had to shovel and sweep himself a path to the car. Then he started the engine, left it running, cleared the windscreens, he put the snow chains on the wheels and now that the mountain pass was closed, took the route through the Forêt de Sanissac. It kept starting to snow and he could go no faster than thirty kilometres an hour with his nose against the windscreen, peering into greyness for two or three hours at a stretch, until he parked at the hospital in a complete daze, climbed the stairs and found the ward where Magda, incomprehensibly shrouded in exactly the same grey-white gauze as the snowy wastes, greeted him calmly.

On one occasion, halfway between Asclier and Saint-Martial he had had the idea of pulling over to the side of the road. He got out, lit a cigarette with his hands cupped and, leaning against the side of the front bumper, started staring at the snow-covered tundra. Almost immediately his senses managed to free themselves from his thoughts. Somewhere shots were being fired, somewhere dogs were barking, there was the repeated ringing of bells, the wind rose. None of this registered with him. Nothing attracted his attention, determined as he was to limit himself to this one, unfathomable, emotionless moment in time, just long enough until, with childlike satisfaction, he knew that he was too late for the sombre building, for the sofas full of visitors, for the snow-white uniforms dashing past and not wanting to be spoken to, for the pestilential smell of medicine, stretchers, pain, flowers and food, for the brooding warmth of the ward full of women with the unrelenting desire for a child of their own, for the tube in Magda's arm, for her well-groomed, contented body, her phantom, her reproduction, for the sinister liquid in the bottle next to her bed, for the trivial words they will exchange, before saying goodbye, for the lift and the chance meeting with the doctor who at an inevitable moment will strap her for the umpteenth time to his operating table.

But when the latter happened, at the most hopeless moment, on the brink of life and death, it was already spring. The red and blue blinds were already being lowered outside the cafés. Pots of flowers again marked the front doors. Robert and Magda drove out of the town, turned right and began the climb up the Triballe ridge. Do you see that, asked Robert at one point and Magda said yes, yes, how lovely. She could see: everywhere water was bursting from the rock face. How lovely, how lovely, she muttered when they got out of the car in front of the house, because now they could not only see it, they could hear it too, from all sides, the water that had come to life somewhere at a great height, and was taking the liberty of glistening, rushing, leaping, tumbling into the ravine on its way to the river.

Chapter Five

There were days when nothing worked. You mix a colour, put down a few lines, a few strokes, you step back and screw your eyes up. Back you go! You've got to change it, you've got to change it, if only you knew how, you haven't the faintest idea and stare full of distrust at the partially wet canvas, the colour sequence of grey-blue-crimson-red-orange-blue-grey definitely does not reassure you, on the contrary there is something ridiculous going on, your chin sags, it is obvious that your powers have vanished, your indispensable instincts have gone, you assume for good.

The heat was extreme that day. As he came out of the studio a red-hot weight instantly descended on his neck and shoulders. As a result he made his way along the path past the mulberry trees slowly and even dragging his feet a little. With a feeling of having reached a dead end, he pushed open the door of the house with his foot.

Silence, semi-darkness, a strip of sunlight, a mirror. He could just make out the young black dog lying flat out on the tiles at the bottom of the stairs. He listened intently. If Magda were not there or did not want to talk or did not want to look at him, he could still jump into the ravine.

She was in the bedroom trying on a straw farmworker's hat.

'Where are you going?' he managed to say.

'To the village.'

The brim of the hat hovered just above her bare shoulders, she was wearing a halter-neck dress.

'You mustn't go,' he said.

She turned and looked at him in surprise.

'Why not?'

'It's too hot.'

'I'm going on foot. I'll take the path through the woods.'

71

'Even so. The heat is killing today. I don't like you taking risks, I think it's best if . . .'

'Oh, Robert, stop it, stop it!'

'Why are you interrupting me? Why do you rush off the moment I show my face? You don't want to tell me where you're going, do you?'

She opened her mouth, unable to speak.

He got angry.

'There's no need to laugh.'

'I wasn't laughing.'

'You were, you were laughing, but it doesn't matter.' Plaintively and suddenly quietly, he went on. 'Let's have a drink . . .'

In disbelief she watched him take her sunglasses, open her handbag, close it and look in the mirror again.

'I'm going.'

'Rosé? White wine?' He blocked her path with arms outstretched. 'It's cool in the kitchen. It's very nice. I have just come through it.'

'Robert, get out of my way.'

She was going simply to walk right past him. Furious, he grabbed her wrist. 'What do you mean, get out of my way! Do you know what you're saying? Look at me! You're just going to walk out on me, aren't you? Look at me!'

'No' she cried. 'I've had just about enough of this!'

She twisted her arm, kicked his legs, but obeyed. Then, as he showed her the fever in his eyes, and his look of an escaped animal, the twitching of his eyebrows, the way he had looked ever since childhood at moments of dire extremity, he let go of her wrist and laid his hand heavily and familiarly on her shoulder, and after he had seen that she swallowed and brushed her lips with her tongue, and after he had also noticed that she could not control her laughter, for a moment, the way someone retrieves something astonishing from the desert of their memory, he put his other hand under her armpit and led her with slow steps like those of an Argentine tango past a chair with a red velvet seat, past a table with drawers smelling of eucalyptus, past a mirror at head height, back into the room where he let go of her for a moment so that, completely of her own accord, she could fall backwards onto the bed, so that the farmworker's hat was pushed to one side and the honey-blond hair came loose.

At that time I once drove to the highest point in the area. There were about twenty people living in the shepherds' village of Saint-Armand-des-Neiges, mostly men, the youngest of whom was nearly sixty. The road was steep. At the end I was moving no faster than a mule. Not much of a village, walls with flowering creepers growing through them, a dog asleep on a balcony. Desolation populated with rumour. I reached the highest point in the region. Café Saint-Armand-des-Neiges. The men sitting at the tables under the trees throwing their dice, paid scarcely any attention to the foreigner getting out of his car in a cloud of white dust.

Inside, at the bar, I drank three glasses of wine, then ordered a pastis, a Brizard, another pastis and finally went outside holding a *marc de poire* in each hand.

Against the stone balustrade a man was playing dominoes by himself. He was an old fellow, with a face which in the filtered sunlight looked trustworthy and almost happy.

I went over to him, dazzled by the panorama at his back: a slate-coloured landscape of slopes and crevasses, unchanged since the fifth day of Creation. I put the two glasses down, sat directly opposite him and said in the thick accent of the region, 'What sweltering heat! Excuse me, but tell me, have you got a wife?'

The old man cast an interested glance at me, but said nothing. When he prepared to lay another domino I began drinking in calm fury.

. . . I can't stand her smile any more. If you ask me it's not a smile at all, but a characteristic wrinkling of her skin. I can't stand her step, her breathing or the way she smokes and drinks, puts cream on her hands, pierces her ears, shakes her hair loose and later, in the early evening, at just the wrong moment says, 'I'm tired. It's hot. Why don't we just go to sleep?'

I find her absent-mindedness unacceptable. You were very different once! When I leave the table, grab my cigarettes and announce that it's time I was getting back to work, her eyes stay fixed on a random object – a candlestick, a pewter plate with fruit on it – as though there were another past besides that which she and I share together. 'Is it cold, is it warm, is it raining?' she asks innocently when I come back hours later and goes on calmly digging her fingers into the dog's fur. She has a very gentle and friendly smile, but I distrust the expression on her face. I know that underneath she is consumed by something strictly personal. I can't stand your double game any longer!

'What do you want from me?' she once cried out. Nothing, nothing at all, dear child. I intended to devote my life to you, to dedicate my work to you. To forget forever my longing for an untamed woman. Sometimes she snuggles up to me half-asleep, I wrap my arms around her and while she lets me have my way, I can feel how she has changed. You are a thing. A hard fossil. An old memory of love.

I want to know how long this is going to go on for. I did have a few plans for us. Didn't I do all I could? I fertilized you more than once. I have given you into the care of strangers. Afterwards I have taken you back without hesitation. You are insulting me, wife, with your silent grieving!

'Please, fill my glass would you . . .' The most intimate words you have whispered to me for months. An hour later I had to watch as she waddled solemnly into the moonlight . . .

The old man had used up all his pieces. Between us lay an elegant black and white labyrinth. He picked up the glass I had set down for him, took a sip and looked at me earnestly.

'Yes, Monsieur,' he said. 'I have a beautiful wife.'

I bent forward. The table creaked.

'Good. I'll take your word for it. What I would like to know is, have you ever thought of wringing her neck?'

The old man gave a surprised look. He scratched his head under his cap, thought for a moment – or pretended to – and then let out a gentle sigh.

'Yes, Monsieur. I have thought about it very often.'

Our eyes wandered towards the summer sky.

His embraces are rough. Through a curtain of tears he immediately pushes his tongue deep into her mouth, although he knows that she really hates it. He grips her hips with his knees. He presses his fingers into her shoulders and then in hasty panic removes them in order to fiddle with the zip of his trousers. He pays no attention to her face, he does not listen to the sounds she makes, there is too much to do. At this blinding hour, in this cell of heat and fury where he has lost all patience and is as abrupt as the blade of a knife, Robert Noort, idealist, artist, utterly exhausted man, thinks his wife has been gone too long, that he has permission to rescue her from her underworld and at the same time to look back, that he can even grab her, that he can bury his head in the sweaty scent of her armpit, that he can drag her back by her hair to her warm beating heart, her skin, her hair, her eyes – your body is what you are, return to it, come on! so that we can learn everything about each other that is worth knowing – and bathed in sweat, his trousers around his ankles, he tries with actions that are essentially simple and, moreover, as old as the world, to restore order.

The confusion you are born with.

Chapter Six

She does not come back. She does not ring. No telegram arrives. In the village people start staring at Robert with curiosity: he's the man whose wife has disappeared, or pointing at him, yes, that chap, the thin blond bloke who goes down the path along the dunes every morning and evening with her three dogs, he gets up an hour earlier and goes to bed later than he used to, he has begun a new lifestyle.

Robert gets into the habit of spending his nights on the sofa in his living room under an overcoat heavy with years of dried rain. After opening the French windows, he smokes a couple of cigarillos, lying in the moonlight that floods in with summery clarity, and usually falls asleep with the thought that the whole disordered mess is after all just temporary.

'I just don't understand it,' said Hélène a week after the disappearance.

In her kitchen, amid the smells of simmering strawberry jam, Robert hears that Magda had turned up late one morning, had joined them for lunch when the children got home from school, listening right and left to breathtaking, half-finished stories and over coffee had reacted sensibly to her sister-in-law's philosophy of divorce. 'She looked very relaxed and, yes, perhaps a bit mysterious,' Hélène tells him. 'It was as though she was thinking of something nice the whole time.' She had been wearing a red dress, a raincoat, because the weather was not too good, and she had only her shopping bag with her. Finally she said, 'Right then, I'm going to pop in to see Mother.'

He visits the old woman. A new white leather chair. A footrest. A mother who forgets that her son has drunk his coffee black for the last twenty-five years.

'I've always thought she was odd.'

He is given the necessary information. Magda had stayed no more than an hour, she had drunk a cup of tea and listened to, oh, what was it they had talked about, she had been very quiet and as she was leaving must have lost the red coral bracelet, the family heirloom which she had been given as a gift when she first met her mother-in-law and had worn constantly since, until the antique chain, as they are prone to, gave way at a chance moment. 'When I was going to Lucassen's to get my hair done it was lying under the hallstand.'

Without a word Robert looks at the stained corners of her mouth, her twitching eye, at the arm of the chair and the skinny hand covered with diamonds, which is the same as the chubby hand covered with diamonds, which cuts the pudding, wrings out the flannel, grabs the nail-clippers, which finds the poems of a sixteen-year old boy and leafs through them trembling with anger: 'So, his lordship has been kept down a year! . . .'

What he was afraid of, her pity, is not forthcoming. For an hour he undergoes the old woman's steady, constantly angry gaze.

Then there is Agnes Rombouts. A woman with copper-coloured hair, youngest daughter of a drunken father. Anyone meeting her on the beach noticed that all natural colours became even more gentle than they already were. She lives in a provincial town now. Her beautiful body in decline. A flat, a carpet, a housecoat with exotic flowers on it. For as long as Robert manages to convince himself that Magda's absence, while incomprehensible at this moment, will soon, in retrospect, be completely plausible, Robert continues visiting his mistress. As long as he is able to conduct his crazy telephone conversations from the boardroom and on meeting friends and members of his family to forestall the pity by promptly inquiring about everyone's health, Robert clings to his double life.

'What did you dream about last night?'

His question – a fixed component of their secret compact – heralds the climax of the evening. They had set out to drive to a waterside restaurant. Agnes had chosen fish in butter, steamed potatoes and four vegetables in season, he went for the menu of the day. They conferred about the wine.

'Poligny-Montrachet . . .'

Eight-year-old aromatic liquid which sparkled palely in crystal. Talk about this and that. A stifled yawn. By about eleven they were back in the flat. Robert tossed his jacket over a chair. In a warm mist of alcohol, of unfocused comradely feelings and of nostalgia with no place to go, he looked at the woman baring her white shoulders. Only later did he start talking about dreams.

She does not answer at once, but continues walking about the room humming. She bends over the ashtray. Her face is so indifferent that he thinks that she has forgotten he is there. When she is finally lying beside him again, she begins. I was walking through a town with two animals behind me that I had to rescue. An empty town with lots of towers. I heard the pattering of the animals' feet behind my back, but I did not know what kind they were. Perhaps dogs, perhaps wild animals. The towers were metal. They gleamed. I climbed a staircase, higher and still higher. When I reached the top, only one of the animals had been able to follow me. The story is as usual so pathetic that he has trouble keeping his laughter in check. When she has finished, he in turn puts on a serious voice.

From the start it was obvious that he did not wish to discuss certain things with her. Not Magda. Which she understood. Which, even more than for him, was out of the question. In addition, any allusion to what either of them had experienced earlier in their lives must be avoided. No revelations. No trivialities that could be treated on a level with the psychologically coloured clichés of God knows who. In order, nevertheless, to find the necessary matter for conversation, Agnes hit upon the idea of dreams.

But one day in autumn he is lying under her duvet. The day was overcast to begin with and now rain is lashing the terrace. He says, 'I have no idea. I don't dream any more these days.' She turns away from him as though he had struck her.

*

A little while later a missing person's report appears in the newspapers and after the news an appeal for information is broadcast on both TV channels. With pain in his chest Robert looks at Magda's face smiling out at him from the screen. The eyes more carefree, the hair blonder than ever in a bygone summer shot through with the light of the screen. If I wanted I could smell the perfume in her neck . . . The weather has been bad for days, there is ground frost at night. Do these facts matter? A red cotton dress, a nylon coat, a shopping bag. My wife.

When he goes into the office the next day, the infernal background noise from the shed is absent. While he realizes that his employees have not gone on strike but are discussing his life in groups, his eyes meet those of the porter, the two secretaries and a technical draughtsman: they greet him with alarmed respect. Are they about to offer me a bunch of flowers?

Halfway through the morning Zijderveldt appears. They get straight to the point: the problem that is getting in the way of the take-off of the new subsidiary. The finance for Alcom is fixed, but a trifling little revolving part which is necessary to calibrate aluminium matrixes has a delivery time of three months in the US!

Robert rubs his chin and observes the calm face opposite. This – as far as I can recall – is the first time he has slipped up on business matters. He doesn't seem to be very upset about it, and nor am I for that matter. Suddenly he hears his fellow-director say, 'By the way, I hope you'll join me for dinner this evening.'

He is not sure he has heard correctly.

'I'm inviting you for dinner at my place. You won't be disappointed. I like good food.'

Zijderveldt turns out to have a private life. A house on the Galgewater canal, a dark blue apron, a cat. In a glass case is a collection of stones which prompt a digression on a hiking trip in the Andes. That evening Robert witnesses a complete transformation. Zijderveldt bursting out laughing (apelike, shoulders heaving), putting on his favourite music (the score of *Bedazzled* and especially the Nuns' Chorus), performing deftly with the cocktail shaker (two kinds of brandy, egg yolks, lemon).

'A Waterloo Fizz.'

In the dining room the table is laid. There are daffodils on the dark red table cloth. After the first glass Zijderveldt stretches out his hand and says, 'Please call me Kas.'

Robert shakes the silky soft hand and waits – flabbergasted – to see what will happen next.

'Kas. Short for Kasper. Quite a common name in Lisse. There were three of us in my class.'

'Robert,' says Robert.

The evening is warm and friendly. The food is good, the wine is good, but after a moment's solemn silence, the host gets up, leaves the room and returns with a still-life painted by his late mother. His eyes are moist. However, the goose pimples with which Robert wakes up the following morning are completely unnecessary. When Zijderveldt comes into the boardroom a few days later he says, 'Mr Noort, I believe I have a solution for you.'

Robert pushes back his chair a little and stretches his legs. 'I'm listening.' He thinks, I knew it. This little fragment of the world, this fantasy, Alcom Ltd, will go on existing. Everything will come right, I knew it would.

He learns that Zijderveldt is on the point of leaving to see his former employer in Pennsylvania. The aluminium company, which is contemplating setting up in the Netherlands, wants to be assured of its market in advance. Therefore it is looking for independent manufacturers to finish its products. When Zijderveldt rang, it turned out that they remembered their former colleague's wheeling and dealing very well.

Robert hooks his thumbs into his waistcoat. We must start producing that part ourselves, he thinks vaguely. I'll suggest it to him later. He sees that Zijderveldt is spreading out his fingers on the desk. How I would love to touch those soft little knuckles for a moment. If it's OK, he will drop his voice right now.

In a muted tone Zijderveldt says, 'If the discussions work out

– and they will, Mr Noort – they guarantee I shall be bringing back that wretched little gadget with me in my hand luggage.'

They look at each other for a moment. 'Fine,' says Robert getting up. 'I admire your quick thinking.'

Zijderveldt has got up too. The question has been discussed to their mutual satisfaction.

Spring 1981. His mother dies.

A motorcade glides along the Oude Zeestraat in the direction of the boulevard. Children with wreaths of flowers are standing in the wind. Magda has been gone for almost a year. Occasionally Robert, who has long since reverted to sleeping in his own bed, starts awake in the middle of the night, turns on the light and seeing his clothes over a chair, says to himself in all seriousness, 'I am not a happy man.' In confidential conversations in the village shops his behaviour is described as growing stranger every day.

Chapter Seven

The end was not exactly peaceful. The old woman slipped in her bathroom at night. She must have become ill after a dinner in the restaurant of the sheltered flats where she had been served a crab cocktail and oxtail stew, food that she has never been able to resist all her life, she cannot have suspected the irritated workings of old intestines, and in her panicky haste must have struck her head on the stand of the washbasin. She was found two days or so later. At her cremation her son, who did not love his mother, makes a strangely mournful impression.

In the atmosphere of the floral tributes. In the middle of the final chorus from the *Matthew Passion*. At the head of a small bunch of people which is keeping as quiet as possible behind his back. Out of the need to focus on a fixed point, he directs his gaze at the parquet floor around the coffin . . .

. . . It was desperately bad timing. Precisely now that her behaviour had become a little less hurtful recently, just when her lips and nails were again dark red, Magda received a telegram from Canada. Only the day before, as a joke, I had listened to her heartbeat. A calm thumping sound. You're your old self again. Now she pulled a chair back and sat down like a withered woman, moving her feet and shifting her lower body as though the oak were no longer reliable enough. Had I ever seen this before? The skin around her nose was indeed as white as chalk. She looked up. 'I dreamed about her only two nights ago.' Silence. The bay leaf smell of the heat. Her feet in black espadrilles.

He has forgotten these urges to cry for years.

About ten days later he met her from the airport. As soon as they were driving along the D 999 towards Quissac, he asked, 'How was it?' As though she were not looking exactly as he had imagined her the week before.

'Magda?. . .'

Someone had pulled back the two halves of her face a long way, her lips were pale, narrow and extended.

She made a weary gesture. What could she say . . .

'What can I say . . .'

The situation was not particularly suitable for talking. It was getting on for six. The cars on the two-lane road were overtaking at top speed. He accelerated, braked for a moment with a screech and then shot past a truck and trailer with perfect timing. There were plenty of questions racing around his head. How did you arrange things, a cremation, a burial, what did she die of, did you see the body? Glancing at the dashboard, he saw to his annoyance that he had forgotten to fill up with petrol on the way there.

He had slept badly all week. While he was busy whitewashing the kitchen during the day, finding her walking shoes and polishing them till they shone, unblocking the outlet of her bath, mowing the long grass that sometimes brought on sneezing fits, while in brief he made excellent use of his days, his nights had been hopeless. In order to get through the hours he had begun to write to her. She must stop deceiving him. In black and white he pointed out the necessity of gearing her feelings to his with less reserve in future. Occasionally his pen was loving, occasionally great words flew across the paper. You are the sparkle in my life. Unfortunately, her personality prompted more bitterness. For example, he went as far as to tell her that he longed heart and soul for the time before he knew her . . . Finally – yesterday – he had crept into the night with the pile of A4 sheets. In the studio there was deathly silence, he had not set foot in there all this time. Whistling through his teeth he began to nail the sheets of paper at head height among the other works of art. Feeling more cheerful and a little dizzy he had surveyed the result. Letters to My Wife.

He cast a quick glance in the rear-view mirror and then at her. She seemed to be searching for words in bewilderment.

'Did you see the body?' he asked gently.

At the same moment he pulled over sharply. A petrol station had caught his eye, that was lucky, there was no other customer waiting, he made a snap decision. The car pulled up sportily. An attendant in deep ultramarine who appeared at once was ignored for the moment.

'Tell me . . .' he insisted.

The look in her eyes was so distant that it was just like an imbecile's.

'She was in cold storage. She was lying on a bed of ice.'

Now his eyes met those of the heavily built fellow by the front bumper. At once he turned aside, got hurriedly out of the car and slammed the door. With his shirt open to the waist, he gave his instructions at length.

'Would you check the oil while you are about it?'

He had seen the mother repeatedly. Born in Prussia, widow of a Czech Jew. After the war she had left for Canada with her child. She was delicate, blond, but completely different from the daughter. He felt that those blue eyes had understood him at once, her daughter is in love with a European, now she too will disappear for good. Poignant arrangements are made: the mother will move in with her married daughter at once, in a year, in three years' time, a separate house will be built on a farm in the Cévennes. Some two years later he had seen her looking – she had come over for a couple of weeks, the small, heart-rending mother – at the dimensions of what used to be the barn, the friendly boulders and the mulberry trees which she remembers from another life. Her smile of consent soon faded. The mother was smarter than the daughter. Magda made serious calculations, divided up the accommodation, the kitchen here, a bath there, her mother gazed out of the window. Later, when they paid a return visit to Canada one Christmas, she pointed to the snow-covered back garden and told them how comfortable she was. But Magda flatly refused to give up her past and continued to cherish the wonderful plan.

'Two hundred and forty-four francs.'

He looked up in annoyance. A pushy fellow was breathing in his face.

'Pardon, Monsieur!' he exclaimed indignantly. As if he were not the one who brought in the money here, who funded this stupid man and his stupid wife and his fat, spoiled children, as though it was not him who kept this little petrol station from bankruptcy!

'That'll be two hundred and forty-four francs,' said the voice.

His fury was wasted. The man stood waiting with an indifferent look on his face. Robert took three bank notes out of his trouser pocket, snapped his fingers once, pocketed the change and a few seconds later had squeezed his way back into the traffic on the autoroute. How quiet Magda still was.

In order to control the silence between them, his headache and his irritation at the heavy traffic, the low sun, the idiots in their fat limousines and everything else that caught his eye, and especially in order to get home quickly so that he could look after his wife, he resorted to an appropriate remedy: the accelerator.

Then he felt her hand on his head. The scent of her body penetrated his ear. 'Do you know what, why don't we stop for a bit?'

The greenish light under the trees of the lay-by was composed of birdsong and rushing water. Unsteadily, now he had no intention of taking his arm away from her shoulder, they walked down a slope towards a stream. They sat down on a boulder. Afterwards he listened with the earnestness of a comrade to her story.

I had thought there would be some time left for her and me in the future. I mean, not visiting or writing to each other occasionally across the ocean, but being able to share some ordinary, everyday experiences again permanently. I meant the warmth of the sun, the cold in winter, the sound of the wind in the mulberry trees at night.

I had quite a lot of domestic chores in my mind, which if you take them absent-mindedly enough, are symbols – handling baking trays, saucepans and grills, jingling knives and forks, and clinking the glasses for the white Lubéron, spreading out the bed linen, flowers, a beautiful old or brand-new item of clothing – I had imagined conversations whose everyday subject would be an integral part of what we would by then know very well: that all these devotions are in fact something else, a sophisticated form of dialogue, a duet for two female voices, a set of responses on love and death.

I had thought that I would have been the obvious one, when the time came, to notice the first warning signs in her, the tiredness, she must have been ill for a long time, she did not want any examination or radiotherapy, at the end the tumour spread to her brain, I would have taken her to our old doctor, Desouches.

It seems that at that point, to her utter astonishment, she experienced whole excerpts from her life again, no, not as memories, actual events, in her nose, her mouth, so I was told, the disturbances in her brain made time into a fluid and backward-following medium. If you start thinking about all those faces, those gestures, those love scenes, those children's tears, those Sunday lunches, the sun, the fires, the firing, when the Russian soldiers left our house my father was already gone, already dead, but oddly enough they had left my mother alone, more than that,

I can remember the parting gift on the garden table. Half an oriental rug and a round loaf of bread, but I'm rambling on, she died in her sleep.

The little Catholic church has white limestone walls. About twenty people about whom I can remember nothing except that they wanted to pay their last respects to my mother, kept me company, there was a speech about God, the organ played and outside in the autumn sun a long black luxury car was waiting, she is buried in the cemetery at Gaspé.

In the days that followed I tried to understand why she had left nothing but utilitarian objects and why she had kept nothing, nothing at all from the past in her house. Last night, in the bed I slept in as a girl, I felt ill, the silence and the darkness merged: she took not only her own past but a large part of mine with her.

The woman's voice fell silent. With inexplicable reluctance he turned to look at her, but she remained staring straight ahead, and seemed to expect nothing special from him. He sat up, began scouring the ground, bent down, stood up to his full height and then thought in a flash, this woman will always keep something back from me! Then he made a scything motion with his arm. The pebble skimmed across the water in two or three bounds.

This happened at a time when I was beginning to come off worst in my trial of strength with the things around me. When my paint dried up, my brushes went hard and the fragile limewash on the walls of my studio began crumbling so that my canvases, which had become increasingly large, empty and colourless, were coated in a white layer of dust. Something had gone wrong. I needed only to look around me to realize. The mountains, the trees, the objects, the light: what self-confidence! What indifference to my principles! The view of the world that I was offered was no different from what any fool was presented with.

And, in some obscure way, the same thing happened with Magda. She no longer sat moping, that period was over, but the cigarette in the corner of her mouth and the devotion with which she bent over to bank up the fire in the hearth, all too often gave me the feeling that she was playing dumb. She got on with her life and incidentally kept the peace. Was it so strange that I should put her to the test a little now and then?

Friends are visiting. The table is laid with the best cutlery in the house. On the tablecloth are three bottles of Château Yzan and a vase of deep red pine branches. The twentieth of October 1973. Magda has received her guests with open arms, she serves, talks and laughs in such a way that everyone admires her and she reaches across the table for the pepper so that the sleeve of her old black sweater slips down over her fingers. Robert thrusts his head forward.

'Why do you dress like a scarecrow?'

She passes him the pepper mill.

'Would you like some?'

He puts his glass down, wipes his mouth, inquires politely if she is perhaps prepared to salvage this birthday party and then in an undertone prescribes the following clothes: your tight-fitting trousers which cling to your arse and have tapes around your calves: your black pumps, your low-cut blouse, your red earrings. I'll see you in a quarter of an hour . . .

She looks at him, completely relaxed.

'Darling, lover, why don't you put on *Sketches of Spain* for us?'

Robert, whose thirty-fifth birthday it is today, is wearing the beautiful bow tie with which his wife surprised him in bed that morning.

It is their custom after doing their weekend shopping to call in at the popular café Au Vieux Relais. Especially in summer they meet people they know there. Robert does not like the look of a young Englishman, his good-natured red face or the topics he is discussing with Magda in muted tones. Suddenly he sees her eyes wandering in unusual earnestness while the man continues looking at her from the side. But when Robert signals to her and suggests leaving, she crosses her legs. And while he expected it to occur to her too how at this time of day the sun is sinking behind the chestnut tree and the dog is stretching out in the courtyard, he can see that she is thinking: go on, go on, I'll finish my Campari and I'll have no trouble in getting a lift home!

Her indifference is more than insulting. If he has a headache she goes ahead and puts on the television because the match between Olympique Marseille and Lyon has started. If he comes into the house with bleeding fingers, she glances over her shoulder, asks what happened – the bloody chisel slipped – and says she hopes there is still a plaster somewhere to be found. He is worried about himself and starts making coffee, he knocks the milk over, spills sugar over the floor, she doesn't even bother to get angry but suggests driving to Combes, someone has promised her a kid goat. In bed he has few complaints any more, she kisses him, caresses him, allows him to drive her to ecstasy, sighing and smacking her lips, yet he can still remember the days when there was no question of water, soap, towels and God knows what else, afterwards. From underneath his arm he looks at what she is up to. The mythical creature is sitting in front of the mirror inspecting the surface of her face. He briefly gives approval to the sheen, the blush, the half-open mouth and the subtle significance with which it is all charged.

Then she stretches and yawns. Teeth, lines, tearful eyes and finally an appalling emptiness. You certainly know how to give something and then take it back again!

Chapter Eight

A man in his mid-thirties with a gaunt face. A man who has no trouble disposing of a consignment of inferior picture frames to a German company with its own contacts. A secretary manages to arrange for him to bump into her in the sauna. He is a persuasive businessman. One overcast day he sits opposite the importer of a shipment of English pianos. An instant before the contract is signed his blue eyes seem to reveal something to the other man which the latter has to his cost never thought of. But the deal has been struck, and a week later the load has found a home in Belgium. Robert, for the sake of appearances, is bound to invite a raven-haired woman to lunch. On his way back from Denmark, where both he and a collector of old coins have learnt a thing or two, a tall girl in a dark sports jacket walks up to his car at a petrol station. She opens the door, sinks into the seat and informs him that she has to be in Amsterdam by three o'clock that morning at the latest. 'Have you eaten?' asks Robert after they have been driving for half an hour and hears that the reticent, low-pitched, sanctimonious intonation of his voice is the same as many years ago in his first encounters with women.

When he and Magda settled in his birthplace in the summer of 1974, he wanted to draw a line under his previous life. He felt like doing things completely differently now, and when he thought of the last days in the Cévennes, he could not help laughing. Laughing at that feeling of impoverishment, deceit, that all-embracing feeling of loss, uncertain whether it was the cause or the result of the deterioration in his eyesight, of always having to look twice: Oh, there's my wife, Oh, the dog is eating, the car, the road, the beckoning ravine, and which looking back on it could very well have been a banal case of fear of death. The nervous problems, though, had quickly disappeared once Magda had finally given in. We are going north. From today we shall speak Dutch at home.

But one autumn evening he came home from a business meeting. He took a bath, listened to the gale blowing from the sea and a little later bent over Magda's sleeping face. She is my wife. After ten years of marriage, Robert resumed his affairs.

Small affairs. Over before they had really begun, and he never made the first move. But as long as it was not necessary to tolerate their noses in his business affairs, their eyes in his, their heads on his shoulder, he saw no reason to reject to the compliments of his girlfriends. Shortly before he decided to put things in order at his father's factory, the ailing company of Noort & Co., he bumped into Agnes Rombouts in a shoe shop. After that it was as if the organization of his double life and the deep satisfaction that its success brought him, released the purest, keenest business instincts in him, and without scruples he made a bid for his sister's shares.

'Ha!' Agnes Rombouts had once exclaimed at the beginning. 'You should have seen how my father could skin a rabbit by his sense of touch!'

But Robert studied his nails. He had no interest in his mistress's blind father, younger sister, favourite dog from child-hood, previous admirers, breathing exercises or real face. He sat at her table, thought absent-mindedly of her big, purple nipples and had no intention of investigating the secret behind her affection for him.

'Is something wrong?' she had asked.

'Of course not. Nothing.'

She was a stimulus, a scent that happened to waft past. She was a space between the houses, where occasionally, with a very small part of himself, he came for a breath of fresh air, too absent-minded to ask himself what on earth he was doing there, and then left miraculously complete, grown-up and broad-minded in the knowledge of having a home of his own, where he could sleep, eat and drink, and where his little triumph – she doesn't know a thing, not a thing – and the insignificant feeling of guilt (because was he doing her any wrong?), and the aroma of coffee with boiled and whipped milk was sufficient for him to forgive his wife her good humour, her study at a language institute, her first translation job, her women's afternoons with Nellie, her affection for the retarded Gaby and the letters she sent all over the world on his behalf. To forgive her all that including finally the naivety with which she trusted in his male faithfulness, because wasn't there all things considered, in her calm certainty that she was the only woman, the only love, the only all-embracing landscape, a touch of complacency? And he realized he was able for the first time in ages to enjoy simple things, from his shaver by the washbasin to his old shoes with their mended soles at the bottom of the stairs, and he even understood why there are people who believe that they have to live their lives precisely for these sorts of trivial things and hence confer on them an aura of sanctity. And hence at the end of a day full of meetings, after kissing the contented mouth of Magda who thinks our marriage has entered a pleasant, peaceful phase, he is able to pick up the paper, go into the garden and in the mild sea air, catch up on the latest news without giving a single thought to the compact of long ago, which had led, ultimately to this moment. In exchange for your present, your past and your future, Magda, I will offer you a love of which you have not even dreamed!

The two-lane road. The wind brushing his elbow. The Chic Choc mountains on his right are a spur of the six-hundred-million-year-old Appalachians. With eyes screwed up he was following the glittering St Lawrence on his left, which changed very gradually, kilometre after kilometre, from a river into an ocean. Beyond Matane the far bank could no longer be seen, the colour of the water became deeper, the lapping waves more languid. After having spent a year among the artists of New York, he was now – in June 1963 – driving north in a Ford sedan. He had lowered the hood of the convertible, a high wind was whistling over it.

The day before he had left Quebec City. He had crossed the

bridge, had followed the signs for Highway 20 East and within three hours had reached the little town of Rivière du Loup, where the four-lane freeway changed into the quiet 132 East (132 Est). In Rimouski he stayed in Motel Rimouski: a French-style meal, a conversation in French and a bed with a lace bedspread. He folded his hands behind his head. Listening to the sounds from outside, the lapping of the water, the call of a nocturnal bird, he thought of the arbitrariness of freedom, on an impulse he had decided to drive right round the Gaspé peninsula.

About fifty kilometres before Matane he had to choose. The road forks here, he could have turned left and driven across a treeless plain to the south coast of Gaspé. His loop around the peninsula would then have followed the opposite course and it is possible that in that case he would never have met Magda. Without a second thought he decided to go straight on.

There was something intoxicating about the winding road which climbed and descended and which indicated in a modest and confidential way that his destination was worthwhile, because just look at the collection of austere houses, the lampposts, the gates: people dragged out their days here, look at the bays, down below on the rocky coast: fishing boats and expertly spread nets, just imagine the life in the woods and sun-drenched mountains on the right: caribou, moose, bears, all in the wild. Sunk back in his leather seat, legs wide apart, eyes bright blue, he whistled through his teeth. The horizon, sometimes close and sometimes far away, made him feel giddy, but his driving remained impeccable.

A sandwich in Sainte-Anne-des-Monts, a glass of beer near Manche D'Epée, an hour or so's nap on the beach. When he raised his eyes he was looking at the face of a man, short, heavily built, who was standing grinning at him with rotten teeth. He paid no particular attention to the Indian. Not for a moment that day would he fall prey to astonishment, there was only enchantment. He was still about a hundred and forty kilometres from the town of Gaspé where he planned to stay for a few days.

Higher cliffs. An increasing expanse of ocean. Once in the

north he decided to take the route around the cape. He drove past the National Park, ignorant of the fact, of course, that only the day before, Magda, accompanied by a friend, had seen a black bear there. The animal was scratching about among the leaves, grabbed something, raised itself sniffing onto its hind legs, and disappeared into the trees with an indifferent gait – he would not hear that story until this evening.

Now he saw the lighthouse of Cap-des-Rosiers. He saw a boarding house with a red painted roof and a row of closed shutters on the first floor. His eye fell on the ground-floor rooms shielded from the sun by a red and white verandah, they looked out for as far as the eye could see, over the ocean, or nearer if one wished over a pier with globe lights and a wrought-iron roof, beneath which at that moment a honey-blond girl was sitting chatting with some guy or other, swinging one leg gently and holding a cold frosted glass against her cheek: Motel les Mouettes.

Almost blinded, he chose a ground-floor room, washed his hands, felt a raging thirst and walked with the uncertain step of the sailor on the point of drowning to the jetty at the water's edge, where with no prior warning he encountered Magda's mouth and two eyes. He sat down and ordered a beer.

She came in just after eight. He stood up, not surprised, he had not doubted for a moment that she would come. He had booked a table by the door to the terrace and had sat down with enough time in hand to drink a whisky, get used to the yellow lamplight and reject the flowers and have them replaced by fresh carnations which with their heavy midsummer night scent did very nicely.

'I expect you are starving, like me,' he said earnestly when they had both pulled up their chairs. And immediately afterwards, 'You should wear green, you know, the faded green colour of an old rabbit hutch.'

She read the menu, looked up and said as their eyes met in a covert kind of craziness, 'I'll start with *fruits de mer*.'

'You're having oysters,' he replied and when she burst out laughing, it was as though his heart beat twice as fast. A hint of anger swept through him.

He had quite simply asked her out this afternoon. When her boyfriend left for a moment he had seized the opportunity without hesitation.

With his shoulders pulled back he marched up to her.

'Have dinner with me tonight.'

The softness of her face had astounded him. He looked at the minute silvery white hairs on her cheek beside her ear. It was as though a tiny fire were glowing beneath the surface of her cheeks. Fine. Eight o'clock suited her too. Her eyes did not pretend to understand anything of what was happening. When her friend returned all three of them introduced themselves formally.

The food and drink arrived. With great sophistication, both of them set to work with shellfish, forks and lemon. People occupied the other tables and the monotonous grumbling and buzzing which began to cocoon them and the calm which that brought led him to become less formal.

'I like sitting here with you,' he muttered.

And she put down her glass and asked absent-mindedly, 'Where are you from?'

He gave some insignificant answers – Holland, New York, the Great Lakes – just enough to be able to turn the tables completely with an innocent voice. He looked at her heart-rending brown arms and wondered where to begin. Perhaps simply with the origin of her grandparents, with the story of her father, her mother, perhaps she was studying something, she rode, played the flute, maybe she had a favourite animal . . .

He said, 'I'd like to know what is going on between you and that boyfriend.'

She assumed an obedient expression. Oh, that. He listened. While his attention focused on the incidentals his eye fell on her fingers and crystal blue earrings. All quite innocent. Obviously she had no inhibitions. The boy was a sweetie, of Scottish origin, he

95

still had relations near Aberdeen, she was spending her vacation with him, no, not in this hotel, they were staying with her mother in Gaspé, they were both studying at the University of Quebec. Yes, you guessed it, French language and literature and yesterday, for example, they had made a nice trip through Fouillon Park, where they had seen a bear scratching about right in front of them, just imagine . . .

He interrupted her.

'How long?'

'What do you mean?'

'How long have you been with him.'

She had to think, then shrugged her shoulders, oh so long, ages, he saw her attention wandering. Delighted, he suddenly raised his arm, Garçon! and ignored the water that was pouring into his lap from the carafe he had knocked over.

Outside the window the last rays of the sun were gleaming. The occasional cigarette was lit up in the dining room. Suddenly, after coffee, he was incapable of uttering another word.

'What is that?'

When they had lapsed into silence he had asked for the bill. She seemed to wake with a start and announce that she was going home at once and she meant it. He had taken her arm and they had gone outside. Now they were standing on the jetty. He looked around, stiffened and pointed into the distance. The ocean in the moonlight. A green, glistening path. And a number of huge creatures moving around in it, turning, diving, flailing the water with their tails, rearing up dark grey and dropping back again, blowing fountains of mist and air at the moon. He turned to face her and asked for an explanation.

'Those are whales,' said Magda. She moved a few steps away from him.

'What kind of whales?' he cried. She scuttled away from him like a crab.

'Hard to see. They could be humpbacks. Yes, I think so. Just look at their clumsy bodies.' The humpbacks go north at this time of year.'

'There's my car,' he said with something like despair in his voice. 'A Ford sedan. The hood is down. I'll take you home.'

But before he knew what was happening, she had got into a bright red Cooper, had started up the damned thing, wound down the window and shouted something he could not understand. She drove off very fast.

'I'm not putting up with this!' he screamed into the night.

Dreadful days followed. He could not leave. He was stranded on a cape above the sea, above a pretty beach covered with lobsters, jellyfish and cockles, and behind sunglasses the faces of those who later in the day would shove him aside in the corridors of the hotel, on their way to the shower, jingling their keys, fretting about what muslin dresses, what pathetic T-shirts with buttons they would shortly wear, with shoulders slightly hunched and arms like those of hunted jackals, would rush into the room to have their banal passions serenaded and, if possible, inflamed a little further by a band with a clarinet and drums.

With a carafe of sparkling rosé inside him he was standing in a souvenir shop with a tropical shell in his hands when he saw Magda strolling past in espadrilles. Within a quarter of an hour he laid his hands against the sides of her breasts, moved the tips of his fingers over the surface of her shoulder blades, her neck, her lower jaw, the inside of her outstretched arms. Your body is what you are, I want to make you submerge completely in the springy flesh around your navel which if you ask me tastes of hazelnut, he pressed his mouth against the line of her stomach. My proposal is that you compress the whole of yourself, all your freedom into a few vital spots which I can then take possession of. He felt the hard bone under her pubic hair which had surprised him by being as thick and dark as a privet hedge. I love you, he said several times, in alarm. Later, when they had started talking again, it was as though the hotel room had been turned upside-down. Her espadrilles on the bedside table, her white blouse over the telephone, his holdall which had fallen over, his books and road maps.

He looked at her indignantly.

'The whales had gone the next morning!'

She laughed repeatedly and suggested going out and having fun.

Is it so strange to get so worked up about your lover's feelings? But precisely when he expected an explanation from her she turned her head aside and began hunting for cigarettes. She chattered non-stop, told him amusingly and in great detail about how the red Cooper and its owner had returned to Quebec, but only after long interrogation would she let slip that she maintained her opinion of the boy's eyes, the sweetness and bluest she had ever come across. He spied at her face and went pale. On one occasion she took him with her to Gaspé. She opened a garden gate, led the way to a conservatory and introduced him to her mother. A little later he had asked why her mother had stayed so young. So young, so sad, so fragile in her wicker chair. She did not answer but asked if he was coming with her to the harbour to buy some squid. Once they arrived they quarrelled and he left her standing there.

That night he called her up. Instead of making you laugh, I am tormenting you, he said meekly. She too, with a sleepy voice, was very nice to him. He had asked her what she had been thinking about at the moment he rang. But I was asleep, she protested. He hung up.

She came round. The next time she steered him into the garden and house where she grew up, she put a photo album on his lap. While her mother pruned the roses in the background and now and then flashed an emphatic smile at them, she supplied him with information, leaning on his shoulder. In this one I am eight, in this one I am ten, this is our dog, this is my mother and me on the beach, in this one I was ill, yes it was bad. She told him meekly about the hallucinations, the bed with bars around it and the

98

terrified eyes of her mother who had to wear a face mask when she came to visit her. I wanted her to stay away, her and everyone, I was really perfectly happy in the clammy mist.

In the afternoon they went scrambling over the rocks. Again he asked about her mother. Because he noticed that her back stiffened as soon as the subject of her mother came up, he asked about her. Magda talked rather haltingly because of the climbing. Her mother was German and in 1936 had been fortunate enough to marry the one great love of her life, a Czech engineer, a Jew. Eight years later she had not been able to protect him. She had not been able to hide him far enough away in their house in the Moravian hills with a mulberry tree and a swing in the courtyard, a dog, rabbits, chickens, an airfield close by. He translated the English radio bulletins for the partisans. One September morning the lorries, the jackboots and the black caps came and she never saw him again. Don't bother consoling me, said Magda before he could lift a finger. It's my mother's grief, not mine. Look, there's the sea.

But shortly afterwards he witnessed what was going on inside her unimpeded. She could not turn her face aside, not disguise her body language. She could not palm him off with something trivial, this time, because she was asleep, the trembling in her legs had woken him. At first he lay and listened. Then he opened his eyes, saw the moonlight streaming into the room and sat up in order to examine the face next to him gasping for breath. He knew what she was seeing. He knew the places where she was now wandering. A concrete corridor with a bend she could not see around. A courtyard where a regularly sweeping light never lit up one of the corners. The bend of a staircase which led to a room with a table and the back of an empty chair. She had told him. She had told him that it was she who had had to open the door that September morning. It is often like that: a cool-headed child opens the door, evokes a surge of distant innocence and gives the grown-ups deep in the house a little time to complete their secret business. Ever since Magda was pushed aside by the German soldiers she has wondered what exactly the result was of her pulling back the bolt on the door. She recalls her father's room and wants to know what he went through. He brushed her hair out of her face. He rubbed her temples very gently. Without waking her, he laid his hand on her skull. Now she is being reassured, consoled, a dream which you interrupt almost always comes back and the dragon has yet another ugly head. She rolled onto her side, her breathing became much calmer. He had sought her out in the place where she was and had talked her round, from this moment on she would cease her blind searching. He saw her face relax, she moved her hips and spread her legs. With a feeling of having fought a primitive, inhuman battle, he got up.

The cliffs began to the left of the hotel. In the moonlight he found his way without danger. The tide must be out. The surf was scarcely audible. Then he saw the cape with the lighthouse on it. Down below lay the bay. He went down and with each step felt the restlessness in his body mounting. A few metres above the beach he slipped. He jumped, landed on both feet and began racing along the seashore like a maniac.

Chapter Nine

He gets used to her absence. In the course of the second year he becomes used to living in a house, sleeping in a bed, to which she may return any moment but for the moment does not. A languidness has descended on him which borders on idiocy. On Saturday morning he goes round all the rooms with the vacuum cleaner, he shops and even – without any interest – buys flowers. Every day the three dogs are groomed, fed and taken for a walk by him. Why should her dresses and shoes in the wardrobe make him melancholy? She is not dead.

She is not dead. In the autumn of 1981 a letter is delivered to the institute for which she does translation work. In her beautiful spiky handwriting she informs them how sorry she is not to have completed her last job. Offers her excuses and sends her best regards, the letter was posted in Paris.

'No, no I wouldn't dream of it,' he says to his sister Hélène and smiles indulgently at her astonishment.

Erik and Nellie cannot understand either. 'Why not? Why not?'

He puts his elbows on the table and closes his eyes for a moment. 'If you like, I'll go with you,' he hears Erik saying.

What counter-arguments can I use, he thinks and reviews a few possibilities. That I am convinced that Magda is not or is not any longer in Paris. Surely they, Erik and Nellie, agree with me how stupid it would be to rush off and start wandering along the boulevards, not that it is not a nice city in autumn, the tourists are beginning to go home, the trees are still full of leaves everywhere, in the cafés famous regulars start debating with each other, as they have always done, but be honest, can you really see it? Magda at a table in the corner, with a glass of wine or a cappuccino, looking up and beaming when she sees us . . .

101

He gets up resolutely. Or shall I simply say what the heart of the matter is: I've become accustomed to the gnawing feeling of ignorance. Maybe this is my idea of calm. I have lost any need to act in this personal matter. I often walk along the beach. I often listen to the rain at night. If my wife haunts me at moments like these, then it is at most in the form of our Saturday breakfasts, with a clean white tablecloth, the aroma of coffee and bread and the warm limp weight of the dogs' bodies against our feet.

'You're very sweet, Nellie, sweet and beautiful, and thank you very much for the tea.'

Step by step he goes down the dune, in the rising ground mist, in the falling dusk, it must be about five o'clock. At the end of the path the wind catches the tails of his coat. In the violet blue light of the street lamps his figure has something of an old private detective who has been repeatedly sent up the wrong path, to the point of distraction.

The days become longer, when he enters the boardroom of Noort & Co. in the mornings, it is growing light outside the windows.

Though in the village his appearance may make a crumpled impression, in the factory he is sharp, lean, impeccably dressed in a shirt with cuffs which half cover his hand. The staff are used to his expertise. He wants to see the figures, the growth in sales, the state of the monthly budgets, the same man who previously with the help of delicate, limited material – canvas, paint – made an assault on the immensity of things, now wants to know exactly what is happening on the shop floor. For that matter, there have been no more redundancies for ages.

Both the mother company and the subsidiary, Alcom Ltd, are on an upward course. On the premises of Noort & Co. new buildings have sprung up. Thanks to the previous activities of Alcom, Robert Noort has been able to make a successful entry into the automobile industry. Now more than eighty plate workers enter and leave the factory gates every day.

At Alcom it was a close thing. What was to be the decisive

factor for the customers of the matrixes – a fast delivery time – threatened to fail completely: an indispensable part is not for sale in Europe. Zijderveldt travels to see his former employer in Pennsylvania and signs a contract which is beneficial to both sides and on his return places a small metal object made of an unusually hard alloy on Robert's desk. With their hands behind their backs the two men study the precise form and the deep blue steely glint. Robert says, 'Mr Zijderveldt, we are going to produce that thing ourselves.' And, sure enough, they are able to come to an agreement with the American manufacturer. The subsidiary activities of Alcom soon turn out to be thriving surprisingly well.

He becomes more reclusive every day. In his time off he sits at home. Rather than summoning up Magda's face, he watches television. Sometimes, when there is a gale blowing, he walks along the beach with the old dog to the mouth of Rhine at Katwijk and back again. He is only prepared to go out occasionally in the evenings on company business. However, one day he accepts a new invitation from Zijderveldt, he doesn't know why, while he really wants to refuse, he finds himself accepting quite eagerly.

In an extravagant Chevrolet with mother-of-pearl blue fins his friend drives him along the back of the dunes to Wassenaar, where a twelve-man saxophone orchestra is performing in a villa hidden among the trees – Zijderveldt belongs to a club. Enthusiastic drinking, enthusiastic talking with Tom, Dick and Harry and the dazed question where on earth he remembers this music from: the orchestra is playing arrangements of nineteenth-century scores.

At the end of the evening they say a touching farewell. In the middle of the Oude Zeestraat, while the eight cylinders are purring gently and both doors are open they shake hands and slap each other on the shoulders.

'Look after yourself, old chap.'

'I'll be OK, mind how you go.'

When Robert stumbles into the house, his sole wish is to hang onto this dull, fragile drowsiness.

Everything comes to an end. The rift with Agnes happens by

itself. For some time the red-haired shoe saleswoman has left him cold, but if he stays away too long she rings his office, the secretary knows her voice, puts her through and he agrees to come. What interest does she have in all this nonsense? He looks at her dimly lit living room, the sofa, the cushions, the ominously large television set.

'How you must have been in love with me, when you were a boy,' she says on one occasion, 'and what a lot of years have gone by before I was able to get any enjoyment out of it.'

The scent of her perfume wafts towards him. She sits at table like a stone, defended by her hunched shoulders, her arms, her thick loose hair. He doesn't answer and thinks: What she says about being in love is probably right, it's just that I can't remember a thing about it. Nor can I remember the few pitiful things which I wanted to give you instead of it. Your monotonous voice and the lines around your eyes mean nothing, nothing at all to me any more. She looks up and asks what he is thinking about. 'About Magda,' he says and begins a story which as the evening goes on becomes more elaborate and more confidential.

'If you don't go now, you'll be too drunk even to hold onto your steering wheel.'

She accompanies him to the hallway, gives him a friendly pat on the arm and says 'So long' to his back.

Old friends. Confidences and confrontations from his earliest childhood. An invitation, no, a summons to Sunday lunch. The lady of the house has always been a bit in awe of you. The master of the house too. He climbs the stairs, hands Nellie a few branches of broom from his own garden and takes a glass of whisky from Erik. In the front room the son Gaby is sitting reading and pays no attention. Robert feels empty and bored, but when Erik no longer avoids his glaze after two glasses, begins conversing animatedly. Topics include the warm weather for May, the removal of the eye clinic, the music of Bach, the aesthetics of dreams, the Cabbala, which maintains that letters preceded words, the collection of poetry *The Face of the Eye* and the brains of whales. Erik has

104

read that even in relative terms the bottlenose dolphin has a larger brain than man.

'It is no doubt more intelligent,' says Robert. 'I wonder, I wonder,' says Erik. 'What about their science? What about their *Mona Lisa*?' At this Robert assumes a passionate expression, pretending that the question interests him, and feels like saying the following. The highly developed culture of whales cannot be observed by us, because the logic of their minds is of a completely different order to that of ours. All we can say is that the culture of the whale, unlike that of man, is not focused on making things. If you agree with the view of Paul Valéry, that the work of art is only an interruption in the creative process, then it makes me think that the whale does not consider interruptions in tangible form at all necessary.

They exchange friendly grins. When Erik leaps up to take a heavy tray from his wife, Robert also gets up. He wanders into the front room, pulls up a chair opposite Gaby and asks, 'Do you still get so much mail?' The young man does not react. From close by Robert studies the face with its small, dull eyes which seem to be fixed in their sockets, which have scarcely any white around the iris, which seem to be able to turn only with difficulty.

'Oh yes!' says Nellie, moving past with flowers and glasses in her hands. 'He gets astronomical maps from Paris, Potsdam, Harvard. Two weeks ago the Quebec radio telescope sent him a nice prospectus.'

'Can I see what you're reading?' whispers Robert a little later with a lump in his throat. Because now Gaby has opened a page in his file with on the left a black-and-white photo showing spheres, nebulae and dots, and on the right the page of a notebook stuck to it covered in handwriting, the firm, spiky handwriting of Magda.

It is strange, when the ring-binder is handed to him, when he sees the astronomical photo from the *New Scientist* and reads the English caption and prefers to avoid the note on the right, it is the strange haunting voice of Gaby which gives him the feeling that Magda may drop in at any moment, apologizing for being late, but, thank heavens, not too late for a meal with friends. Without faltering once, as though all he had to do was to read off the text from the inside of his eyes, Gaby says, 'Eta Carinae is as far as is known the brightest star in our galaxy. The intensity of its light is probably ten million times as great as that of the sun. Its mass is approximately a hundred times the mass of the sun. The star is seven thousand light years away from us and is located in the extensive Carina nebula. Its surface temperature is twenty-nine thousand K. Two neighbours of Eta Carinae, the stars HD 93129A and HD 93250, have surface temperatures of no less than fifty-two thousand . . .'

'Are you two coming?' says Nellie's voice, rather urgently.

In the week preceding Magda's return he sleeps restlessly and dreams furiously. On Monday he starts awake just before sunrise, he looks at his opened fists in the morning light and dives back under the covers in order to cry. Yet he remembers a dream full of light and warmth with a Magda running through a fiery red field of tulips, and a dog behind her. When she stops at the edge of a ditch, she calls something. Her face becomes big, cheerful and rounded like on a photo which is taken too close. The moment that he wakes up this all changes in a flash to helplessness.

A few nights later he imagines the deathbed of Madame. His affection for her is great. She doesn't mind getting up from her damask sheets, putting on her coat and accompanying him on a walk through the town, she is wearing a white summer hat with white ostrich feathers. However, this lady, who is greeted with respect by all the passers-by, arouses his irritation because of her obstinate cheerfulness, she says, 'I fell asleep counting the stars,' and bursts out laughing. He sees that it is a laugh like that of a bird, so that it looks for all the world as if the two of them are on their way to some ·spring fair. 'Stop laughing,' he says, 'that's something from the past. Now that you are dead you must cry.' She raises her face towards him, and obediently covers her mouth and eyes with her hands. But he is not fooled: between her outstretched fingers he can see how she has to bite her lips to suppress her amusement. 'Then I shall take you back to your deathbed,' he says calmly. With knee-length stockings around her ankles she follows him like a ten-year-old daughter, stifling her giggles.

On Friday, in the early evening, as he drives into the Oude Zeestraat and sees his house where the road curves, he notices that the faded red striped blinds have been let down. The attic window has been thrown open. In the front garden a sprinkler is describing a transparent figure of eight over the roses. She is home.

He parks his car in the drive, gets out and bends down to stroke the Pekinese, which have charged out of the house to meet him. It has been very warm the whole day, suddenly he feels the patches of damp on his shirt. Calm. Calm down now, boys. He scratches the fur of their heads, under their mouths, between their paws, until the creatures, more impatient than he is, leap away from him again. The next moment he is on the threshold of the kitchen. There is Magda.

She says, 'What do you think, shall we eat outside even though it is full of wasps?'

She is standing by the sink washing her hands. She smiles at him over her shoulder. She comes towards him wafting garlic and roast meat.

He does not panic. He recognizes the green shantung dress and sees that his wife has not grown one centimetre thinner or fatter. Her hair too, blond as that of a Scandinavian fjord horse, seems very familiar, it falls over her shoulders as it used to. Yes, he sees, everything is perfectly normal, her bare arms, her bare legs, the faded espadrilles which I expect she dusted off when she fished them out of the wardrobe today. There is a time to go and a time to come. I am being told, in this special case of rebellion, that it would be better if I can think of two moments in time as juxtaposed. The contented expression on her face, the chaos in her kitchen and even her dog lying panting in its usual place like an old black rag, are trying to fool me into believing that nothing at all has happened to Magda in the last two years.

He returns her kiss. 'As you like, as you like,' he says. For a moment their eyes meet rather restlessly, it is possible that they will now cry, squeal, wail: circling around the truth. 'But I'll take a quick shower first.'

With the eyes of someone who is slightly off his head, he looks at himself in the bathroom mirror. Nowhere has he been able to discover a case, nowhere an airline ticket, a railway stub or a postcard showing the lounge of a hotel. A journey that has left no trace, which has vanished like a dream, ethereal, idiotic and chaotic, without bearing even the most pathetic witness to anyone at all.

At first the situation reassures him. Magda is back – unchanged – and everything resumes its usual routine. On the roll-top bureau in the side room there are again piles of dictionaries and reference works. When he comes home a little earlier than usual he can see her sitting at the window, smoking and thinking, with a cup of tea within reach. Sometimes the telephone rings and she has an animated conversation. Who rang, he asks a little later. Tomorrow morning all the gas appliances in the house are going to be checked; the geyser in the bathroom, the geyser in the kitchen and the small stove, she explains earnestly. He nods and his thoughts have already wandered off, distracted as he is by the taste in his mouth, which has recently been troubling him at the most unexpected moments. It is a persistent, slimy feeling, maybe thirst, maybe fear, which begins at the side of his jaw, and spreads over the whole of his palate and mouth on its way to his throat, and nose, and which often can only be stopped with a swig of whisky direct from the bottle.

It is lively enough again at home. People ring at the door. Here is your clean washing. Here are the heather plants for your garden. Good morning, I represent the Organization for the Propagation of Faith. He can't quite understand why the tradesmen and the people in the village – initially – are so friendly to them. It is disturbing. Isn't everything normal? It is a normal fine summer and often they swim in the sea in the early mornings. Come on, says Magda, emerging from the water next to him, you are going to have a raw herring for breakfast. At the stall on the promenade he gapes at her the way that you look at a bear at the fair. The salt water has turned her eyelids, lips and nails luminous pink. Is that by any chance a reason for the fishmonger to make her a present of a gherkin with mustard? And what does it mean when, after they have bought lobsters and brightly coloured flowers in the market, he is tapped on the arm? The lady goatkeeper offers him a pure white, home-made cheese. When the dirty, senile old woman points significantly to the dill leaves on top and then – with her hand and elbow – makes an obscene gesture, all he can do is to thank her with a bow.

They enter autumn, winter. Now when he enters a shop with Magda, conversations about the strangely calm weather begin to falter, people no longer talk about the temperature which has not been so high for years and which means that a lukewarm mist is drifting into the village from both the sea and the land, a mist which, mixed with traces of salt, dung and earth, is attacking the outside of houses and is penetrating them mercilessly, causing algae to grow in the cellars, no one likes it.

Secretly he is astonished at Magda. She seems completely untroubled. She lies asleep while he, with eyes open, tries to regulate his breathing. It's always useful to think of Noort & Co., anyone who has the gift of managing such a company with so cool a head must be capable of keeping his muscles relaxed at night, in the clammy darkness. Imagining the river, the quays, the lorries and the infernal noise and fire would not be such a feat, if only he could manage to leave the mystery inside him alone: this sleeping creature beside you, who smokes a different brand of cigarettes, who sits in the evening dusk without looking at anything in particular, who has more energy in bed, from where precisely do you get the impression that this is not, definitely not the person whom you once knew intimately?

In February it suddenly turns cold. The village gives a sigh of relief and sprays a layer of water over the tennis courts of the Casino. But he, Robert, goes on a business trip to Algiers, conducts his negotiations in the heat and is back home when the bulb season begins, earlier and sunnier than ever. The village is inundated with tourists. They walk in procession through the fields and throng the streets round the church with their arms full of flowers. Shortly after Easter the sea is already so warm that the duck-boarding is put out in front of the beach restaurants. But an offshore wind attracts monstrous quantities of jellyfish towards the coast for weeks on end. When Robert drives down the Astrid-boulevard at the end of the day, he sees the swimmers sitting on the beach and looking in astonishment at the blue translucent creatures.

Like many others he is completely exhausted by the end of the summer. When he and Magda are sitting outside one evening with a couple of old friends, he finds the visit a burden. He has to make a great effort not simply to say nothing in reply to a remark of Erik's. What he would most like to do would be to keep out of every conversation, avoid all company now the heat still refuses to subside and his attention in the false mixture of moonlight and neon light, with the buzzing of gnats around his ears, cannot possibly focus on anything except facing the question which now besieges him day and night, which is like a fist in his chest and from there takes over everything that he hears and sees, the garden smelling of decay, the dogs gasping for breath under his chair, the harassed faces of Erik and Nellie and the cool gestures of Magda. He puts out his hand: she gives him a glass of whisky on the rocks. He takes a swig, nods as if he agrees with an argument put forward by Erik and pulls a face. Isn't it in fact ridiculous, this crawling over the floor, this whining like a dog, this wringing of hands in order to suppress a question which people ask each other on many occasions and receive a perfectly ordinary reply to – oh, well, to the hairdresser's, in the street, to the cinema – but whose four clear, precisely delineated words in this case, in the case of Magda who has disappeared off the face of the earth for two years, do not constitute a question, but an ambush, an abyss, a poisoned arrow, which held against the bow with the string at full stretch, is finally, with the power of a charging horse, released . . . 'Where have you been?'

PART THREE

Chapter One

Ha! Even when I was already in the bus to Leiden, I did not know exactly where I was going. That may seem strange, for all I know, but if anything left me cold that day, it was the difference between strange and not strange, an attitude which has been my credo ever since. All right. I got on the bus at the start of the route, the roundabout in the dunes. I said to the good-looking driver with a moustache, 'A single to the Hartebrugkerk,' after which I installed myself by the window, pleased to be the only passenger. I had no sooner unbuttoned my coat than the doors closed. The engine roared. Despite the ear-splitting noise I must have fallen asleep, because I can remember nothing of the first part of the journey, the route along the Astridboulevard, all I remember is the horse I was dreaming of at the moment when the bus braked unexpectedly: a mare with friendly black eyes. We were stationary for a minute or two. Because for some obscure reason waking up was quite difficult, I made no attempt to find out what was going on. And anyway the wheels began turning again. Having come to my senses I looked out of the window.

There, at the edge of a greyish brown plateau, lay the village where I had lived for years, I was still close to home. To the light clear world of water tower and bunkers, to the sand from the dunes which piles up against the pavements, to the row of fishermen on the promenade which is photographed by the tourists every year. If I tried, I could still hear my footsteps along the streets, resonating, booming like a platoon of soldiers, what a lot of walking you do in your earthly life. Especially when it was raining I liked looking at the houses. My favourites were the ugly gloomy house fronts, which prompted me to imagine the smell of the hallways hidden behind their walls, the staircase, the granite bathrooms, the bedrooms with dark wallpaper and meanwhile to shiver: If I had to, Robert, I really could stand it here together with you!

I didn't know whether I had left him. I sat in the rocking bus, saw the village and the dunes disappearing out of the corner of my eye and didn't know if I had left my husband. How could that have happened? Someone who has cherished the same love year in, year out, will discover sooner or later that they never get into a lift or a train alone, never look at a flower or a summer sky without being shadowed, never listen closely to what a friend is saying without feeling that somewhere, in the dark, your hand is being squeezed, no, I didn't know. All I knew was that I had woken up that morning with the fixed intention of packing my bags.

Let me put my red dress on, I thought when I opened the curtains, let me see if I can find my apricot petticoats, those things may have fallen into disuse, but they are exactly what you need for a damp spring day like this, and I bent over the windowsill to close the window which had been open during the night. For a moment I saw reflected in the glass a woman's face, eyes sleepy, the mouth giving a chilly smile. That's you, Magda, who in a life of sunlight and warmth have experienced a number of extraordinary moments, but who now, on the point of leaving, are astonished how little there is to say goodbye to. I turned and began making the bed, a simple chore, because during the nights when Robert was away I usually lay dead still between the sheets. Don't let me forget to drop by the bank later, I thought under the hot shower.

Ten past nine. A bit late for the dogs. When I came down with wet hair, the three dogs were waiting for me at the bottom of the stairs, I threw open the back door and they charged outside. For a moment I stood on the threshold. I had had the biggest hand in the deep greenery, in the flowers, in the newly mown grass of the garden. It's a dreadful job fighting the sea wind in this village, everyone complains about it and many people finally give in: all right then we'll have shells, tulips, pots of begonias which go into the shed in the winter! I looked at the bed next to the drive. Thanks to Robert's mother's beech hedge my phlox and dahlias would come halfway up it in August . . .

This was also her kitchen, her fireplace, her red and yellow tiled floor. I opened the larder and in a primeval smell of beans, lard and unbolted flour, grabbed the bag of dog food and the bread. When I became mistress of the house here years ago, I had no objection to continuing the grasping and finicky gestures of my mother-in-law, not at all. I can still remember the cheerful occult mood of those days, walking up the staircases, clearing out the chests-of-drawers, everything gave me the feeling of having found my way into something old and enduring.

'Where are you!' called Robert when he came home unexpectedly. He had no sooner said this than my voice came from under the floor, 'I'm coming!' and the trap door at his feet opened and I appeared, covered in dust and cobwebs, smelling of a batch of star apples which had disappeared years ago. 'Oh . . . Robert! What a lovely day, what sunshine! It is as though summer is coming again!'

There was sniffing behind me. The dogs had returned from the soaking wet garden, they were hungry. I stepped aside in order to avoid the Pekinese who were jumping up at me. Anatole was well behaved, the Bouvier sat staring at me in complete confidence by the kitchen door. Should I, now I have the chance, spoil them thoroughly for once? I have cut up the heart, boiled the milk and mixed maize and vegetables. Anatole has much better table manners than a human being. He takes careful mouthfuls with his lips, shakes his head slightly, chews a few times with his mouth wide open and makes a movement with his neck. Swallowed, gone. His bowl is empty in a moment. He licks his nose and grey-black hair clean at length. I knelt by him and began stroking his back, in reply he wagged his tail a little and glanced at me understandingly. This creature knew me, it knew me through and through. What did the chaos between me and my extraordinary smell matter to him?

Now it was time to have breakfast myself and then to pack a few trifles in a bag. By the hallstand, with my coat already on, I

115

became confused for a moment. Oh God! What a strange light there is in the hall, what a glow the wooden panelling gives off. A dream house, a dream life, can't I at least try to capture this moment, this lucid, cool amazement? Then there were footsteps outside. A pile of post was pushed forcibly through the letter box. A fan of unknown communications lay on the mat. I turned on my heel. Come on, I thought, let me take the dogs to Nellie's.

A woman's hand with a sapphire ring on one of the fingers. A body which moves so lightly that its weight is above suspicion. She put a beautiful coffee cup in front of me and sat down across a table. Of course I was quite aware that she was peering at me a bit.

'Why, yes, of course,' said Nellie. 'How long for?'

I shrugged my shoulders.

'I'm not quite sure. Robert will be back in a few days and he'll collect the animals from you.'

'What are you going to do?' she asked.

I replied, 'Visit the family.' And because she kept looking at me, I added in a mumble, 'Hélène. Mother . . . I'll see.' My eyes glided over the biscuits, the roses . . . She pushed a crystal ashtray towards me.

Lost in thought I pulled on my cigarette. When the wind which was blowing against the windows dropped, you could hear the ticking of the clock. Why was it so necessary for me to be talkative? I've known Nellie for sixteen years, that makes us friends, doesn't it? Friendship for her warm house, her arid garden, for the bottled mussels that she serves at her parties, for the husband that she twists round her countrywoman's fingers, for the sensual effect of her bracelets and the porcelain in the shop where she walks among the showcases in a black two-piece suit, for the son who is supposed to be mentally retarded. I feel friendship for the imagination with which she is able to arrange all this into a daily life. But why have we never lain crying on each other's beds, from time to time? We really had reason enough to.

116

She asked, 'Why are you sitting there grinning like that?'

'Was I grinning?'

'You were grinning like a fruit-machine gambler who's hit the jackpot.'

'Give me some more coffee.'

'Of course.'

As soon as she was sitting down again, I said, 'I can't help thinking of the time when we first met. Do you remember?'

'Robert brought you over to introduce you. The twenty-second of January 1964.'

'There was a language barrier . . .' I stuttered, taken aback by the two things which she immediately mentioned on impulse. My husband. The eve of the birth of her son. 'We couldn't say a word to each other . . .'

She laughed a little and turned her head away. And of course, as though that had mattered! As though that was necessary! We didn't need to say anything to each other that evening. What we had to say was outside us. In quite obvious signs, the way that the weather, wars or natural catastrophes are. It was clear from the beginning what course our friendship would take. The enthusiasm, the restlessness, the hunger of a man who is used to saying: come to me. The elusive gaze of a child that thinks: leave me alone. At their intersection our friendship. I stretched my legs under the table and was about to say: how is Gaby, when the door opened and the boy, he was sixteen at the time, came in.

'Magda?' he said to the rainy sky behind my head. He laid an open magazine in front of me. *New Scientist*, volume ten. Then Nellie gave me a note pad and I began translating – the mystery of Eta Carinae . . . – and I knew that my writing hand, my pen and the pointed words which flowed from it, contained my whole name and person for the boy who stood bending over me sniffing and sighing.

'There you are,' I said in a friendly voice.

When he had left the room again, Nellie walked to the window. I looked at her back. She stood very still and said nothing. Now and then there was a gust of wind. Then the windows rattled in their frames. The curtains on either side puffed up and sank back again. Sometimes I could hear the wind in the distance, rising and subsiding, and still further, whistling gently, reminding me that there was world out there full of mountains and seas, churches and boats and of creatures to whom I owed nothing. Circumstances meant that I was free to go.

She turned round.

'Well I'll be damned if you aren't sitting there smirking again!'

Suddenly in a hurry, I pushed back my chair and got up.

'Do you know what time the buses leave?'

'Yes,' she said. 'They leave every hour from the terminus.'

You have decided to go on a journey. You have got into a vehicle, you have unbuttoned your coat and sat back in a seat with your knees relaxed. Even after the first few metres you are a long way away from the ordinary world. Now you see everything growing smaller, the view becomes wider. One plane disappears to make way for the next. Bulb fields turn into greenhouses. The water tower: the P. de Jongh and Son cattle-feed factory. The crossing by the traffic lights features a woman on a poisonous green bicycle. She is carrying a child on the handlebars and a dog on the luggage rack, as soon as the bus pulls away all this changes into a man with a walking stick. Ah! That rocking of public transport which is taking you heavens knows where!

Of course I hadn't been alone for quite some time. At the end of the Oude Zeestraat the driver had let on a whole group of passengers, including a fat schoolboy, a fisherman's wife and a man whom I considered slightly simple because in passing he confided to me, 'Didn't sleep a wink last night!' This pattern continued. As we approached Rijnsburg I was next to two farmers who were independently making calculations with blunt pencils, from which they kept looking up and saying to each other, 'Right?' and, 'Right!', a husband and wife who had put their heads together to fillet a huge mackerel on a piece of grey paper, and two young women who carried on a conversation behind my back the confidentiality of which was doubtless inspired by the warmth of the speeding bus.

'What could I do?' asked one voice. 'I took off my stockings and crawled into bed with him. He immediately put his head on my tummy and that was enough for me. Wife! A little boy who could already draw so well! The next morning I didn't say a word about it. While he was paying the bill at the counter I ran out of the hotel and waved down a taxi.'

'Tut! Tut!' said the other, consoling or impressed.

In the suburbs of Leiden a woman got in, a shabby type of about sixty, who after she had paid immediately focused on the empty place next to me. 'Come on, dear,' I said softly. As soon as she was seated, she bent forward in order to dig up one of the purchases from her bag, giving me a particular kind of glance: yes you can look too . . . We looked at a brand new photo frame, with the price still on it, two guilders fifty and not a cent more, and at the photo which miraculously fitted the glass to the millimetre.

'As though it were made for it,' I said helpfully.

'Yes.' She nodded. 'I had taken the photo to the shop just to be on the safe side.'

A blurred snap, taken with one of those cheap automatic cameras, of two cheap people in their cheap living room. She and her husband. He is wearing a hand-knitted pullover and a nice shirt but how thin, the face grinning from ear to ear which he is burying in her neck is so thin. In the background: a vase of roses, a candlestick and bowl of apples on a tasteless sideboard.

'It's three months now,' she said and began telling me the whole tragedy, from the first doubts, there was nothing wrong, to his shame a few months later, I've turned into a skinny old man, to that last grey afternoon, when his grimace and crooked smile kept making her turn away to what, if she was honest, she remembered most clearly from that afternoon: the washbasin, the towel-holder with the light green towels and the limply hanging curtain.

Voices, smells, the proof of a love which would find its way to a place next to a vase of flowers in a frame. There must have been a sympathetic and at the same time cheerful expression on my face. That was all right by me. I may have awakened from my favourite dream, these small fragments of alien life certainly played upon my passions just as effectively. Not being the mistress of the house any more, not being a faithful wife, not being an old friend, fine, you can certainly be a more relaxed. Meanwhile we'd reached a town. I remember looking at the rainy sky breaking open above the houses and thinking: well now, it's a long time since you felt so sensible and noble!

Now I had gone on a journey myself, I understood the tourists peering through their lenses on the Astridboulevard. What you are looking for is a flat, untouched world. Set the timer, set the distance, and the background remains background. I felt the arm of my travelling companion on mine. Around us hung a smell of soft green soap. Why should I know who she was, outside this moment? Like savages and the dead, travellers pay no attention to past or future, we couldn't care less about the lessons of history, laugh with me, eat with me, that will link you to those things too! We'll see each other again, won't we? Yes, yes, of course, tomorrow, the day after tomorrow, never . . . The row of fishermen on the promenade. Behind the impassive faces: bursts of anger, bragging, stubbornness. You brush respectfully past them and deftly interweave looking and knowing . . . Tears formed high up in my nose. I saw how my travelling companion was sitting knitting a sweater in great haste, soon it would be too late. Would I be able to feel more for a blood relation than for her, sitting next to me in a wine-red coat with worn-out seams at the shoulder?

The bus began slowing down for the Hartebrug stop, we both got out. While we stood swaying to and fro at the exit, she asked, 'Where are you going to? and I replied, 'To my mother-in-law's.' Whereupon a calm, cheerful, mocking smile appeared on our faces. The doors folded open. In the drizzle we separated without saying goodbye.

Chapter Two

I was very quick. With my ticket in my hand I ran up the granite steps, platform five, platform five? Yes! I had been told and, sure enough, the grey-green express appeared before me, I felt rather than saw that it was already slowly moving off, gliding out of the station, this was the train I had to catch: in the open door of the luggage compartment there were two dark men with moustaches who grabbed my arms and helpfully smuggled me aboard, had you ever run faster in your life? A hand pulled back the dividing door for me and I sank into a soft red plush seat, second class, smoker. Ah! Ah!

Breathlessness. How comical this is, how delicately we are tuned, we plants and animals, a difference of a degree, a molecule too few and we become extinct. But never at once. Before it gets to that point, there is the slight lack of oxygen, the slight intoxication which is so illuminating, so stimulating. When I think of how I lay back there, in that compartment, chest heaving, hair loose, eyes which in spite of all the fuss absorbed the view, which was certainly well worth looking at, I really have to laugh. As we emerged from the station the friendly cows, the friendly sheep were immediately there in the polder landscape which through my marriage had become part of me. Five o'clock in the afternoon. Pollarded willows. Ditches with a light orange film on their surface. A shame that soon the face of my mother-in-law loomed up behind all this, heavy and pale, with which she had opened the door a fraction to me that afternoon, the old woman did not like unexpected visits and she knew that I knew.

'. . . Oh . . . Magda, how nice, how nice, well, all right, what brings you here . . .'

She had led the way into the kitchen, where without a word she began filling her whistling kettle. She was wearing her

121

cashmere dress and gold jewellery, but she no longer at all resembled the woman I had looked up to for years, but was like a robust, iron-constitutioned old lady whose appetite has something frightening about it.

I am going on a trip, I thought while I pushed a cup of dark red tea towards her across the table. I am going on a journey and saying goodbye to Mrs Noort's very thoughtful daughter-in-law. To the Monday morning telephone calls, the white bouquets on special days and anniversaries of deaths, and to the instruction: 'Two glasses of fruit brandy, Robert, before we sit down to eat, just look at how it makes her eyes shine!' Could anyone explain to me how this young woman had got to the point of investing so much of her gentleness, her affectionate nature in someone who did not love her?

Stormy love affair with the son. A prey to a troublesome, insistent desire that takes away your certainty and your breath. The grimaces in front of the mirror, sticking your tongue out, puffing up your cheeks, sobs, laughs, staring at the heels of your red shoes and at the lather on your soapy tummy, you were completely lost, my girl. French Canada. The boiling hot summer of '63. When I met him I was a student weighing twenty-five kilos with nails bitten down to the quick and a lover called Terence. He had been blessed by nature with the forehead, the nose and the sky-blue eyes of an angel, a male creature who felt well enough disposed to you to pull you away from the edge of the ditch, for your own sake, and then to take your head in both hands to let you look at the stars . . . 'What are you thinking about,' he whispered at night, in the tangled bed in the moonlight. 'You!' I invariably whispered back. Is it possible to be congenitally in love?

In 1938, the year that my mother was pregnant, Czechoslovakia was already beginning to disintegrate, but the country was not yet occupied. In the south of Moravia the summer lasted far into October. I picture my mother walking quite calmly there in the hills between the whitewashed walls of her houses surprised at the intense heaviness of her body. And in the early evening, under the violet blue of the sky, she stood looking at her husband – he is dragging the newly pruned branches of the ten-metre-high white mulberry tree into the lee of the south wall – she looks with absorption at the way he moves, how he is dressed. Old linen trousers? An ivory-coloured shirt? In any case I remember the eyes, deep black, where something irresistibly cheerful smouldered. I was a love child. My mother's love was in my blood.

Have I ever been free of it? No, not as far as I recall, never in my life. Not even when I go back so far that I find myself as a toddler, somewhere along the sweltering street in my native village, I am eating a peach and, war or no war, I have a little circus parade pass me, ghostly creatures are carrying musical instruments, they are clashing and beating, animals with plumes on their heads leave their droppings behind, until I have found him, there at the very end, a barefoot boy lost in dreams who is carrying nothing with him but his own warmth, his shirt and his trousers . . . 'Did you see that horse?' cries my mother as the uproar disappears over the bridge and she doesn't notice that I sigh hesitatingly and only much later say, 'He had an armband on . . .'

And then, on the other side of the ocean, there were others, again and again, I can recall them easily giving me those little signs, familiar and strange like stars above a wet shopping street, that it would be good to look round, walk slower, to wait a moment despite the cold . . . The teacher who beats time for the class in her angora sweater, the boy who cycles past with a cigarette-end in his lips, the tall, dark, handsome father of a girlfriend and the first boyfriend, the first man who, when I was thirteen, had the idea of showing me something interesting in his room. 'Well?' he ordered, after opening his white trousers. Whereupon I, with a brand new feeling, replied, 'I really think it's stupendous,' and went to the mirror to brush my hair.

Oh, my premarital loves! That squabbling, that looking at birds against inky blue skies, the physical complications and that record of Aznavour on the gramophone . . . *Je ne ferai pas mes adieux* . . ., none of it was unpleasant but gradually it ceased to excite me. Certain loving urges were quite simply innate to me. Yet looking back it seemed incredible: just at the time when I had a nice boy to eat and sleep with, a loving boyfriend who made me burst out laughing often enough, called me 'rabbit' and once took me to the café-billard Mon Plaisir in a lorry full of apples, just that summer, I mean, that I should have given my whole, free, mysterious life like a pack of cards into the hands of one single man, a Dutchman with a head of sun-bleached hair. Please, you open the bidding, you lead, what do you think of my pictures and signs? Not bad, are they?

A lustrous summer went by, full of gleaming. At the beginning of autumn he proclaimed, 'All real painters come from Europe.' I nodded and looked outside. My mother was crouching at the foot of the magnolia, her hands full of peat.

I sat there like a ghost. I smiled, crossed my legs and drank tea in a little drawing room where I did not belong. Opposite me an old woman was trying to command me with her eyes, her cup was empty. Did she have to *ask* me to take hold of it? And while my hand glided towards her, the rest of me was going round the room, from one piece of furniture to another, the plants, the knick-knacks, there were the colour photographs of the children and grand-children, her violent love, her expansion, framed and hung next to a clock with weights swinging to and fro. There were no sons – or daughters-in-law, one had been dismissed for bad behaviour, the other had not given life to anyone. At the window I laid my cheek against the glass for a moment. Cool, smooth, the faint smell of methylated spirits attached itself pleasantly to the seagulls and lampposts outside, was it going to rain, no, I don't think so.

'Shall I take your cup?'

And I sank down to make a little more conversation with this woman, the mother whose nesting instinct had long since faded. I said, 'I dropped by to see Hélène this afternoon too.'

She nodded absent-mindedly. 'Hélène . . .' she repeated. Her mouth contracted. It was as though she was listening to something in the distance. 'How was she?' she asked.

I laughed and spread my hands. What a question. There was, as always, a large cordial sister-in-law who embraced me, brushed her curls over my cheek and pushed me into the living room, the dining table was laid, come on, sit down, come on, the children will be here in a moment, here's some currant bread, and here's some milk, and cake! Wait, hold on, I've still got half a whipped cream cake, how nice, how nice, Magda, till she finally came to a halt, legs apart, looked me straight in the face and blushing, her eyes moist with affection, she exclaimed, 'How's my brother?!'

I picked up a fork and began eating the tart. 'Oh, well,' I said. 'He's on a trip to Vienna. Do you know that he rescued a cat last week? He didn't even take his shoes off but he waded into the duckpond just like that, in his nice summer suit . . .'

'What!'

She began laughing her head off, exaggeratedly, crazy with happiness you might say. I looked at her with curiosity. And suddenly it was as though I could see how the image of a beloved, dripping wet brother merged in the confusion of her hundreds, thousands of childhood memories, bonding with them as if in a chemical reaction, subverting them, slightly discolouring them, corroding them. That's how it is, there is nothing strange about it. But I had to get up to find a fixed point to look at: the shed in the courtyard shone with bright green paint, on the handlebars of a bike sat a sparrow. I must be off, I thought. A silver chime sounded.

A silver chime sounded.

'Half-past three,' said the old woman with a frown, she showed her irritation and she was right. I must be off, I must get the hell out of here, soon I shall have a headache. A delusion held me here for years. I was determined to make do with these loved ones, these skies, these street scenes. They were the secrets surrounding me, small, pale but derived from a man for whom I had deep but unfortunately rather pathetic feelings. Today I am restoring the distance between me and these accidental things. If I get a move on, could I still catch the train to Paris?

I got up, walked around the table to kiss my mother-in-law on the cheek. 'You stay where you are. I'll let myself out.'

For a moment the lavender and the smell of her neck evoked a ready-made sentence in me. Tomorrow Robert will come and pick you up before dinner. But I clenched my teeth and left the room with a sweet smile.

For the third time that day I put on my raincoat. Holding the two sides apart I looked at my figure in the mirror, one metre sixty-eight tall, not too slim, in a red dress and shoes with ankle straps. My face had a pensive expression. Did I perhaps want to find out what was left of me? When I put my hands to my hair, I felt the blood coral bracelet slide off my wrist. The following moment the old chain, on which the beads were strung one by one, had snapped.

Not until Roosendaal did I wake with a start from my reflections. The compartment door slid open, three people had come in to share the compartment with me. A short bald man, a young man in army boots and a woman with a perfect china face nodded at me and took their coats off. There was whistling, hissing, the train moved off with scarcely a sound. We saw backs of houses, an advertising hoarding with a man on a horse, a red-brick factory complex and then the fields gliding, spinning past, becoming darker and darker, the May day was speeding to a close.

Beyond Brussels our party was summoned to dinner by a waiter. In the restaurant car we rested our arms on the dazzling white linen and under the influence of the wine, the poultry and more wine soon lowered our voices familiarly. The bald man informed us that he loved running through the woods and jumping ditches at dawn, the woman laughed and said that she, for her sins, was crazy about pink, pink flowers, pink sheets, pink saltcellars,

126

whereupon I told them that if you walked along the Astridboulevard you had boarding houses with peeling paint on one side and ships on the other. Then the young man started telling us about the court case he had brought against his father, about the verdict of the court that morning – he had won – and his absurd behaviour in the presence of Justice.

'I sat there crying my eyes out!'

We refilled his glass and went on to listen to the man's life history, which he concluded in astonishment with the words, 'Yes, I have really done everything wrong, just imagine, everything . . .!'

'Everything is a lot,' admitted the woman. She studied the tips of her fingers. 'But nothing, well, that's rather little.'

After I revealed that I had spent my childhood in Canada because there was nothing to keep my mother in Europe since she lost her husband, that the houses in her village, the inhabitants with their customs and the members of her family who belonged to the German enemy meant nothing to her any more, in no way, to think that such a thing could happen overnight, and that you simply leave the house . . . we decided to return to our compartment. There the woman put the light out, pulled down the blind of the door to the corridor, and nestled into the cushions. The two men also stretched out. To the accompaniment of their friendly snoring and wheezing I turned to the window.

The spinning space. The night sky. A rising piece of land, blue as the ocean and equally impassable. I had not known such solitude since my childhood. I hunted cautiously for a cigarette, I wanted to let the others sleep, I wanted to smoke by myself and stay awake looking at the clouds obscuring the moon. I was exceptionally calm. I remember my calm, my emptiness deep inside. Trees . . . fields . . . a farmhouse like a boat under the stars . . . suddenly it occurred to me that my life with Robert had been a poem. Everything that mattered to me personally had taken a new twist in the light of that chance meeting. My eyes and skin: designed for other use. My past and my mother's: captured in words. My future – look: a sun-drenched plain that we were going to populate with mountains, trees and rivers that belonged to both of us. I stretched my legs. I looked tenderly at the sleeping young man, his forehead pale as wax in the light coming from outside. What I want to know is this. Would it also be possible to take that poem in my hands and drop it onto a stone floor? So that it smashed into fragments, into crude slivers . . . For years we fished in the river. We put on hiking boots, got lost amid the boulders and when we returned home crawled under the covers. There was rain, snow, sun, once a hurricane that blew the roof off the kitchen extension into the valley, but what could you do, besides that there were September nights, unstoppable crying fits and let me not forget the dialogues, they were crazy, those conversations, contrary, sly, on art, God, love, the evolution of mankind, the upkeep of our house and about art again. We were masters at interweaving our dreams that we dreamed aloud. What I want to know is this. Among all those things it must surely be possible to find something which could not be swallowed up?

Northern France rushed by. Towns and villages became more numerous. More and more light. More and more small stations, where people were standing waiting next to their luggage, with all their being, they had disappeared before they realized, grey, amorphous, misunderstood by a drowsy company wishing to move A to B as quickly as possible. The train negotiated a series of points, the whole compartment jolted and the man opposite me woke up. 'Half-past ten,' he said after a glance at his watch. He coughed sleepily.

Fine, I thought, in three-quarters of an hour we will be at the Gare du Nord. I know where the taxi rank is. Hôtel Gaspard, I shall say from the back seat. They have rooms with stained floors, a view of an old-fashioned Métro entrance and a bed which was far too soft for Robert and me together, back then, we rolled into the middle and woke in each other's arms. Hôtel Gaspard. I intend to take a bath, sleep like a log and tomorrow after breakfast continue on to the Cévennes.

Chapter Three

Racing the sun. Travelling west and postponing night a little. Seven p.m. One August evening I took off from Charles de Gaulle airport for a flight across the Atlantic. The temperature in the aircraft was a relief, the weather had been heavy and oppressive. I knew that the parks and streets below me were still teeming with people who because of the heat had no intention of eating yet. After a quarter of an hour I unfastened my safety belt. I moved back my reclining seat. Speeding onward between heaven and earth I surrendered to the calm in my limbs, the chaos in my brain and the invisible crew who, basing themselves on exact reports from Iceland, Greenland, and Newfoundland would land this machine in Quebec, on the same August evening, at 9.30 p.m: the time when French Canadian children are called indoors to eat at the end of a glorious day. The sun would have stayed an hour and a half ahead of me.

I looked up. A young woman had approached me across the carpeted floor. Did I want anything to drink? Certainly I did. With a smile I was handed a pretty little personal bottle of champagne, a transparent cup and a handkerchief drenched in perfume. Everything OK? Dinner will be served shortly. Dark, inquiring eyes. I nodded and smiled too. Sure, sure, everything is OK. In the most incomprehensible way, I drink, I listen to the organ sounds of this simplified, air-conditioned world and already cannot understand how I came to hang around in the Cévennes for sixteen months.

Forgot the time. On the umpteenth occasion in your life you forgot to keep an eye on the clock. Like a child with no interest in time, but all the more so in the space where it finds itself, I had kept stopping to stare open-mouthed. Blue ravines, yellow terraces with overgrown chestnut trees, faces at windows which were being closed, abandoned dining tables covered in breadcrumbs, corks, the piercing heat of the afternoon, the suddenly silenced shriek of an animal caught by another animal far off in the night, the fingers of a man on the skin of my breasts, his dark morning face and his kindness ... was it any wonder that I had lost my sense of direction a little? I had set out in seach of familiar, if necessarily rather disordered images. I needed them for my autobiography. But I don't know, in some way, I kept just missing those few points and lines that I had marked out in my former world. And instead of wandering around in my former house, looking under the beds and snuffling in the cupboards, one day I had taken off with a total stranger, a refugee, a criminal with a false name who could not take his eyes off me and who talked to me once after I had finished work. He lived in a cottage clinging to the overgrown slopes of the Triballe. The Cévennes are hospitable to those who want to hide, he had whitewashed the walls and built a stove of fire-proof bricks. I wasn't cold once that winter. I realized that just next to the life in which you happen to find yourself there is another that, with no problem at all, you could have lived equally well.

I was lying on the bed in the maid's room of the Hôtel Roland. The window was open, over a chair hung my dress, the sheet on the triple mattress felt as soft as silk. I had lain down on it for a moment after showering. It was late morning. I did not need to be downstairs to serve light potato soup and the broiled rabbit of the region for another half hour.

Saint-Martial. A village three kilometres from our former farmhouse. When I arrived here in May 1980, I moved into the only hotel in the surrounding area. In the quiet streets, between the houses, there was an air of enchantment, something languid and exceptionally friendly which made me sleep without dreaming. After a week I realized I wanted to stay, I consulted the manageress of the hotel, a woman of my age with varicose veins which made

130

it difficult for her to walk. She looked me up and down with the eye of a farmer at the cattle market.

'Can you cook?'

She led me past the trout in aspic, the smoked duck's breast, the kilner jars with their soft pink and yellow contents, she pulled open the drawers in the kitchen, pointed to the saucepans and explained to me what knives could be taken from the rack for what clearly defined purpose.

'Anyway, it's better to hang a guinea fowl than cut its throat.'

Finally she gave me the key to the attic room. I was to serve in the afternoons and in the evenings help with the oven. Whenever I wanted I could take the green van.

Occasionally I did so. Occasionally I drove past the mountain on which I had once lived and hesitated whether to change down a gear and start the climb at full speed. I remembered that the new occupants were an architect and his wife and daughter. But I stared straight ahead, went down to one or two farmhouses to buy a batch of goat cheeses and drove directly back to Saint-Martial, where during the day one could look out over slopes covered with grapevines, meadows full of sheep and mulberry trees, where at twilight you could wander down the spiral steps to the cinder field full of dogs and children, where you slept dreamlessly at night, and where when you woke you threw open the shutters and stood eye to eye with the small, walled graveyard on the other side of the road, which descended so steeply that the dead who were carried there in their pine coffins must become completely disorientated and must be relieved when they finally reach their destination on the shady side of the mountain ridge so that they can keep their eyes focused on their native village for at least a few centuries.

I sat up. The church tower clock chimed. The amusing double bell of the Lutheran church, high-low, long-short and dull, chimed twelve times. I slid off the bed, stepped into my dress and put on flaming red lipstick. When I entered the dining room, three things immediately struck me. Six of the eight tables were occupied, which was a lot for the month of September. One of the customers, a man with a shy, arrogant face, was making his second visit of the day. And at the back sat a family that recognized me and greeted me very cheerfully: the architect with the blond hair, his wife and his little daughter, who had grown up. She seemed to me to be about nine.

'You must come and have a look soon.'

After the dessert they had offered me a *marc de poire*. Most customers had left, only the man in the corner had wanted another coffee, it was OK to sit down with them for a moment.

The architect turned his bespectacled gaze on me. He lent forward and informed me that it had been no easy task to make the kitchen window wider, the lumber room ceiling higher, the bathroom floor warmer, the walls white, and the doorposts bluer.

'Excuse me.'

I got up and went over to the corner table with a smile.

'Monsieur?'

But I was wrong. He had not waved me over. Rather surprised, he looked into my eyes and then, to please me as it were, ordered an unusual brand of cognac. His accent had already given away the fact that he was not from these parts either.

When I rejoined the family with an interested expression on my face, I was no longer concentrating at all. The well in the courtyard may have been cleared out, swallows may have nested under the eaves, the faded blue rabbit hutches may have been got rid of, I could feel pinpricks in my back. And while the architect's wife spread her fingers to count the flower beds she had laid out – 'Purple dahlias, Japanese roses, arum lilies, a swing and a sand-pit . . .' – I sniffed restlessly: right across the dining room a sharp smell of tobacco wafted towards me, as though through a narrow tunnel, it made me joyful, joyful at everything that was about to happen, in a little while I shall impudently turn and look at him, I thought.

The daughter looked at me.

'I've got an elephant on the wall next to my bed.'

We got up from the table laughing. It was time to go, they had eaten and drunk their fill, the bill had been paid. With his siesta already in prospect the architect repeated his invitation in a drawl. 'Be sure to drop in soon . . .'

'Oh, of course,' I said, lowering my voice to give an impression of how curious I was about my old house. 'I'll definitely come.'

Wasn't I lying through my teeth? I knew that nothing would come of it for the time being. I shook hands, smiled and knew that I had other things on my mind because a man who had been through a lot in his life had meanwhile started coming towards me past the chairs and tables, at any moment I would feel his hand on my elbow and without being in the least surprised hear him say, 'Can I ask your name?'

The ravines are wild. From high rocky slopes rain and meltwater rushes down, uprooting trees and washing away animals and houses. The standard description of the Cévennes is inhospitable. I am not the only one who knows better. Besides eagles and wolves, a fair number of people find refuge amid the granite and pine trees. *Terre de refuge*. The population is Protestant, very stubborn and has an aversion to central authority. Missing person's reports are traditionally ignored here.

I never knew what crime this man had committed. I never asked and he never gave me any indication in words. But I realized that with those small dark hands, the smell of wood and smoke, something dreadful and unforgivable was stroking my body, from the moment when, stretched out on my bare back, I closed my eyelids and muttered urgently, 'Yes . . . yes . . .'

He took me on his moped. On his moped! There is something irresistibly comic about the sight of that man and woman, both middle-aged, chugging uphill and downhill in the sunshine, she in a waitress's dress, he in a shirt flapping in the wind and with long, albeit rather thinning hair – now and then he shows her his profile to say solemnly, 'Just a little further . . . this is the last slope . . . now the path . . . be careful' – on their way to a hard canvas bed in a mountain hut among the trees.

He turned off the engine. The path became too steep and too narrow. We had to walk the last bit. I watched him pushing his moped ahead of me with short steps. I also directed my gaze upwards and to the side. Trees, ferns, dead branches. Despite the stitch in my side I liked the green warmth.

'We're here,' he said and I saw the dirty white hut clinging lopsidedly to the mountain.

Dusk between four walls. A bed, a table and a window which in my half-blinded state I went over to for a moment. Another blue panorama after all. Why? Why this playing for time? This afternoon there was no question of what in the past had surprised me often enough: that you cannot touch a particular man, that it is inconceivable and that's all there is to it. He does not have yellow teeth, does not spit when he talks, and is not draped over a three-person bench with a hollow crotch thrust forward. Yet there is a concrete wall between you and him. Are there perhaps other experiences clinging to him which repel you like lemon does a gnat, or elder a fly? This criminal and I had come to an agreement hours ago. There was no reason at all not to turn around immediately, pull open my dress, press close to him and feel the four walls of the shabby room receding into infinity as if on the edge of sleep. Ah! Sexuality! Drifting away, making love in this way, without any context, nothing has happened between us that can secretly interfere at this moment, no sickening fuss, no reproachful looks, no cock-and-bull stories beforehand designed to merge our life histories into something shared. Why? Couldn't I see perfectly well despite my fidgety arms and legs what he was like, this man? I saw his face, his naked shoulders and chest, his sex, erect, the black hair which climbed up in a line from his belly and then branched out luxuriantly – he is mean, sweet, sensual, indifferent, loyal, violent, dishonest, naive . . . and I saw that in all my splendid solitude.

Now you are racing ahead of dusk, reclining with a magazine on your lap, the summer and winter days of the past years converge into a single colourful hour in which there is ample time for every event. Room to spread a snow-white tablecloth while lost in thought, to listen to the hotel manageress talking about the war years as she fills a hogshead, to sleep so deeply that you forget your dreams, to make friends with one or two villagers: shall I take the green van in a little while and drive to the Triballe? At the beginning of the forest path there is a parking space where I can easily leave the van till tomorrow morning.

Again I had a man who drew! I did not know what to make of it when I first glanced at his table and discovered paper, ink and paints among the domestic rubbish.

'What!'

He turned and stood behind me to see what it was that I was surprised about: the detailed drawing of an enchantingly beautiful creature, an insect with a deep red shell, six pitch-black legs attached to a pitch-black body and two deep red antennae on its head.

'A click-beetle,' he said and pointed. On a sheet of blotting paper lay the original specimen. Small, motionless, dead.

That afternoon in the forest he looked at me, with a finger on his lips. Listen. We sank to our knees. A bright green beetle bent its body first forward and then backward before shooting into the air with a loud click.

'There it is.'

He had caught it in his hand.

I looked. I was standing there in the undergrowth, my left foot forward, holding my breath, looking with intense interest at a green beetle one-and-a-half centimetres long.

'This creature belongs to the *Elateridae* family, which contains at least eight thousand species.'

I nodded. What a lot.

'Behind their breast they have a thorn, which fits into a groove between the hips.'

A butterfly zigzagged between us, it was hot, but thanks to the four glasses of red wine I was not bothered about anything, anything at all, I listened to the most mysterious information, when the insect bends backwards the thorn is pulled out of the groove, and examined the man's two folded hands to discover where that tenderness came from, sleepily I noted the form of the knuckles, the nails, the hairs which were of course much darker than Robert's. Robert, I am thinking of you. I am thinking of you but I am sensible enough not to go on about it too much. I'll just mention your impulsive way of doing business, which I liked, your fear of being hurt and humiliated, which caused me a lot of bother and, how shall I put it, your omnipresence. I am sitting at my desk, and there is your car coming up the drive. I am lying in the bath, and you bring me an espresso and a macaroon. I walk into a boutique and buy a red dress with a tight skirt and buttons at the front. With a stab in my heart I remember how at night when there was a storm blowing, I lay with my cheek against your shoulder thinking, just let ten, twenty, thirty years go by, I don't care. I have to confess that when I acted so impulsively with you sixteen years ago, the unheard-of, extremely attractive idea took hold of me that in future you'd be my whole existence. Today I am glad to be able to put this boiling hot afternoon between us . . .

'The beetle that has jumped often falls back in the same place, or not very far away,' he said and threw the creature over his shoulder into the bushes.

We looked at each other, I raised an eyebrow.

'But why do they do it?'

'It's a flight reflex.'

They were strangely disconnected days. Mornings and evenings, sun, rain and wind followed each other in light-hearted succession. It was laughable trying to think about the future. Things happened, caused short-lived astonishment and disappeared again. Snow began to fall. There was a silvery strip above the mountains. There was a smell of burning everywhere. When it froze, it was sometimes difficult to reach the hut on the mountainside.

He might have been an entomologist in real life. In passing I learned a lot about bugs and butterflies. The *atalanta* migrates south in the spring, the *parnassius* has wonderful reflecting spots in its eyes. This fugitive easily acquired the money he needed. The region had become familiar with his abilities. He laid on electricity, branched telephone cables, discovered water: with arms half-outstretched he walked in circles over a newly mown field. I look at his empty, indifferent face, he rubs his thumbs and fingers together as if counting money. Then the impossible miracle happens.

'Water,' he says. His arms sink. 'Between two and three metres deep.'

There is no doubt that we get to know each other in depth. But our secrets do not intermingle. I laid my clothes on the warm stove. He made coffee on the primus. I listened to the screech of a female eagle. He was more interested in the drifting snow. I could tell him my most intimate thoughts, let him take my hands in his, let him listen to me full of understanding, he was not capable of absorbing the least thing except for what he was bound up in.

You should have seen me looking at the house I used to live in. Yesterday, in the early evening. It was bitterly cold. Before I could drive off I had to mess around with snow chains for a quarter of an hour, but I was determined: let me go and visit those friendly people at least, it might even be fun. And if that smell of wood and ash was still there, it might be nice to squeeze my eyes shut for a moment and see myself as I was in the rocking chair behind the kitchen door, on the stairs to the loft . . .

The steep path shone in the moonlight. A layer of cinders had been strewn over it. I drove up in first gear and covered the last leg as I always did when it was icy, with sideways steps, resting my hands on my knees. Then I caught my breath. There it was. There at the edge of the clearing, next to the bare mulberry tree, was the house, still, the walls blurred by the driven snow, but with warm lights in all the windows. I knew at once. Stop. Don't make yourself known. You don't belong there. And I took a few steps to the side and hid behind a pine tree, the bark of which felt like the skin of a warm animal. There I stood, imagine, in total concentration, staring at the front of the house, that roof, those windows, as though at any moment I didn't know what might happen . . . when the front door opened.

A square of light on the snow. A blond man buttoning his windcheater. 'Dominique!' In one hand a lantern, in the other a milk pail. There was the girl, 'Papa!' My eyes followed the pair along the wall, past the built-on goat shed, through the gate in the fence, everything had changed, I couldn't recognize a thing, now a bright arc lamp went on, goats came out, ghostly, pure-white creatures blew clouds of steam into the mist, they scrambled, bleated, in the shed milking was in progress, I heard the father and the daughter laughing and carrying on a monotonous conversation. Papa! Dominique! Papa! Dominque! My heartbeat slows. Was I freezing as I stood here? With my head resting against the mossy trunk, in great calm, I felt one event slipping away to make way for another. Paler light, hollower sounds, my pupils slid back. I was lying in bed. A moment ago a bed with bars on it had been wheeled into a white ward at great speed. Someone was softly stroking my cheek. I raised my eyes. Robert was sitting on a stool next to me. He looked alarmed and embarrassed and wanted to know if I was in pain. I reassured him – no, not at all, not a twinge, a bit disappointed, of course – I put out my arm and a firm hand enclosed me. And then?

And then a puny grey devil behind my forehead. Then glasses that shattered between my fingers, a dead nightingale in the garden, dreams of cats. Then grief that I managed to keep smouldering for a whole year by dropping on my knees in front of it and gently blowing on it like a fire.

Until one afternoon Robert blocked my path. 'Where are you going?' he asked as I put on a straw farmworker's hat and said, 'To the village.'

A second summer went by. Wasn't it time for me to take my leave? I had travelled back to look for something. I had thought I would be able to adjust my memory on a number of minor personal points. Other mysteries had loomed into view. They had amused me, preoccupied me, made me fall in love. Most of all they had made me sleep with the abandon I remember from my earliest childhood. Once I dreamed of my mother. One day I began thinking of my mother. Not in the everyday way which is not really thinking, but snuffling about among lost fragments of knowledge. I began thinking of her in indescribably sharp images. I saw her standing in the bay window of our house in Gaspé, a smoking cigarette in front of her face. I saw her with her face cocked to one side shoving a pile of school exercise books into a briefcase, with the dog at her black-booted heels she is running along a beach at Cap-des-Rosiers, she stops and points something out to me, but I must have looked at her wrist and head against the marbled sky.

More and more often after my work in the restaurant I would climb up to the attic room, lie down on the bed and after glancing at my watch think: getting on for four. That was the time that she and I came out of school, we opened the French windows and stretched out in the red-and-white striped deck chairs. The dog rolled on its back, spreading all four legs, its jowls sagged to one side. We were silent, squabbled, had conversations: she looks at me and laughs, her melancholy lies behind her like a motionless field, she does not want to bother me with it at all. Parties, girlfriends, a first love who threw me over unceremoniously, she never stood in my way, when I came home there were sometimes funny purchases in my room: a T-shirt with a bear on it, a book with pop-up reptiles, a pen with invisible ink. For as

139

long as I lived at home a portrait of my parents had stood in the living room.

I lay on the bed half undressed. Groping around I found my cigarettes. I enveloped myself in smoke and thought of the time when my mother had come over to the Cévennes for a month. In the springtime, with the sleeves of her beige dress rolled up, she had stood listening with a calm expression to my plans to convert this barn made of blocks of stone into a proper house. How was it, did one need a visa to get into Canada?

Chapter Four

The voyage began in Naples.

The Swedish troopship *Goya* left the quayside at Naples in the summer of 1947 with my mother and myself on board along with two thousand other emigrants. We stood at the railing, early in the morning, packed in the throng on the foredeck, I remember that my mother did not move a muscle and said nothing and that I waved with both arms. Because I was going overseas for the first time, I waved at the cranes, at the ships, the gulls, the whitish coastline with its houses and palaces and got the fright of my life when the *Goya*, having reached the open sea, belched out its final farewell. I was a skinny blond girl of eight.

We had not had to say goodbye to a soul. In the Bagnoli reception camp, where we had stayed for one month, everyone was passing through. Czechs, Poles, Greeks, Italians lived in a laconic understanding on the boiling hot site of a couple of bombed-out steelworks. I liked it there. In front of the barracks they talked deep into the night, there was singing, people cooked at all hours of the day – it was really crazy, in the kitchen, on fires, grills, in tins: people were constantly occupied with food – and there were children, scores of them, who never divided up into opposing camps, because before it could reach that point they disappeared again, embarked on their way to Australia or Canada.

I had never seen the sea before. Only at Bagnoli near Naples did I see the sea. My mother took me to the beach. Before taking off my leather shoes and my dress and realizing that the sea in the postcards was made of water, but salt! Salt got into my hair, eyelashes, lips, my knickers which sank down to my knees – I stood transfixed. I thought that the expanse of beach surrounded by land on three sides was enormous. Weeks later, when we sailed out of the Bay, I saw that there was lots more water behind that water, water and coasts. Sardinia, North Africa, the Straits of Gibraltar, Portugal, where we saw the last European harbour. Then the sea. Space. Knowing space. This swell, this dark green, these white horses would last till our eyes were completely empty and our heads too. Old town centres? Variety theatres? Victorian chests of drawers with letters, powder cases, glacé gloves? Europe had become a smell and you only remember smells at the moment of rediscovery. My mother must have said goodbye forever at that moment, on the ocean.

She had looked for her husband everywhere. She had consulted every list, every agency, first in Czechoslovakia and later in Berlin. She followed up every lead. He was supposed to be imprisoned in such and such a camp, supposed to be in such and such an institution, out of his mind. She found the administration of the Theresienstadt camp, one afternoon she looked at the exhausted faces of men who had completely lost their way. Later she told me that she had been certain that her wandering was useless, but that she could not help it. The obsessive searching had kept her together until she heard about UNRRA, a division of the United Nations which helped people to leave Europe.

We shared our cabin with four Polish women. Their frizzy hair fanned out over their shoulders. Their holdalls were full of garlic and vodka. By the light of the night lamps their blue-and-white thighs walked back and forth in front of me. I slept in the second bunk. Mostly they were completely indifferent to us, they yawned, ate and drank as though they were in their own farm stall. But sometimes one of them turned round and pushed the vodka bottle at us, which my mother invariably accepted and put to her mouth expertly. One night it was the smell of the garlic which they ate like apples, which together with the heat and the pitch blackness of the cabin and the moaning and grinding of teeth of the sleeping women and the vibrating of the ship which drove me to the point of a screaming fit. I hoisted myself up to her bunk.

'Mama.'

She immediately turned on the light.

'The hammock. Where is the hammock? Didn't you bring a hammock?'

She sat up. She looked at me and understood what I wanted.

'Do you want to sleep on deck?'

'Yes.'

'Wait – I'm coming.'

A moment later she was walking with her daughter in bare feet down gangways, up stairs, to the top deck: quite a few people were sleeping there.

'Put your head here,' she said. 'And your feet here.'

She had attached the hammock to the palings around a mast. She put a blanket over me and stood for a moment looking at me.

'Goodnight.'

A kiss.

'Goodnight.'

And she had gone, leaving me behind in the cool air under a black sky full of stars.

If one wants to get to the far north-eastern tip of the Gaspé peninsula from Quebec, where the town of Gaspé lies in an estuary eaten out of the granite coast, one can take the plane, the DC 9 of Brewster Airlines flies one there in no time, the only service run by Via Rail takes one straight through the interior, past the town with the Indian name Matapédia, to the end of the line, the station of Gaspé covered with an old-fashioned tarred roof, and one can go by boat, one can take a boat and for six or seven hours, lose oneself and find oneself again while one lets oneself be carried downstream along the banks which recede hour by hour, the banks of the river which is still called the Saint-Laurent by the French-speaking inhabitants of Gaspé. Water. Sea and land birds. Fellow passengers. What in heaven's name is my reality?

As always happens, I had got into conversation on deck. As I was about to smoke a cigarette, I was politely offered a light by a man of about seventy with sly, cheerful, light-brown eyes behind spectacles. He also had a beard. I heard at once that his French was a bit awkward. Where did he come from? Originally he came from Holland.

'Alphen,' he said. 'Hoge Rijndijk, 19. Downstairs my father on his sick bed, with a crucifix above it, a white bedspread over it. On the first floor my family, wife, eight children. In the attic my office, accountancy . . .'

He glanced at me cheerfully then screwed up his eyes to scan the horizon again.

'Oh, accountancy,' I mumbled.

'Yes. If I had not left the country, they would have run me in.'

After a silence, I felt I should reveal something about my life. So I began talking about my Czech origins and the sea voyage my mother and I had made from Naples. Travelling and telling stories, as I had already noticed many times, go together. In the moving world, without terra firma under your feet, you emphatically place yourself against a background of a Central European country, a mother, ship's fittings, masts and ropes, and you tell how once, with a gently beating heart, you woke up outside, because you felt someone looking at you over the edge of a hammock – a ship's officer – dark shoulders, eyes just below the peak of a cap – hands you a bright green apple.

'It must have been a Granny Smith.'

You hit on irrelevant details which may even be false, but nevertheless in the midst of those details, there you are. The Polish women pout and flick the garlic skin high in the air with their tongues. A plague of flies on an ocean liner, is such a thing possible? You had to bend down in the cabin to avoid a fly paper that hung too low. Now your hair sticks to it. You feel your mother's gently moving belly against you, she says: Stand still, otherwise I shan't be able to get it free.

I turned my face towards the man next to me at the railing. 'Suddenly I wonder what language my mother and I spoke in then.'

'It was probably Czech.'

No. Not Czech. It was German. My mother must have spoken the language that she no longer liked hearing. Not only had she never really mastered Czech because my father spoke fluent German, but the year before we left we had lived in Berlin with her family.

Berlin. I can remember that city, that house particularly. It was in the district of Reinickendorf, close to the railway line, in the French sector. Everything in that house was rusty red, the rusty red colour encapsulated you, moved towards you from the carpets, the curtains, the panels of the doors which did not shut properly, even the daylight joined in, in my memory, by entering the living room from the west and striking the copper candelabra and with her back to the window sat my furious granny, my Nazi granny who could not reconcile herself to the capitulation. Apart from my mother and me, my mother's eldest sister Mimi and her son Walter also lived with my granny. Walter, who was already ten, and I decided to ignore the rusty red colour of the house. In fine weather we played among the peeling house fronts of the city. Bus shelters, urinals, floors on the point of collapse covered in plaster dust and slivers of glass. When it rained we lay on the sofa. Peace, slumbering, exploring hands. None of the three women around us dreamed of stopping us, because in their way they were all somewhere else: my granny, who was mostly silent but who would sometimes explode bitterly, 'God, oh God, oh God! What a mess! French uniforms, insignia! Insults on the radio!' My aunt Mimi who went to work every morning in thin stockings and a short dress, and my mother, where was my mother? She was gone, for days on end she criss-crossed the city in search of the authorities or wandered in a disguised gesture of flight across the Jungfern-heide which had been churned up by army trucks. At night she crept into bed with me with cold feet.

I felt good. The boat moving calmly onwards along the river. The old man dreaming and smoking next to me. Although the Saint-

Laurent was already so wide by now that you could no longer see the other side, I stared straight ahead, it was halfway through the day, September 1981. What do those facts matter now that you have focused your gaze on a pack of clouds with light edges which are gliding silently along with you? The wind played through my hair.

When I presented my passport at Quebec airport a week ago and took my large yellow bag off the luggage belt, I felt my journey had been too quick. The dividing line between my life in the Cévennes and my present – Quebec, Gaspé: the scene of my girlhood – was minimal. I decided to look for a bed at once. Taxi! I called in the dusk.

While I was being driven to a pension, the name of which just happened to occur to me, I closed my eyes to the brightly lit squares and streets, the old houses, the fortress walls and the Grand Théâtre of the city where I had once studied and which I knew like the back of my hand. You can eat, dance, walk in processions till all hours, in the winter, during Carnival, you can take part in canoe races on the river strewn with ice floes. Tomorrow, I thought, and registered at a counter, took the key from a beautiful tanned woman, climbed up a highly polished staircase, opened a door and saw a bed with white sheets with the covers drawn back in a room where in two deeply recessed windows the blinds had been half drawn for me. Ah! I let myself fall forward with my arms and legs outstretched.

The next day I picked up the telephone book, I just wanted to know how my old friends were doing. But in seventeen years people change names and addresses. I tried Alette, Jonathan, Lise . . . Yes, her most especially, suddenly I began to miss her furiously, a voice mentioned a name, another voice mentioned another name, no, they did not know her. I insisted: Lise, a girl with brown curly hair and as mild-mannered as a camel . . . Then I dialled a number that might belong to my friend Terence, no answer, finally I got through to his mother. Magda my dear, go and visit him, he'd love to see you, he teaches French, his wife is a psychologist, his two sons are the apple of my eye. By the way: it just happens to be his birthday today!

The weather was beautiful. I walked down the winding streets of the seventeenth-century city and at midday ate a fish dish with which I drank quite a lot of white wine. Then my legs started moving again, in the park children played and neatly dressed women walked to work from one exit to another staring straight ahead. I climbed the steps to the Citadel, went down to the wooden footbridge of the Terrace Dufferin, where I sat down on one of the benches with a view over the river, to be able to assume at my leisure the guise of a resident of this city, a woman with a nice job, wife of a French teacher, with whom, because of his dark blue eyes, his infectious appetite, his songs during car trips and the good-natured gesture with which he had once grabbed her numbed hands and tucked them deep under his winter sweater in the warmth of his body, she had really been in love.

'A gentleman rang for you,' said the owner of the pension when I got back. 'He asked if you would ring him back on this number.'

Nine-thirty p.m. The front door of a house in the rue Saint Jean was thrown open for me. Terence! An embrace and immediately afterwards the festive living room, where among the sports jackets and low cut dresses I recognized the faces of Alette, Jonathan and Lise. So you were all here! I laid my cheek against Lise's, her coffee-brown hand patted me gently . . . Lise, you haven't changed a bit . . . and in amazement I noted that Jonathan, Alette and several others have been scarcely affected by the passage of the years, only Terence seemed to have put on a bit of weight, which did not matter at all. Not a bit, in a sky-blue shirt he introduced me to his wife, also well fed and cordiality itself. At her insistence I agreed to come and have dinner with them that same week, whereupon husband and wife looked at each other earnestly and immediately fixed the menu. I was to be given artichokes, halibut in cream and tarts filled with Benedictine.

'What do you do for a living?' I asked the very next person I found myself standing next to like a complete idiot.

'Michel Toussaint,' said the man, bowed formally and then informed me that he worked for the astrophysics laboratory.

What? Astrophysics? Astronomy? Who was this in front of me, a man of the heavens, a stargazer, a student of the dark-blue ravine that is a thousand times too large for our pupils . . . Gaby!

'You work at the observatory . . .' and while I stared at the astronomer, another vision loomed up, very, very clearly in front of me, the young man with protruding ears and eyes that were like flat brown stones.

'The old observatory is scarcely used by the university any more,' said Toussaint.

I had seen him grow up, that child, that rocking, wriggling, hand-flapping, gaze-averting child, that night owl that cannot bear his feathered body to be touched. Nestling on one side of the darkness he peers through a telescope at the other side, he has no objection at all to restricting his attention in this way: what are my coordinates in eternity? I thrust a marvellous journal under his nose. For a moment his unaccountable gaze passes over me.

'Why not?' I asked.

'Think about it. The lights of the city, the air pollution, the small number of clear nights in this part of the world.' And he told me that the Canadians had built a joint observatory with the French on Hawaii. He had once done some research there, in the mile-high air of Mauna Kea, it had been a shattering experience. After working for a few days with the computer-controlled telescope, which no longer required a human eye, he had gone down the mountain to the intermediate station, and for a whole day had not been able to utter a single word, to anyone.

'I went berserk,' he said and I could see that he was still astounded. A lean, pleasant man, he looked at me with deep-set eyes. 'Come on, let me go and fetch another glass for you and me.'

A little later he promised to show me the old observatory the following day. I would see that the 35cm reflector telescope was still in perfect order.

The reflector telescope still in perfect order? He had understated it. It was – my God! From a leather-covered four-wheeled arm-chair, the back of which had been adjusted by a lever so that my body lay at an angle of one hundred degrees, I looked through the soft green cylinder of the 35cm Schmidt telescope at the northern sky . . . the firmament, the dark purple wall with the dots, how familiar, dots indeed, but also an immense spectacle of nebulae, veils, dark river-like patches and six or so blue-and-white flame-throwers.

'The Pleiades . . .'

Long after midnight, when it was pitch black, Michel Tous-saint had first opened the door of the observatory for me. A deathly quiet vestibule. A pillar which must carry the telescope right through all the floors. A case of books.

'Hey!'

I had found a treatise written by my host!

When Toussaint offered me a copy of *The Formation of Galaxies* as a gift, I said yes, I'd love one, and asked for a favour as well. Have the university send the book to this address. I gave the name, street and a locality on the Dutch coast. Gaby. The phonetic form fixed itself behind my eyes, unspeakably familiar, and continued reverberating there, even when after climbing up three flights of stairs I lay down in a leather chair while Toussaint, behind me, opened the cupola of the observatory by means of a two-wheeled mechanism and the sky became visible. Gaby.

Halfway through the ocean journey, in the week when there was not a breath of wind, two people died. The first was an old woman, a grandmother who had given her blessing to her grown-up

149

children and then went calmly. The second was a baby. When my mother told me that they were going to throw the baby into the sea the following day at dawn, I said I wanted to see.

It was a mild morning. Very early. A few rays of sunlight were just peering above the surface of the water. With my hand in my mother's, I went down to the lowest deck, to the bow which was as large as a dance floor, a small crowd had gathered there. Passengers, officers, a row of sailors at attention with the baby in a white cardboard box on a table. When I got close, I looked carefully. It was a sturdy, pretty baby, with a face that looked calm and even a little proud. Under its long-lashed eyelids it succeeded very well in hiding what it is like to be dead. Contentedly I noticed the dark pink roses laid around the body.

They had been made from sanitary towels. I had seen the women at work, the previous afternoon. They had carefully pulled apart the sanitary towels, which consisted of a pink and a white layer, they could use only the pink layer to fold wonderfully ingenious roses, twist them round and secure them at the back with a tacked stitch. Tell me, I asked the baby softly, is it true that everything first goes grey, then white, then blue, and then you fly to the stars? By the way, what do you think of those roses? I think they are the most beautiful thing I have ever seen.

A man recited a prayer. There was a scream. Two sailors closed the box, placed it on a plank, a smooth, light brown plank, which they began to push across the deck towards the waves. Before I knew it the baby had disappeared from sight.

Chapter Five

When a voice from the cockpit announced that one of the engines was being given an extra boost, just to be sure, and that instead of leaving the Boeing would be staying at its gate for a little while, five or six figures immediately stood up in the cabin. They walked forward with their hand luggage, said goodbye to the two air hostesses at the door and left the aircraft without a fuss. Most passengers dealt with their fear of death more laconically. They continued talking softly, stared straight ahead like animals, or thought back over their lives.

I could have stayed in Gaspé, I certainly could. I could easily have switched to the life that seemed to have been waiting for me with the smell and taste of my childhood.

First, an old acquaintance of my mother's had got me a job. When I wandered among the books in the Bibliothèque Gaspéoise, ran my eyes over the computer screen and my fingers over the microfiches and looked through the crystal clear windows where I could see the market square in the autumn sunshine, fiery red maple, prams, a ladder against a house front, passers-by going for bread and a newspaper whenever I wanted to, I thought: this isn't an excursion, this is a life which gives me enough scope to serve out my time.

Secondly, I had been proposed to. In January, when a whole group of us were skiing in the Laurentides, Michel Toussaint took my hands in his, one icy afternoon. I looked at him in alarm. We were sitting in a mountain hut under a yellow lamp. We were wearing winter sweaters and padded windcheaters, but had still stayed a little too long in that grey-white abstraction of lines and surfaces and the cold had put me in a vacant mood. I saw the eyes under the jet-black eyebrows. For months my relationship with the astronomer had been as light and pleasant as the world. Now

151

he made this kind gesture and I shot upright: I've been here before, this combination of cold, winter sweater and affectionate impulse is a fragment of time about seveteen or eighteen years old. Terence, my mother, my white figure-skates and still no sign of Robert . . . I'm dreaming, I'm dead!

'I am already married!' I cried, but of course he knew that. Looking over his shoulder he ordered hot tea and then started talking about how easily these chores could be arranged nowadays across an ocean.

'Are these your parents?' he had asked a little while ago. Interested, he bent to look at the portrait which stood on my table on the left, close to the wall, between an ashtray and a dictionary, I lived in a grey-painted rented apartment at the top of a house overlooking the harbour of Gaspé.

I didn't answer at once. In my bare feet, my hair still damp from the bath, I was putting a sweater in a holdall. It was late. Michel had come to collect me, we were going to drive the following day to the radio telescope at Greenville. Flushed with amazement I would look at the row of enormous dishes, estimate their diameters, about twenty-five metres, count them, ten, ten elegant constructions could be transported on a track, over a sandy plain, along a line three kilometres long in order to make their observations. I would look at the sky and see stars, I would look down and be consoled by a number of firmly tightened bolts, in the extension I would be able to see the screens with the radio maps. What is your research? The galaxies. What would you like to know? Why they are distributed so unevenly through the universe. Is that so? Every four hundred million light years they are so close that we talk of a wall. A wall! Yes, a wall six billion light years long . . . Shall we go and have a bite to eat? OK.

I pushed my holdall aside with my foot. 'Come to bed,' I said. 'I've opened the window a little so let's pull the quilt over us. Yes, those are my parents. They adored each other for ten years and then suddenly it was over. Would it make any difference, do you

152

think, would you be more careful if you knew in advance that you were going to have ten long complete years and not a day longer?'

He got up, bent as he went past to lift my hair up a little and then drop it and walked to the bathroom whistling softly.

Why in heaven's name didn't I stay there? I certainly wasn't bored with Toussaint. It was in his company that I got lost in the wilderness near Black Mount, it was his dry clothes that I put on under a piece of canvas, opposite his fiery narrow face I once collapsed in Grand Café Leblanc to lick my fingers after eating a portion of Rockerfeller oysters and slightly drunk, started talking.

His calm question: 'What are you thinking about?'

I shook my head, smiling, confused, and started telling him about my childhood. What it is like to grow up with a mother who doesn't understand why one half of her life was unfathomable happiness full of sun, beautiful blond hair, mulberry trees and man who hunts and rides like a Cossack, and the other half a silent film in black-and-white, taking place in a French-Canadian coastal town, a house, wicker furniture, a snow-covered garden and a daughter who in her childhood was twice hit by a car but apart from that was very sweet and amenable.

My voice dropped. I put down my glass.

'She knew about my feeling of guilt. When Robert started talking about our future in Europe, she wasn't able to do anything more than put on a light-hearted, interested face.'

He poured me some more wine, gave me bread and a light and now and then asked me something. Why didn't she fall in love again? And while I answered honestly, I felt that my mother, with all her story, remained mine – the map of Europe in her classroom, the melancholy, repeated every year, of the first few days of September – nothing changed or disappeared. Once I got to the point of giving her away with my words. In order to free me of my grief about her Robert had wanted to know the facts and subsequently, had returned them to me seen through his eyes. Now I said, 'No chance of that. She may have seemed delicate and dreamy, but she was as stubborn as a mule!' And there I saw her in front of me, as clear as anything, with her cyclamen-red shawl, her sturdy hands, her warm breath. Spirit of my spirit and no one else's.

'Are you like her?'

'Yes. Terribly.'

And I shrugged my shoulders and pulled a funny face. I knew that nothing that I talked about would be retained by this man, he would not steal one single fragment to pass it on out of my control to a shadowy woman, a you, the second person in a love poem. I ate and drank with him as with a comrade and later in the street in the treacherously chilly evening air took his arm in order to strut home past a trail of red and green lights, to a room with a wooden floor where I, in a theatrical swoon like a tragic actress, a queen, took off my stockings on the edge of my bed, bent my neck, lifted my legs to be suddenly overwhelmed by an old scent, an old promise, a long since vanished sensation . . . What's wrong? What are you looking so happy about?

. . . Robert! this is no ordinary meeting, this is a two-step in a palace floating above the ground!

The beach near Cap-des-Rosiers. I am lying next to a wonderfully built Dutchman with blue eyes and a mysterious character. I am dreaming and looking at the same time. The sky changes colour, becomes as dull as copper, it must be about seven, the people on the beach are gradually retreating homewards. Just as I am thinking: he's lying there as though he's drunk, he sits up on his elbows. I notice there is not trace of a smile on his lips. The wrinkles next to his eyes are white.

. . . We saw whales playing, Robert, we drove in a cabriolet in the wind, we slept with each other and looked at the full moon and the strips of light on the wall opposite our hotel bed. Did all of that bring us something which we didn't yet know? Full of disquiet we dressed and undressed, we didn't comb our hair or wash our feet without ulterior motives. What lent the enchantment to two damp towels on the bathroom floor? Do you remember that excursion to Forillon? The wooden cottages, the villas, the horse and the pig in the meadow: we drove past them, at a sedate speed, and suddenly everything joined in with us, it was as if a coloured pencil line had been drawn around us, which gave us a quality of sweetness, something like a child's drawing. We were lying on the beach at Cap-des-Rosiers. The tide was beginning to come in. The area of sand became smaller and smaller. I began to laugh and pointed. 'Do you see that dog?' For a moment you stared with me at the animal which was digging with its black front paws, its whole body was jerking, the sea water kept coming and destroying the hole, I know what it's like. Then you grabbed my wrist. You frowned, I knew that you were worried about my thoughts. The tall boy with sailor's eyes looked at me, stared at me as if he had looked right through me and discovered a ship on the horizon. 'It was pure chance . . .' you mumbled. Right, so I was in love with you. But what disquiet! Where were my holidays at my mother's place? I have to go, I said to her, I'm young, free, I've got an urgent appointment, and I left my coffee where it was to go hurriedly to my room and to look at my swollen lips in the mirror. Was I perhaps putting the world in order in that way? I seemed to think I was. In the room at Motel les Mouettes I lay flat on my belly in bed. While you had gone into the village to buy squid and lemon, I thought of it. You are not the first, Robert, who has forced his legs through my legs, unbuttoned my dress and squashed me flat and God knows things will have taken a very strange course if you are to be the last. In feverish haste I fumble with your clothing, I take you in my arms and between my knees, I enclose you with tiny movements and counter-movements, you are not the first. But when you come back in a little while, I will look at you with a shocked expression: we can stay together, betray or abandon each other, but, if you ask me, this is for always. I

155

raised my head. The summer afternoon was almost over. In the motel people were slamming doors. Everywhere showers were rushing. My tears ran into my mouth in two little lines.

The giant orange bird had been repaired. Experts had given the go-ahead. Off you go, things have been fixed, if it's up to us, none of these passengers will die prematurely. The air hostesses began walking down the aisles. The plane taxied away, I looked at my watch: 6.30 p.m., one hour late according to the timetable.

My eyes met those of the passenger sitting next to me. The small grey-haired man had noticed my gesture.

'There is a westerly wind over the ocean,' he said. 'Sometimes that makes an hour's difference. It's quite possible that we will be on the other side right on time.'

I smiled at him. How nice. What a nice reassurance. This delay isn't a delay. You have been able to reflect for an hour, for form's sake, you have been able to toy with the idea of still retracing your steps, but that's as far as you get. Everything will go perfectly normally. And in the departure lounge there really won't be anybody waiting. We had said goodbye in the most tender way.

'Life is ridiculous,' said Michel.

'Yes,' I conceded. 'In a word. It is ridiculous and incomprehensible. A mishmash of anguish and pleasure that nobody can make head or tail of. Let's have a last glass of wine, over there, in the corner.'

At the bar in the passenger lounge there were a number of couples like us: one of the two in light travelling clothes, one of them keeping an eye on the time, one of them leaving. You will come back, won't you? Will you write? Telephone? Promise me you'll look after yourself.

I thrust my head forward threateningly.

'Oh dear, there you go again!'

We had been through it all. I am not going anywhere and I am not leaving anywhere. I am doing research, I'm collecting and composing. While writing my autobiography I am often over-whelmed by experiences that I don't know what to make of. And so I go on, correcting and adding.

'You look very nice in that dress.'

'Really?'

'I shall miss you terribly.'

'And I you.'

He accompanied me to passport control. There was a whole queue of people. Spare yourself this shuffling queue, I said.

Just before I reached the counter, I turned round. Immediately I found his eyes in the crowd. We waved once more and then he went into the early May evening, through the glass door and only when he stepped into the road between the parked cars did I see that there was someone on his arm, a female figure, a giggling, knowledge-hungry offshoot of myself, complete but with a very strange lifeline. Then they crossed and disappeared behind a gushing fountain.

I glanced out of the window. We were flying over eastern Canada. I saw the St Lawrence River, the Gulf of St Lawrence and I saw the elongated form of Gaspé, the peninsula that I was now saying goodbye to for the second time. Then I was sitting in a DC10 next to a young man whose voice and attitude were not at all indifferent to me. Now a small grey gentleman and I unfastened our safety belts and I realized that the Boeing 747 was far from full, the rest of the seats in our row were empty. Then, in bursts, awakening from my erotic dream, I must have thought now and then of my mother, she had seen us off at the station at Gaspé, her head cocked to one side, shoulders covered by blond hair, on her face was the expression of pained surprise that I can still see in my dreams. Now I asked myself wide awake what I had recovered of her.

I wandered around the cemetery with flowers. Her pink granite headstone was by now in the middle of a row. I had talked with a friend of hers, a neighbour, her former headmistress. My mother lived to be fifty-nine. She taught until she became ill. She loved her work. She was always in her classroom ahead of time to look after the flowering plants in the windows, to draw calendars on the board and to unroll maps. The children arrived to find a space already inhabited. She liked the town of Gaspé, and visited the regional museum not only because of the exhibitions on history, but also to drink tea and to look out over the bay through the bow windows. She read a lot, keeping to her habits she took a bath at about ten o'clock, put on a beautiful kimono and then lay in bed for hours reading, smoking, with a glass of whisky to hand; when she went to sleep she took the ashtray away and opened the windows. After the death of our Labrador she hadn't wanted a new dog. Still she was accompanied on her walks along the sea shore by a cheerful, playful animal, the mongrel spaniel of the neighbours: Mickey! Mickey! But the creature was already rushing at the seagulls who were standing motionless looking at their reflections in the metal-smooth sand along the tideline. Her daughter had gone back to Europe. She must have accepted it as inevitable. She telephoned, wrote and was as pleased as Punch when she got a letter, with a couple of photos enclosed. But why didn't I find any of those letters, not a single photo, or a single photo album from my childhood in her house after her death? No one could tell me. In their view my mother had not been a sad woman, but very absent-minded. She listened and talked with a wrinkle between her eyebrows, just as if she were looking inside herself with rapt attention. You might take her to be a woman who had gone blind who was training her memory.

A wrinkle between her eyebrows. Yes, that's how I see her in front of me. It is February, cold, as cold as can be when you are sixteen, and I have had to trudge home through the blizzard from school. My face is full of tears, she and I have had an argument and afterwards made peace magnanimously. I follow the movement with which she rakes up the fire in the wood stove, she is sitting on her haunches, half-turned towards me, a thick woollen skirt spreads over her legs like a monk's habit, suddenly I begin to glow with warmth. I look at her face, her skin moves with the play of the flames, and then I feel, as clearly as if I'd put my fingers against my

158

own face, the shape of her nose, her forehead, her jaws . . . I wait, taken aback, until the moment passes, the moment in which I feel in my very blood cells what I have in common with this German woman, this immigrant, this outcast in a small town . . .

'Mama . . .' I say slowly, deep in thought. 'How is Walter getting on, and Aunt Mimi? Why don't we go and visit them?'

When she looks at me that wrinkle is there. I know that she is thinking: Child, what have I got to do with them any more? But she doesn't say that. She smiles very sweetly, at her daughter who has suddenly thought of her blood relations, and says, 'Yes, perhaps we will do that one day.'

Nine hundred and fifty kilometres per hour with a following wind. The darkness slid ahead of us faster and faster. The passengers in the Bӧeing were served an aperitif in the twilight, and were just able to stub out their cigarettes to start dinner late in the evening. Everyone was hungry and that was logical. What is more reassuring than the individual, well-tried tempo of that inseparable duo hunger and thirst? I bent forward and beckoned the steward again, flashing a smile at my companion. He was certainly younger than I had first thought him to be, because of the grey, swept-back curly hair. We introduced ourselves. He was a doctor specializing in cardiovascular transplants, on his way to a conference in Istanbul. I was a biographer and translator, on my way to relations in Berlin. We began a non-committal conversation. I brought up: my happiest moments . . . the débâcle of my life . . . the joys of wandering . . . my other, freer self . . .

I ate lightly seasoned lamb and rice.

I saw film images on a screen that had been let down in the middle of the cabin. A desert landscape. Two smiling women. A donkey.

And I thought of the hurricane behind the window next to my head, of the awful, water-filled chasm beneath me, of the completely unreal world which somewhere, having drifted off in time, must still exist: my house in the Oude Zeestraat, my husband and my three dogs.

I began sweating furiously.

'I'm not getting any oxygen any more,' I stammered to the grey man next to me. 'Good God, what's going on . . .'

He looked at me with a kindly expression. 'Wait a moment, madame, I'll help you breathe again.'

And he reached up and adjusted the ventilator above my head so that a fresh breeze began blowing on my cheeks, air, real air from outside. Oh, the girl's dream! The novel about doctors! The healing eyes and hands. I calmed down. I calmed down and laid my head on his shoulder and a little later on the knees in the soft flannel. The doctor's fingers stroking away the hair from my temples. The plane which now and then jolted and jarred like a ship. 'I wonder what time it is . . .' I mumbled, drowsily.

And so I travelled back to Europe, with my face in the crotch of a complete stranger. Half an hour ago I would have been able to think that I ought to make arrangements for my life, that I ought to send a telegram at once. Now I realized drowsily that in each human being there is a blue, Mediterranean area in which the events of life move around, criss-crossing each other, like chickens on stately legs, pecking and looking around without hurting each other. I moved my hips. With my hair spread out, my blouse unbuttoned I abandoned myself to the rhythm of the night.

Half-asleep. Abstractions. Short lucid reasonings. After having wandered the world for nearly two years I knew my route, but not my place. I was still curious. Can you revise the past? Of course you can. Is it possible to walk away from your own image? I have seen towns, climbed mountains, more than once I have descended into a river. Very likely I've managed not to be the same person any more. Not the same person as who?

When during an endless hot summer I bumped into Robert, it had happened to me more than once that I knocked over saltcellars and needed people to say everything to me more than once. But it was different that time. My beauty was unparalleled, my words were heavy as gold, beside myself I signed the shameless contract of the great love. Now I have to give myself entirely, that was clear enough. Overawed by the situation that I found myself in I listed my preferences and antipathies, my holiday memories, my childhood illnesses, and girl's secrets, and then, once I got going, I dragged in my childhood friends male and female, my old loves, my dog, my mother and my father.

But what was that? Everything changed colour and was cast adrift. Some things became larger, others much smaller. One thing only disappeared. The nightmare disappeared. The nightmare which had pursued me from childhood, full of corridors, staircases, sparsely lit rooms, was swept from my consciousness. A few nights after I had told Robert that I was looking for him, my father, in all the prisons, in all the courtyards, in all the rooms with concrete walls in this world I dreamt the following:

I am walking hand in hand with a man through a rocky landscape. I am a child. My hand is completely hidden in that of the man of whom my dream shows me nothing except that hand and a part of his arm covered in a white cotton shirt sleeve. Nevertheless I know who he is. He is my father. And at the same he is Robert. As we climb up among the boulders, I suddenly realize the reason for the journey. I must stop searching. I must stop peering through railings, wandering through corridors and looming in doorways. Your future lies ahead of you, not behind you, remember that. Then we stand still. Suddenly there is a panorama. The hand lets go of me, points, and immediately I also see it. In a crevice in the distant rock face, quite undramatically, is a knife. We look at it in silence. At our leisure we study the elegant form and the metallic gleam of the object, which reminds me of the long narrow leaf of an exotic plant, carried along by the wind and deposited in the sun.

*

161

I raised my eyes. Around me there was an atmosphere of calm and a rushing vibrating movement which I could not immediately place. Then I recognized the droning of the aeroplane. And I felt someone in the specific grey light of a day which had not quite dawned, looking and smiling at me.

I lifted my head off his lap. Rather sheepishly I sat up.

'I hope I haven't been too much trouble to you.'

He sat there just as calmly as at the beginning of the night.

'No trouble at all,' he said. 'It was nice having you close to me.' He hesitated a moment and then said, 'It's been a long time since I had a woman in my arms.'

We laughed and without further ado began a series of caresses – kisses on the cheek, nostrils, upper and lower lips, burrowing with our noses together, gentle sniffing – till I sat up and looked around. The morning after a nocturnal journey. Yawning, dishevelled faces. If I go to the toilet cabin now, there won't be a queue. I grabbed my toilet bag – 'Excuse me!' – and slid past him.

I surveyed my face in the mirror. I tapped my cheeks and pushed my chin. Are you still the same person? You were an eight- or nine-year-old girl with transparent green eyes and flaxen hair. Will it be painful when they see you, as the woman standing there putting lipstick on in the mirror? Walter, let's see, is a man in his forties, a completely imaginary figure from behind whom since the last year of the war an emaciated, dark-haired boy has stood making funny faces at me and beckoning me to come and lie on a dark red sofa pushed into a corner. I stick my tongue out. As soon as she sees me my aunt will probably say that I'm like my mother. Come on, let me put some perfume on and find my seat in the aircraft again.

At breakfast he says, 'Come to Istanbul with me.'

We looked at each other, in complete seriousness, but when I began to laugh and shook my head reluctantly, I could see that he was already resigned to the conclusion of our meeting, to this May morning, with the coffee cups, the sachets of sugar, the remains of

162

toast and the warning signs which soon, in the aircraft which was losing height metre by metre after a flight which had begun slowly but apart from that had gone very pleasantly, would flash up in red letters: *no smoking, fasten your seat belts.*

Chapter Six

'That's one,' said Mimi.

She had sat down next to me on the back seat and reached toward the door which was still open.

'That's two,' she said when Walter, in the pouring rain, closed the door on her side.

'And . . .' she put down her hood and unbuttoned her raincoat, '. . . that . . .' she stroked the front of her coat with her old, heavily veined hands, '. . . is . . .' she put her feet together and straightened her back, '. . . three!' She looked at me with satisfaction.

Birgit, at the wheel, waited until her grandmother had finished all the manoeuvring and her father, who meanwhile had got in next to her, had put his case of cameras on the floor. Because of the rain she had let the engine run a little already, but the fan was still blowing in cold air, for a moment all four of them were busy cleaning the mist from the windows.

'Let's go,' said Birgit.

In the mirror I saw her eyes. The eyes of this serious, nineteen-year-old, like her hair, had the colour and the disconcerting gleam of a chestnut just taken from its shell. Birgit, who since she had got her driving licence, practised as much as she could in her father's car, had offered to drive me to Bahnhof Zoo. The train to Prague would leave at the end of the afternoon. 'Into first,' muttered Mimi, 'indicator on, and, whoops, off we go, now into second . . .'

We drove out of the Wolffstrasse. With a feeling of really saying goodbye I looked at the row of grey-and-white apartment blocks with small windows. Behind three of those windows I had been at home. For no other reason than my blood relationship with the occupants I knew where the telephone was, I knew the idiosyncrasies of the geyser, I had sat with the master of the house and his daughter in a pink dressing gown drinking beer at the

164

kitchen table and when I first came in – three weeks ago – the old woman who lived with them held her hands to my face, looked at me for a very long time and then stammered, 'Now first put some coffee on, then get out the cognac and then talk, then talk . . .'

It was unbelievable! When we turned into the road past the Viktoriapark, the sky went yellow, in the middle of the day the lights went on in all the buildings, on the pavements people began running.

'There's going to be quite a storm,' said Walter.

Keeping to his agreement not to interfere with his daughter's driving he hung half over the front seat and looked good-naturedly from his mother to me. Just as we reached the Yorckstrasse, he was proved right. A flash of lightning rent the sky, followed by a vicious crash, the kind that puts your heart into your mouth, and then it was as though a helicopter were hovering above the city, a monstrous craft which swept people and dogs off the street and blew papers across the road; the trees along the avenue bent in all directions. We watched the spectacle intently. The car shook a little, but it wasn't unpleasant.

Mimi nudged me. She raised her eyebrows and made a sideways motion with her head.

'Watch, Magda, it will be the bridge in a moment. Well, oh, bridge, it's a rusty structure and that only serves for the S-Bahn.' She put up three fingers and counted, 'A great, ugly, rusty wreck.'

My gaze met Walter's. She is upset, he said with his eyes. I nodded, yes, I know. She's upset that I am going. Well, he replied, I don't like it myself either.

'She's been through a lot,' he had said a few days before, half to me, half to himself. He was standing in his darkroom and looking at a series of photos that he had just printed and were drying on a line. Fascinated, I bent to see the studies of the old woman, because yes, that was how I knew her. A face which smiles and looks at you, that listens calmly to you and also tells you very honestly in answer to your questions: her youth was idyllic, full of puppet shows and summer evenings; whatever her younger sister

165

put on, everything suited her; when the Russian troops marched into Berlin, all women were exposed to obvious terrors. I knew my aunt as someone who is a passionate card player, cook, purchaser of vegetables in the market who at some moments seems to want to put something right, a chaos, an obscure dislocation, to count with a look from which all calm has disappeared, to measure, to sum up . . . 'Yes,' I had said. 'It's her to the life.'

As we emerged under the S-Bahn bridge, the rain began in earnest, 'Well now,' spluttered Birgit and switched the windscreen wipers onto full speed. In a matter of a few seconds we saw the asphalt change into a mass of water with trembling, splashing light. We turned into the Bülowstrasse, crawling along, picking up speed and stopping at one traffic light after another and finally found our way into an infernal entanglement of saloon cars, yellow taxis, and cream-coloured buses, there had been a collision, the rest of the Bülowstrasse was totally blocked.

Birgit remained cool-headed. In the wake of a taxi she managed to get away from the junction and did not hesitate to turn into the Potsdamerstrasse, in completely the wrong direction. A poor area. Peepshow adverts, bars, rubbish containers, and a boarded-up restaurant with the name Souvlaki-Johnny.

She looked at me in the mirror.

'Don't worry. You'll get your train.'

And I really wasn't worried. Thanks to Mimi's nerves we had left home more than an hour before we needed to. As far as I was concerned we could drive as far as the Wall. I felt myself become more and more indifferent. The train will soon be leaving from Bahnhof Zoo. What would it matter? No train is ever the last one. Revelling in the warmth, in the company of my aunt and my cousin, who, like me, did not say another word and my niece who seemed to be the only one who was really awake, I was – long – past caring.

I looked at the girl at the wheel. Her neck. The small white ears which emerged from her gathered-up hair with a special kind of significance. Birgit is studying biology and last week, with a breaking heart, ended a love affair which she told me all about. Velvet eyebrows, slanting eyes. More than any intimate conversation, her appearance and her way of behaving initiate me into her secrets. Now she takes one hand off the wheel, brushes it across her cheek, adjusts the indicator with three fingers and casts a glance over her left shoulder, I think she is indescribably sweet.

We turned left, then right again. A little square. A tree with a fence around the trunk. The rain was hammering monotonously on the roof of the car. My eyelids were becoming heavy. I put my elbow against the window frame to support my head which kept dropping. A wailing ambulance overtook us, we had to stop for a moment, I stared at a bus shelter where, in a corner, a number of people and dogs were standing together like a ghostly apparition, vague, immaterial. When we slid a metre further, the bodies gave way to a wall with captions in fluorescent paint: *Yankees, raus! Chinesen raus! Türken nicht erwünscht!* I glanced at them without any reaction. As far as I was concerned this city could be any city, a system of caves, a sewer that can only tolerate its own stench, I had nothing to do with it. The only thing that counted in this world was the purring of the engine and the deep breathing of my relatives . . . I felt my muscles relaxing.

'We're almost at the Nollendorfplatz,' said Birgit's voice suddenly.

I raised my head. The lucid statement brought me back to myself in a trice. Wherever I may have let myself be dragged around, and for however long, I now just shifted energetically in my seat and noticed that pale afternoon sunlight was streaming into the car. I looked outside. There was the theatre, the metro station and the house fronts decorated with bent metal balconies around the square which was precisely on the route to the station. Aha, I'm here. And the downpour is obviously over.

The other three also seemed refreshed. Mimi tapped the end of a cigarette on her thumbnail, Walter gave her a light, Birgit said, 'Look at that . . .'

Up to their ankles in the water of an overflowing manhole a

group of Jesus freaks were standing singing. With the hem of her dress clinging to her calves a woman tramp was trying to fish something out of her bag, and she had it: a leather travelling case. At the counter of a red-painted snack bar, men were drinking beer and eating sausage with ketchup, closely observed by a troop of soaking wet sheepdogs. A taxi stopped at the kerb and let a boy get out clutching a mysterious dark purple case.

We watched in silence, all four of us, like people who had not, as we had, sat dozing and sleeping, but who had just had a particularly animated conversation. We agreed, completely, one hundred per cent, and if it was necessary to philosophize, sulk, rage, or laugh, we would do that harmoniously or not at all. What time was it? We drove past a clockmaker's and glanced at the front. Five minutes to five.

The Kleiststrasse. Café Jenseits. Walter and I had sat drinking more than once in the neon-lit bar. Because the place stayed open all night, you met journalists, alcoholics, cleaners, hairdressers, publicans, lady bus conductors. The day before yesterday a poet had come and sat next to us who after graciously accepting a coffee with a Weinbrand, began reading aloud from his work.

'I thought there was something touching about the lad,' said Walter suddenly. He had read my thoughts.

Later that evening two musicians had stood up in the audience, no one had seen them come in, they were simply there. After the juke box had been turned off – there was a moment's uncomfortable silence – the music began, the harmonica and the banjo, which made the café regulars get out of their chairs, grab each other for a joke and start dancing round, to 'waltz' to the long-drawn-out, exquisite, lonely sounds of a pop song resurrected from the past . . . Walter is a man in his forties who dances with slow steps. He had the veiled look of the professional photographer. A moustache and a leather jacket also form part of his equipment.

'Magda . . .'

Mimi stared at me biting on her lip. She pointed to the fingers

168

of her left hand, but could clearly not decide what to start listing. I gestured outside.

'Look. The Europa Centre. We're almost there.'

For a moment both of us looked at the pink Mercedes star rotating on its concrete pedestal.

We parked. We got out. There was the station concourse and the steps which were counted one by one by Mimi: there were eight. The train which would take me to the Eastern block was waiting on platform one. I said a tearful farewell. When the departure signal had been given and the whole train began gliding away and Mimi, small, blonde, in a coat with buttons askew, ran along with the train for a little way calling out all kinds of things, I suddenly realized how like my mother she looked.

Chapter Seven

Something must have happened. The train stopped again. I hesitated. The idea of crawling out of my sleeping bag for the umpteenth time was not very appealing.

We had been stuck at the border for hours. My passport had been checked more than once. A woman in a uniform jacket which was hanging open had inspected my bed, my bare feet and my face, which was etched with resentment and sleep, without a glimmer of understanding. Because the moment the woman had turned on her heel, the train seemed to set in motion, I had locked the door of my compartment. Hey ho, on to the Netherlands. With a bit of luck I can sleep as far as Nuremberg. And I had taken off my dress and had lain down again. Two o'clock in the morning. The trifling distance from Prague to the West German frontier turned out to be a journey that it is best not to make light of.

Then I heard the sounds. They began in the distance, lazily, softly, exceptionally threatening, they were noises which every human being recognizes naturally, even those who know nothing of the secret language of a blank wall, a door without a handle, becomes restless. The thudding of boots. The panting of animals kept under control. I rushed to the window and let the roller blind up quickly.

It was misty. The train was standing on a gently curving track. The number of carriages was so great that I couldn't see the first or the last. But about a hundred metres away I could see a building illuminated by searchlights with the name of the border post above a door. Pomezi. And in the mist I saw a group of uniformed men and women with dogs which were straining at the leash marching towards the train. I put my shoes on, my dress and my jacket.

I want to go home, I thought. The uproar came closer. I don't want to be prevented by anything or anyone. From the neighbouring compartment I heard orders in a language, my native language, which I scarcely understood. Now I have finally decided to go home, I am in a hurry. My door was thrown open.

Really it was ridiculous. They were looking for someone, a criminal, an enemy of the state. Did they really think that someone like that could hide behind the panelling of the compartment? They banged the ceiling with the butts of their rifles and tapped the empty berths above my bed. They searched the floor on their knees. As they left, I recognized the woman, she gave me a vacant look, it struck me that her uniform jacket had been buttoned up.

I was standing at the train window, wide awake. No man's land glided past. I saw a watchtower, bright arc lamps, a footbridge with rolls of barbed wire at the sides. At the end of a small wood a second station appeared, 'Schirnding' I read, this was Germany. How must I have looked to the lonely official on the platform? A ghostly figure with teeth gritted. A woman returning home, who a few days ago was overcome by a vague impulse – isn't it about time. . . – but who now, after a border incident, with the obstinacy of someone who has almost been frustrated, is driven by a single – blind – thought: you are bloody well going home!

Your eyes glided over deciduous and coniferous woods, over valleys in the sun and walled farmhouses. Despite the beautiful June weather very few animals were outside. You are on your way to the house where you were born. From Prague you caught the train. From there a bus took you deep into Moravia. The closer you get, the clearer the memory becomes of the colour and light of your village. Particularly the first light, in the morning, when the sun rises from behind the hills, you remember, you must have been five or six. The road climbs. You realize that you are not looking too closely at the beech hedges, the cornfields, an enormous heap of dirty agricultural rubbish, perhaps you would rather not know the present state of affairs. First of all move into the inn, which as you know for certain, is at the highest point in the village, where three country roads meet and where in summer, on the square in front of it, fires are lit and festivities are organized during which, under a bright pink sky, you cannot take your eyes off the live cocks who to the sound of bagpipe music scratch around solemnly on tables decorated with ribbons . . .

The bus stopped at the highest point. I had scarcely climbed down the steps or when sure enough there was the inn, Hostinec Na Výhledech. The word, which I couldn't even pronounce, nevertheless set something in motion in my brain. I looked around and began to laugh. Inn of the Views . . . Inn of the Views . . . isn't it comical? At the front a concrete silo fringed with rubbish, from the side windows a filling station. When I tried to open the door – it was locked – I discovered a hand-written message. *Open from 4 p.m. to 6 p.m.* That's how things are. Here people have a drink after work. Here people don't eat and certainly don't sleep. Well. Should I start walking down this asphalt road? Over there, on the other side of the slope, must be the house and the swing and the ten-metre-high white mulberry of my earliest childhood. What's wrong with you? Take that stupid expression, as though you could burst out any moment in a crazy fit of laughter, off your face. Anyway, why is it so quiet here?

How quiet it was. I went down the road along the flower-covered verge, I had already noticed that cars pass you here at full speed without giving way an inch. Against the side of the hill there were fields, some of them under cultivation, corn, hops. I heard the distant purring of a tractor, there was a bit of wind, there were cries of seagulls above a mountain of rubbish, I saw them glistening against the blue sky. How high they built their barns here. Why is it no one is working on the land? Isn't that the farm of Baron Šebek, there, with the tall narrow chimney of the distillery that made the headiest plum brandy in the area? I walked into the courtyard, there was no dog who barked at me, I looked in amazement at the desolation. The walls had crumbled, the out-houses had collapsed, the first floor of the villa seemed to be inhabited. I found the stables by the stink, a white horse looked at me above a half door and bit when I tried to stroke its nose, there were crows with their warm patient eyes, why aren't you in the meadow? Plenty of space, plenty of grass, why are you covered in thick crusts of muck?

A few people were walking along the village street. A boy with a satchel gave me a friendly greeting. Our house was further on, a little while and I would be able to see it. It is a nice house, quite big, we are quite well off. In the living room there are carpets with fantastic curling patterns, there are flowers everywhere and at the grand piano sits my mother, she is biting her lip and lets one hand, a hand which suddenly looks very like a lovable, wriggling animal, creep from one end of the keyboard to the other. She looks up, pulls a face and says, 'Will I ever be able to learn it? Come on, let's go into the garden.' The dog – a wild animal, half wolf, half dog – has understood her and gets up immediately. It is beautiful in the garden. There is a small vineyard, there are mulberry trees, next to a row of apple trees trained on strings are the chicken runs and a pigsty. The barn, at the back, is a place full of tumultuous life: on the left there is the stable of an Arab thoroughbred, in the garage, on the right, there is a dark blue motorbike with a sidecar. My father, who is director of the sugar factory in Oslavany, rides that motorbike or that horse to work, it isn't very far, about five kilometres, I think, along the path by the river. I can still remember . . .

I was there. Yes, I stood in front of the house, what excitement. I got tears in my eyes, would you believe it: how well I know the walls, those walls and that roof. It is just a little strange that a shop has been opened on the ground floor. Let me drift over to the shop window to look calmly and quietly for a moment – sugar, beans, jam, biscuits, toilet paper – and the white words which can be read on the window, Smíšené Zboží, which probably means: all kinds of things. Now I look at the garden. It has become smaller, certainly, and the old mulberry tree has gone, the apple trees trained on strings as well, but the billy goat which comes up to me with bright blue striped eyes, is nice. I pushed my fist against the hard head. The animal pushed back hard. You want a fight, lad?

Then I suddenly heard, 'Hello!'

I turned round.

A few steps away from me was a blonde woman. Her laughter was intended for me.

'Hello!' she said again, pushing her neck a little forward. Her hands were occupied. On one side she was holding a girl of about four, the other was on the handle of a cart on which she was carrying a large jute sack full of potatoes.

She began explaining something to me. She asked me something. She pointed to the house. I stared at her pretty broad face – she must be my age – what was she talking about?

'I used to live here,' I finally said, instinctively in English. 'I left in the summer of '46 with my mother.'

Then the unbelievable thing happened – the grey eyes opened wide – I was recognized.

'Magda!'

She let go of the cart and, without hesitation, the child too. The two arms were needed to wrap round me, to pat my back, to grab my shoulders so firmly that I could be looked at again from a distance but could not under any circumstances take to my heels.

'Magda . . . Magda Rezková!'

Like me, Milena Cepová had been born in this village. We must have played together as children, our mothers were friends. It took a little while before I could understand her English.

'Walk along with me,' she finally said excitedly. 'Look. My house is a hundred metres further on this corner, you will eat and stay.' She bent down to take the child's hand again.

We pulled the cart through the village street, it was a quarter past twelve. We came to a house with a pointed roof and a beautiful detached barn, the wind blew through the cherry and mulberry trees in the garden, under the terrace stood a sofa.

174

Milena pointed to the house and the barn.

'Smith,' she said beaming. 'This house was a smith.'

We dragged the potatoes down the grassy slope to the pantry, the four-year-old girl, Eli, looked at me shyly. Milena opened a door and took me into the living room, where the windows were open and the sun was shining in and to two little boys one of whom – the seven-year-old Kuba – had such a round head and such long lashes and such tender cheeks that you could mistake him for an elfin child, and the other – the nine-year-old Matěj – put a game of spillikins on the table in his fist, dropped them in front of my nose and looked at me with sparkling black eyes. I reached out my hand, let it hover, held my breath and, in a silence that you could cut with a knife, lifted, pulled away the top stick with faultless precision.

Then we were called to table, the children and I. We were given bread with quark and onions, tea and warm dumplings filled with plums.

'Try them, Magda,' said Milena and she pushed the dish of steaming white balls towards me. 'Look. This *švestkové knedlíky*! You like!'

Milena and her husband enjoyed speaking English. When I met the genial Jewish lawyer that afternoon, I understood why. Jiří had been in Amsterdam and London. He had been enchanted by the (diurnal and nocturnal) life of bourgeois society. Having freedom, expensive cars and newspapers is not by definition criminal.

'Oh this country! It is a tragedy!' was the regular exclamation with which Jiří accompanied me across the fields and along the river of my native region and helped me gain access to the houses, the land, the people of my village.

'Who is she?' people asked him.

A farmer's widow let me accompany her when she took a bucket of soup to her pig. She talked to the animal, which took its pale pink snout out of the mess in order to listen and even to grunt back. A teacher showed me his pigeons, each of which had its own beautiful nesting compartment against the wall of the barn. The director of the water mill, who was in the process of giving a coat of paint to the idyllic building which had originally belonged to his family, interrupted his work to open a bottle of sparkling white wine. Jiří explained about me. Then even more doors opened, new bottles were uncorked, people began beaming, occasionally people cried, people remembered my father, my mother and their blonde daughter very well.

'What a tragedy,' cried Jiří as we walked home through a neglected wood and could not find a single chanterelle for supper.

Milena never went with us on these trips. This beautiful woman, who had not become a mother until ten years after her marriage, had made her choice. Early in the morning, when I was still under a quilt behind the stone stove, I heard her busy in the kitchen with her children. In order not to disturb their domestic routine, and also for my own sake, I did not appear until later, when the radio was on softly and the vegetables still covered in dew from the garden were on the draining board, and Milena turned to me in the sunlight while she screwed together the two halves of the coffee percolator. Sugar biscuits. My dress on the line. A woman who is concerned with my safety and happiness. Milena is my friend and my mother, most of all she is my sister: the very first evening when we were sitting with our backs against the warm outside wall talking, we had already discovered that we had hidden in the same cellar in the spring of 1945.

We had let the chickens loose. The bombardments were coming closer and closer, the Russians were advancing towards Brno, they said, our village was on the route to an airfield, if there should be a direct hit then it was better that the chickens should be able to escape as they thought best.

My mother and I found a hiding place in one of the cellars of a friendly wine-grower, whose name was Hrubec. Our wolfhound went with us. With three or four other families we lay on mattresses between the gigantic wooden barrels and listened to the war being fought out above our heads. Everyone tried to deduce from the whistling, the explosions, the rattle of machine-gun fire who was winning. People speculated on the comment of the German telegraph operator who when we arrived at the farmhouse was packing his things. Just you wait and see. When the Russians come, you won't have very much to laugh about.

The end of the fifth day it went dead quiet. We looked at each other in the light of the carbide lamp. The best thing was to stay sitting still. A baby was given a drop of honey on its lips. Better not to let it cry. Then we heard the boots, they thudded along the road, and talking in a strange language, clearer and clearer and louder. Footsteps descended the cellar stairs, we all looked at the door, there was knocking, one of us immediately opened up.

I had never seen such people. The two soldiers had broad faces, flat noses and slanting coal-black eyes, they were Mongols. They came into the cellar and looked at us without laughing or greeting. One of them appeared to be interested in my beautiful blonde mother. He walked towards her. However, when his comrade made a gesture with his sub-machine gun – upstairs, you! – we were all able to leave without trouble.

Outside the evening dusk hurt my eyes. There was a smell like iron which you couldn't get out of your throat. I saw military cars, motorbikes, Mongol soldiers on horseback and women, women who looked imperturbably around them with cartridge belts slung across their uniformed breasts and gave orders like growling dogs.

We walked back to the house in the darkness, my mother, the dog, two little boys who for some reason had been entrusted to my mother and me. Although the distance was scarcely a kilometre and a half, the journey took us at least an hour. More than once I imagined I saw a grey curled-up figure lying at the edge of the destroyed road. There was our house. There was the garden where on the lawn, illuminated by a blazing fire, two tanks were parked. In deepest silence we walked into the garden. Everywhere lay the bodies of Russian soldiers. We counted eight. Then an officer came out of the house towards us. He greeted my mother in French, excused himself for the drunkenness of his men and explained that if we moved into the upstairs floor, not a hair of our heads would be harmed.

His gaze slid from my mother to us, the children. I saw that he began smiling and shaking his head. His expression changed – he grinned like an uncle who is about to do something crafty. He walked into the kitchen and came back with a torch and motioned us to follow him. In a corner of the barn, on the soft hay was a large quantity of eggs.

There are events which do not disappear into the past. They do not happen once, they do not happen repeatedly, they have the terrifying quality of continuing to exist through the years. Not as movement, but as paralysis. Not as fluid time, but as a frozen moment. When one September morning I opened the front door of my parents' house, I was still small. I would be six in a couple of months. I pushed down the handle with one hand and at the same time pulled the copper housing of the lock, because I knew that the door stuck. I was nervous. The screaming and the banging of rifle butts outside and my mother's whispered command, bending, with her hair loose, in the well of the staircase, had made me panic. The door flew open, the event had begun.

My father was betrayed in September 1944. Until then the Germans had more or less left him alone, perhaps because of his marriage to an Aryan woman. When he arrived at work in the mornings, he began by typing out the BBC radio reports that he had listened to the evening before. Then he had them taken to the partisans in the hills. Although he was nominally no longer director, he still managed the factory. That morning everything seemed normal. I had crept into my parents' bed and lay in the down pillows, which were still warm, watching my father who was standing shaving. The foam was still on his ears, his lips were strangely red, he winked at me in the mirror and, at intervals, sung a funny song about the animal orchestra, 'Ptací kapela'. When the lorries stopped in front of our house, I was downstairs by myself. Dressed in a fluffy dressing gown I was sitting in the kitchen with my hands around my mug of ersatz chocolate milk. I listened. Outside there was shouting. The lorries kept their engines running but did not move off. I ran to the stairs and saw my mother hanging over the bannisters.

I am standing in the doorway. Without moving or blinking I look at the Gestapo men. They want to come into our house. I can't feel anything. I see the boots, leather belts and weapons, and don't get upset, but I am blocking the way. Then a hand pushes me aside. The gesture, which is powerful, makes me land among the coats which are hanging on the hallstand. In a smell of grass and rain I follow the extraordinary noises which accompany the arrest of my father. It doesn't take long. Then the group comes downstairs, hurriedly, my father in the middle. His hair is a little messed up, he is wearing his old sports jacket, I can't see his expression properly because he is pressing a handkerchief to his mouth. Without looking up or round he walks straight past me out of the house.

I experienced endless June days. I had no responsibility or duty. All I had to do was look at the grass. At the cherry tree which fills half the sky. The calm, almost timeless family life of Milena bounded my view of the world – there are Matěj, Kuba and their father who come out one by one with wet hair and a clean T-shirt, there are the cat, the tomato plants, the sprinkler – and when I looked at the four-year-old Eli who is getting too big but is allowed by her mother to have a bottle of milk with sugar, I thought: I am very little different from the child. I have recovered my childhood misunderstanding completely, yes, things are eternal. Everything is as it should be. And I rolled onto my side to grab my cigarettes.

It was nice to be set to do a chore now and again. I dried the dishes. I went to the baker's. The more I strolled past my parents' house with the bread, the more warmly it seemed to welcome me. Sometimes I saw a window open on the first floor, a curtain flapped back and forth across the window pane. I began to realize that neither the house, nor I, were responsible for the stupid shop and the tasteless garden. What were the things that mattered? What mattered was the summer air streaming in through the window, which was not only unchanged, completely the same, but which I had never lost, as I had not lost the blue vase full of fiery red poppies in front of the mirror in the hall, or the huge white moon, in the winter, above the hills. And I stood still, in the middle of the road. And just when I was thinking: I am empty, cut loose from my history, I remembered with fantastic clarity my excitement when I was allowed to go to the factory with my father. It sometimes happened, on summer mornings when we trotted along the path lined with alders beside the Oslava, that everything came and disappeared, the bushes, the river, the bushes, the river. Only my father, the mare and I did not disappear, we soon arrived at the sugar factory, the mare was put out to graze in the meadow and my father and I ensconced ourselves in a room with high windows, he in order to telephone with a dark, narrow, animated face and to write and I to colour all the bears and giraffes outlined in black in a large-format book . . .

'Do you know,' I said to Milena who had lain down beside me in the grass. 'It's about time I was thinking of going home.'

Now I did a round of farewells. A trip through the villages because I am leaving tomorrow. I took Milena's bike, seated myself on it in a very sporty attitude and sped down the asphalt road. The wind rushed past my ears, a butterfly tried to get into my blouse, it is ridiculous that I am leaving, these hillsides covered with vineyards are certainly not boring me yet.

At the crossroads I suddenly heard: 'Teto!' I looked round and saw a skinny boy racing up to me on his bike, standing on the pedals. 'Teto!' he called again when he had caught up with me, meaning: Auntie! Matěj wanted to accompany me on my trip.

We got talking, the Czech child and I. After riding along beside me in silence for a while, Matěj arrived at a marvellous solution to our language problem. What did it matter that I communicated with his parents in completely incomprehensible sounds? I wasn't stupid, I was fun. He slowed down, shot a quick glance at me, pointed into the distance and began telling me something that was impossible to misunderstand. He raised his voice, he slowed down, he speeded up, he thought with a frown, a hesitation, a conclusion, a smile. He looked at me.

I also gave a little laugh, full of agreement, and thought: Czech is a sharply articulated language with lots of 'a' sounds.

The road not only started climbing but also grew worse. In various places the asphalt had worn through. For a moment we both had to be careful not to have to get off. There was the highest point. Relief, rather exaggerated recovering of breath, laughter. He resumed talking. I listened. This time his topic required a firm, persuasive tone. Now and again he looked to the side and only continued after my nod. Talking. Talking is not revealing what you know, but what you want to say.

His final sentence sounded like: '. . . straravranakolatch!'

In order to keep my end up, I decided to repeat the last word.

'Kolatch,' I said. He shook his head earnestly and corrected me.

'Kolatch!' The 'l' had to be much thicker.

'Kolatch!' I said. All right. Now he nodded in satisfaction, this word was passable. What if he tried a lower gear? We were riding along a road nestling in a flower-covered plain. The air felt like rose petals and smelled just as sweet. What language should I choose to say the necessary things to him in turn? The exotic vocabularly of Dutch might perhaps equal that of Czech. I thought for a moment, cleared my throat, and when I had captured his attention, began talking about my husband, my dogs and the place where I lived on the coast of South Holland. I don't remember all the things I blurted out, it must have been amusing, because I can still see Matěj's face in front of me, grinning at me with conspiratorial delight.

'The nicest time there is bulb time,' I concluded. 'Then the whole village smells like a cupboard full of linen and soap.'

The Moravian hills. The river Oslava. Farewell and return. I think of Matěj, a nine-year-old boy in a blue tracksuit. If he wanted to speed up a bit, wanted to ride faster than me, he stood up on the pedals. I can see his skinny little body appearing first on the right and then on the left of his bike. If you could imagine that bike wasn't there, he was executing a comic, supernatural dance in the air.

When we got home I asked Milena what 'Kolatch' meant.

'Koláč!' she repeated laughing. 'That means tart!' Whereupon Matěj returned to the subject. He wanted to make a cherry tart for me. So that I would not die of hunger tomorrow in the train. His mother wasn't allowed to do anything except weigh the flour and turn on the oven. They were busy with it for a long time.

Shortly after dawn the train arrived in Nuremberg. A harassed crowd emerged, looking for the sausage stands and newspaper kiosk. Everything was still closed. I let myself be swept along with the stream of travellers passing through, wandered over one or two platforms, saw the still empty track and joined the queue for the coffee machine. When the train came in everyone crushed forward. Together with three Slovak men and two Gypsy women with a baby I looked for an unoccupied compartment in a carriage where the faint sulphurous smell of some noctural journey or other still hung. With considerable effort we found one. We put our bags at our feet, crossed our arms and waited for the departure.

Everything went well until we got near Würzburg. Then we stopped in a suburb and the door of our compartment was pulled open by a huge railway official with blond hair and a thick red neck. The man looked angry. He tapped with his nails on the strips of paper which were stuck to the outside of the glass and inquired whether we could read. No one replied. Then he puffed up his chest and buried us under the weight of his official announcement. This was a mother and child compartment. 'Raus!' he said, summarizing the situation. 'Alle: raus!' and while the Slovaks, the Gypsy women, the baby and I were still vacating the compartment, the mother was already arriving. A beautiful young woman hurried past us with unseeing eyes, clutching her child to her to devote herself to her motherhood despite the privations of the journey. The official slid the door shut behind her.

I stood in the corridor. One of the Slovaks gave me a thin black cigarette. The smoke stung my eyes and lungs but was so good I almost felt like crying. I lent, with my back to the landscape against the window, rid of my exhaustion, of my sleep, of my fear, of my revulsion, of everything except the complete solitude which lay like a blanket around my shoulders. Next to me sat the Gypsy woman with the sleeping baby on a kind of cot, a seat attached to the wall of the train. Her face was dull and withdrawn, so that despite her long skirt and bulging bag at her feet she was, as it were, not with us. The train jolted. The ringing of a level crossing sounded and was smothered again. Straight in front of me, behind the glass door, the mother kissed her child and took a bottle of milk from a thermos container. When the buffet trolley came by, we had to stand on tiptoe to make room for the monstrous vehicle. The attendant in a linen jacket opened all the compartment doors and sold his wares with the greatest ease – the mother also bought coffee and a roll – but he couldn't sell anything to us. We were a different breed. The Slovaks took out a dark loaf, the Gypsy woman laid her baby under the red shawl covering her breast and I opened the packet with the cherry tart cut into squares and wrapped in white tissues.

On my way home with my eyes fixed on the little oasis, at the mirage behind glass, I thought: house, address, locality, what did that mean? I wasn't quite sure any more. There, in that corridor, among poor wretches who were bold enough to go their own way, I remembered – from a vast, grey past – the contempt of the nomad for the villager, for the pathetic prop of having, if not your time, then at least your place in this world under control. The train rattled over a bridge. I moved my weight from one foot to the other. I was still not tired. With pleasure I followed a tiny cloud of cigarette smoke, which was floating away, expanding and dissolving in the sunlight before my eyes like a little seahorse.

It had been a long journey. A concatenation of events, signals, hints which together, I see looking back, form a logical and mysterious story. Of course, nothing has been explained. You must not think, but act. Not talk, but look. Soon you will be back where you started. The bus stop in the dunes. In your mind you are already walking in the salt wind, you are writing letters, telephoning, setting to work and visiting, completely your old self again – I'm coming, Robert! – and smoothing the sheets of the large bed with both hands; the windows into the garden are open. Had I changed? Grown older? Not at all. Everyone will recognize me, my body, my clothes, the inflection of my voice . . . no one will be able to deduce from my familiar behaviour that my eyes have become sharper, that I can judge distances and see in the dark. Shortly when I am sitting reading the paper or having friends to dinner, who will mind me looking out over a landscape that no one knows except me and recalling things that are nice to think about, proud, barbarous, personal things which I shall never be able to share, with anyone . . .

I turned back to the window. The train was travelling through a hilly region. Tomorrow I would be home.

PART FOUR

Chapter One

It is Friday morning. Nellie is lying in bed thinking: What shall I wear today? Something blue, something grey, should I wear a hat? She feels a faint current of air across her face. The wind is blowing behind the curtains. If it starts raining I'll put my cape on. Her ears follow the sound of a passing moped. A street door opens and is pushed shut again. Normally this dozing would give her a headache, Nellie is the type of person who doesn't appreciate lying in and having breakfast in bed. Normally she would have known perfectly well what to put on. My trousers and blouse and this afternoon when I go to the shop, my black linen suit with the jacket which comes down over the hips.

In the circumstances, however, her shop is closed this Friday. All the shops will be closed. The village is on its best behaviour. Since the terrible turning point at the beginning of this week, when the rage that had built up, the resentment, the stifling heat of the summer gave way to a grey blanket of clouds, people are opening their doors to each other, waiting by the till, letting dogs and children cross the road, you'd almost think that the people had become saints, saints or accomplices, people look at each other innocently, unfinished sentences hang in the air . . . poor Magda . . . Nellie turns onto one side. Out of habit she stretches out an arm.

Her husband is already up. Of course Erik is not going to work today either, the eye-sufferers must be a little patient, but nothing can stop him keeping to the rhythm that he has chosen for himself summer or winter, drama or no drama, at six-thirty night gives way to day. At the crack of dawn she saw him standing in the doorway of the bathroom, he was wearing a white shirt and a grey suit, stretching his neck he adjusted the knot of his tie. A nice man. A·man with a beautiful balding skull and a face that exudes calm. Has she ever heard him raise his voice? He has organized his world, things are fixed, why should he be put out? I am his wife, he will be faithful to me till death do us part. A nice marriage. Nellie regards it as successful. Her husband: a respected eye specialist. Her farmer's daughter's fortune: invested in a gold and china shop. Her sex life: enough incense and holy words to put her in very benevolent moods. Her son:

Her son. Sometimes she feels the boy, now a nineteen-year-old who talks haltingly, walks with a shuffle, who despite his imbecility can read well but whom on the other hand it is difficult to teach that waiting your turn in a queue doesn't apply only at the grocer's – yes, he can understand that, he nods willingly, he will do that in future – but also at the post office, the bus stop, the ice-cream stall and the cinema, sometimes she feels this boy as a small, stubborn presence in her blood and her skin. His body temperature is higher than hers. His thirst is sometimes unquenchable. When she buys vegetables, she feels how he touches every carrot, every potato quickly with his tongue before putting his fork in his mouth. Normally her son is the first person whom she thinks of when she wakes up after a night full of insigificant dreams. But this morning it was different. She heard his footsteps on the floor above her. For a moment everything stayed motionless in her head. Then she thought: it's Magda's funeral today.

What shall I wear? I've noticed that one no longer automatically wears black at funerals these days. The dead person might be annoyed by all that solemnity, we'd prefer to see friends and relations behaving as normal, with their hair loose, bright clothes, harmonica music, I can remember a particularly tragic funeral with a widower in rubber top boots.

I was her first friend in this village. The fact that in the beginning she lived in France and I saw her only at intervals, did not stop me knowing about her hopeless series of miscarriages and, during a holiday visit to their farmhouse, despite the fair amount of misery in my own head, feeling the consolation she derived from sitting on the swing in the evening with my heart-rending darling. Later, when she and Robert had moved here, our friendship deepened. I was the one who helped her pick the moonstone-coloured velvet with which we upholstered the sofa in her study one sunny summer afternoon. We toasted it and, through the open widow, suddenly saw the sun on the lawn. Come on, said Magda, we are going to stew in the sun for a bit in our birthday suits. But I shook my head. Gaby is being brought home by taxi at five, I replied. But still I stretched out for a moment behind a hedge of stinging nettles next to her, awkward and cumbersome, not dreaming of taking off my dress and white satin reinforced wired bra.

God, how angry I was at her! Now that my rage has gone, has subsided into emptiness, into the sort of stupid emptiness that you also feel when you have been to a film in broad daylight, I can admit it to myself: I really detested her. At first I was amused by her silence. When most people were already beginning to get annoyed, beginning to think: What airs you are giving yourself, my girl, I still enjoyed the affair. Magda is waiting calmly until we can talk alone. So that when once we were walking along the beach surrounded by the flapping of seagulls' wings, I let a silence fall in our conversation. I glanced sideways at her and cleared my throat. And then I broached the subject of going away on journeys. She didn't bat an eyelid. Slippery as an eel she asked my opinion of the agency which had let a holiday home to us in Belgium.

Other opportunities followed. She resumes her visits to Gaby: stay for a cup of tea, I ask her. We drop in on each other to borrow things and have a bit of a chat: I lean against the doorpost and look at her longingly, she has said: I need your advice, Nellie. When she starts talking about a pair of gold cufflinks that she has seen in my shop, I drop my eyelids and have the urge to punch her in the stomach. In September, Magda had been back about three months, I invited her and Robert to dinner.

It was a hot evening with open widows and doors. It was

getting late. After a pause filled with cigarette smoke Erik and Robert had again started talking with slurred voices. All at once my mood slumped. Opposite me Magda sat drawing a pattern on the tablecloth with her index finger, very calmly, a diamond-shaped pattern, the same thing over and over, her face was entirely impassive. And while I almost expected that at any moment she would start rocking her upper body to and fro, I felt a furious impatience rising in me. For God's sake don't let it be too long before she raises her head, looks at the clock and says: It's late, Robert, we're going home!

As the weeks and months went by I became less and less happy about her spending time with Gaby, I did not know why.

Chapter Two

She hears him walking to and fro above her head. He is already dressed, she can hear the shoes. The young man, in black from head to toe, keeps his restlessness under control by walking across the attic with rhythmic steps. Shoulders and arms hunched inwards, he moves forwards uncomfortably. He uses only the balls of his feet, his knees are rather bent, so that it looks as though something invisible is pushing him in the hollow of his knees, as though he is almost falling over but is able to keep his balance by moving a foot each time. When he reaches the north-facing window, the sound of his steps is muffled. There, on a mat, stands the tripod with the 68mm telescope. Nellie knows that he will touch the instrument for a moment. He will let the tips of his fingers slide along the metalwork, he will move something, a screw, a handle, but he will not bend forward and put his eye to the lens. He is too restless. The ceremony which is about to begin today, interests him deeply.

'Is she going to be interred?' was the first thing that he said after she had told him on Tuesday, cautiously.

Neither his stiff formulation nor his monotonous voice struck her. That was his way of talking.

'Yes.'

She put a beaker of milk in front of him. It was six o'clock. Gaby had just come home. He had listened to her bending over the table resting on his hands. As always when he came from the workshop, he looked ashen. With his eyes fixed on the tablecloth he said, 'She's not alive any more.'

'No.'

'She has no voice any more.'

'No.'

189

'What's going to happen with the articles from the *New Scientist* then?'

'Papa will translate them for you.'

'She has no writing any more. Her writing is going into the dark with her.'

He began rocking gently, without taking his hands off the table he pushed his body forward and back again. Nellie let him be. When his movements became faster, more impulsive, she took his two hands, it was a gesture that he knew, he drew back meekly, took a couple of uncertain steps and let himself drop into the chair which for years had stood with its back to the window for him.

She smiled at him, at his head with the bristly hair sprouting in all directions. If he felt sad, then she would want to console him. But a point had been switched between his grief and her consolation. What's this about, comes the question from both sides at once. She handed him his tea. He groped for the spoon, and began stirring quickly and gently so that the whirlpool, which as always his attention demanded, could be created. Then he asked the questions which Nellie had anticipated. Well-tried questions, indispensable in taming an alien world which was trying to escape.

'When is it?'

'Friday.'

'What time?'

'At ten-thirty.'

'Where?'

'The requiem mass is in the Jeroenskerk. The funeral is at Zuidvliet cemetery.'

After quickly dipping his tongue in it, he drank his tea in one go. Gasping for breath he said, 'Then I'll need black clothes.'

She does not know what is going on inside him. She observes his behaviour, perceives signals which are definitely not alien to her – crying, staring, stammering, lapsing into silence – but he makes different connections from us. Suddenly he is prohibited from speaking. Suddenly his pupils enlarge. In the middle of a warm summer's day a shudder passes through his body, goose pimples appear on his arms and legs.

He liked the black clothes. Since the stock of the clothes shops in the village was still completely geared to the holiday season, she had driven to Leiden with him. She must not go to boutiques for young people, a pair of denim trousers would certainly not do, not only with his skin not being able to tolerate a rough material, it would not be black enough. They found what they were looking for in the fashion house De Faam. Yes, a soft, deep black pair of flannel trousers was held against his legs by the salesman, and almost imperceptibly fastened at the waist. Gaby closed his eyes. He stood very still. When the salesman shot a smile at his mother she smiled back faintly. She felt as though the boy were standing listening, as though he were listening with a sense that was much more ingenious than her common sense to the muted, enchanting sound of black, of woollen material, of deep peace and of Magda who was dead and who was to be buried at Zuidvliet on Friday. Not for the first time she thought: I believe he is looking forward to it.

Gaby opened his eyes.

'I'll take them . . .' he said.

Nellie looked at the salesman with affection. The young but already greying man knew her son. He would never suggest he should turn round to admire himself and his new clothes in the mirror.

'And now we need a jacket,' she said. 'A jacket, socks and a shirt, all black.'

At the end of the morning they drove back home. On the leather-upholstered seats Nellie and Gaby both sat in silence. When Nellie lit up a cigarette, to her surprise Gaby pulled out the ashtray. She smiled. Undoubtedly he felt satisfied, a satisfaction which in this case was completely in harmony with hers, because indeed, they had done well. They took the turn-off to Rijnsburg. It was quiet on the road. Her eye caught the fields and the figures bending over the flowerbeds under a grey-white sky. Something trembled in her, a happiness, absurd, primitive, but as clear as crystal. She tapped the ash off her cigarette and imagined, in the warmth of this moment, the boy sitting chatting beside her.

Sometimes I just can't cope any more. The mass of objects is terrifyingly large. Should I cover my ears up? Close my nose and mouth tight? Wearing sunglasses the whole time is disapproved of by those around me. So I see and hear the distant things. I smell. With things that are close I stick out my fingers and my tongue, I feel and taste, I get to know the things which are close by. Sometimes I feel revulsion, sometimes an urge to laugh. Food I eat up. Nausea. Particularly since I have been able to walk I have been plagued with it from morning till night. The cold and distant objects grow larger and smaller, smaller and larger, they change their shadows and multiply tenfold. Attempts to establish relationships. No chance of doing that. My brain cells say no. I rock, I rock to and fro, I bang my head against the wooden frame of my bed, I cry for all I am worth: it works. The insistent mob lets go of me and recedes.

At first I preferred not to walk. I could lie, sit, stand and wasn't bored. One day a blue ball rolled in front of me. It came from behind and rolled forwards past my feet. I thought of the turning, blue eye of a giant. Since the day that a ball rolled in front of my feet I have been walking; since I have been walking I know that I can't fly; since I know that, I miss not so much the feeling of beating my wings as weightlessness. You fly and have no body. You fall relentlessly through the dark. There is nothing. Nothing touches you. What space. What gentle pleasure.

Of all objects people are the ones which are most commonly first here, then there. Their faces talk and laugh. They stretch out their arms and touch you, even when you think: I don't want them to, even when you think: I'd rather touch my skin myself. Then they ask you things that you can't understand. I avoid that. I repeat their words and ask their names. That is enough. At first I preferred not to talk, preferred not to. I take a metal ashtray, put it on its side and give it a blow with my fingers and thumb. It starts spinning and reveals its secret. Why do I need words? Why do I need a verbal system?

At first I used Mama's words. I talked. She laughed and stretched out her arms. I imitated her. My voice sounded. Now other words aroused my attention, page two hundred and seventy-one, right-hand column, I read and remember fluoridate, fluoresce, fluoresceine, fluorescence, fluorescent, fluoride, fluorinate, flush, flux . . . I feel an urge to laugh.

I prefer night-time. At night, when objects are idiotic and odd, I dream or get out of bed. I put my feet left and right on the carpet and my eye to the 68mm reflector. In the cloudless darkness I soon see compressed white sparks. I look and look and can't stop looking, although after a time I could just as well put out my hands and my tongue because they are so close. In the blackness and silence I feel the urge to laugh. The thought comes over me, irresistibly, despite my organism and my eyes, that perhaps I haven't been born yet.

Chapter Three

Pregnancy and childbirth went normally in every respect. In June she realized that she had missed a period for the second time. She came from the beach and went to the bedroom to examine at leisure in the mirror how the colour of her arms, legs and shoulders contrasted with the area in the middle precisely marked out by the shape of her swimming costume. Pale skin which glows in the light of a summer afternoon, navel, breasts, there was nothing to see yet. She laid her hands on her belly, thought of what was dividing and multiplying beneath it in a systematic tempo, and a little light-headedly began calculating.

'January,' she said softly. 'January, end of January.'

Her maternal love began. Her maternal love did not begin, as in some women, with the idea of conception, or, as in most, a day or two after birth. Nellie began to care about her child when as she chewed unthinkingly on a roll, a little wriggly eel in her insides started trembling. She held her breath – it happened again – and burst out laughing. This incident, which, entirely according to the rules, happened in the fourth month, was followed by a series of benign changes in her body. A fat belly, large breasts, what's wrong with those? Nellie, who no longer smoked, scarcely drank, who twice a week exercised her pelvic muscles with ten others in a room, dressed in black tights, had never felt so well. Glittery sweaters, flannel sheets, flowered sheets, gradually it became autumn, winter was approaching. When she walked through the rain in a wide coat, with an unperturbed expression through the snow, she liked thinking of how down below, in her uterus which was expanding from her pubic bone to her rib cage, the unborn child was living its life, how it was thriving now that her strengthened heartbeat was pumping blood with all its energy faster than ever through her body. A wooden cylinder was placed

194

against her abdominal wall, a doctor shook his head and smiled. You don't need a low-salt diet. He pointed out to the mother-to-be her slim wrists and ankles.

One night in January Nellie puts her hands against the inside of her raised and widely spread knees. She holds on tight. After having had visitors all evening, after having walked to and fro with cream and dessert forks and having counted herself lucky that Erik and Robert kept up the conversation and the new friend didn't understand a word of Dutch, she had lain down on the bed on her back. Outside the windows a blizzard is raging, but in the small detached house there is the smell of glowing wood. After she has obediently endured the passing hours, greeted a nurse and a doctor with snowflakes in their hair, accepted her husband's hand and in muted protest against her pain, of which she was to say looking back: it could have been worse! has squeezed her eyes and throat tight shut. Nellie bends her back and pushes as hard as she can. Then she realizes that her child has been born.

In astonishment she looked at its little hands.

'But those little hands . . .' she managed to say.

They had laid the baby in the hollow of her arm. They had wiped the greasy body a little and wound it in a cloth and brought it to her: a son, a perfect son who had cried powerfully and had ten toes and ten fingers.

The nurse, with a bowl in her hands, half turned round. 'Well,' she said, 'I've certainly never seen one do that before.' Her face assumed a tender expression.

Nellie looked for her husband's eyes.

'Erik . . .?'

He was sitting on the chair next to the bed. From his lost look she realized that he had not yet recovered from the hours that had passed. She herself was completely alert. While the doctor was busy putting a last stitch between her legs and she no longer felt the slightest pain or any exhaustion, she was amazed that the peacefully sleeping baby was holding its hands intertwined with such force that the fingers went blue from the compressed blood. 'Erik?' she repeated.

He got up. Clumsily, like after a dream, he stretched and sniffed, she knew that he was concentrating his attention. Now he stopped and began to disentangle his son's tiny fingers by bending them back one by one till the hands separated and he could take them in his own hands and rub them and knead them until they had assumed the normal grey-white baby colour.

'That's better,' he said, laying the hands back on the nappy in which the baby was wrapped. 'That's better, don't you think, son?'

For a few moments Nellie and Erik looked at the two spread starfish. Then, before they realized, they saw them rise again, grope for a moment, and with the power of magnets, find each other and join together.

'He'll stop that in the next few days,' said the doctor, who had finished his work and looked at the strange case with them for a moment.

But he did not stop. The baby, sturdy, dark-haired and so angelically behaved that he went on sleeping even while being bathed, did not allow himself to be deprived of his support. Not at night, not during the day, not on the scales, not during feeding; when, while being dressed, he had to allow the chain with himself to be broken for a moment, he bent his head and hollowed his back. He stiffened. This also happened when after twenty-four hours he was put to the breast. He refused or did not understand. Sweating, with less and less courage, Nellie continued to press the child to her, the milk began to flow. We'll try the bottle, she decided after two days. Now he lay next to her, apart from her, she pushed his lips open, he accepted the large, tough dummy smelling of rubber, but did not drink. She enlarged the hole. Pale with relief, she saw that he understood that he could drink, that he could swallow the treated cow's milk which ran into his mouth all by itself. From now on things will go well, she thought, his growth, his life is beginning. She bound a tight cloth around her

196

breasts and managed to enjoy the baby's drinking five times a day, the smell of baby oil, the winter light and the blissful haste with which he swallowed when his dark, glazed eyes had focused unwaveringly on a fixed point above her head. 'Do you think he's blind?' she whispered to her husband one day.

Erik – he didn't believe a word of it – examined his eyes at her insistence. He laid the baby on the chest of drawers and found absolutely nothing wrong with them. The iris reacted to light, he told her, and there was no question of a clouded retina. Nellie listened. She listened with a gratitude which was eager to learn, and looked at her husband, who there in the middle of the bedroom, seemed to be enjoying explaining to her the extraordinary operation of light absorption by the retina, distinguishing between light and image – 'Light,' he said, 'is something you see with your eyes. Images you see with your intelligence,' – and who finally looked from the baby to her with a patient, professional smile and said, 'Exactly what he sees, Nellie, we aren't sure. Eyes are conductor mechanisms. They transmit only what the consciousness thinks is worthwhile.'

A spoon. A shoe box. A tennis racket. The corner of the linen cupboard. The corner of the mantlepiece. The reflections of light on the ceiling. He wasn't blind, he moved his eyes round. It must have been after about three months that she bent over the cradle to look at the child which as usual averted its gaze, and that for the first time in his life he began laughing. He drew back his lips, contorted his whole face and even cooed. Incredulous, alarmed, she looked at what he was looking at. The chrome-plated hairdryer in her left hand was gleaming in the afternoon light.

One day she was walking past a toy shop. Clowns, cuddly animals, coloured rattles, she had tried them all, but no, his hands were simply occupied. Suddenly her eye caught two small white bears, identical, which looked so delightful and fluffy that before she knew it she was at the counter.

'Is it a present?' asked the shop girl.

Nellie nodded.

'For a boy or a girl?'

'A boy.'

The bears were packed. First in tissue paper and then in flowered paper decorated with blue ribbons. Nellie came home. She put tea on and sat down at the table. Then it took a long time before she opened the package, took the bears out and went to the room where Gaby was having his afternoon nap, sleeping like an angel. She forced the hands open. Stiffness, resistance, the arching of the back. She folded his fingers around the bears and held onto them until she realized that his revulsion against the unknown, against emptiness, freedom, was beginning to take over. Retreating, she saw a chubby baby with a toy in each of its raised, waving hands.

Now he would not let go of the bears again. What a brilliant idea! The baby and the bears intertwined, and instantly his skin mingled with their white artificial fur, recognized it as warmth, softness: facts, and approved them. What a find! How moving people found the five-month-old baby who lying on its back in the playpen unleashed strange cries at the bears. How striking acquaintances in the street or in the shops found the beautiful child who half sitting up in his pushchair, hugged its bears, seemed to be absorbed in that clutching or in what one could not say, and would not be distracted by any finger poked into his tummy, pinch on the cheek, sweet or biscuit from the extreme concentration with which he preferred to sit and stare straight ahead.

The doctor laughed too. The doctor whom Nellie had asked for an appointment after a year and a half, when her son was still not crawling, walking or speaking, laughed paternally. Immediately sensing that the mother was still inexperienced, still over-concerned, he said, 'The fact is that some children take their time.'

She nodded, with the child on her lap, and looked outside. The windows of the consulting room were open. She saw a sun-drenched garden with gravel paths, jasmine bushes and peacocks which dragged their half-spread tails behind them.

*

In her rooms, her house, indeed in her arms: a small stranger who does not notice the difference between himself and the world. He is sitting playing on the floor, the door opens, everything is now confused, he starts howling like a dog. She carries him upstairs, he is already used to the sinking of the walls and the revolving of space, downstairs in the curve of the corridor. Then he is put on the ground, let go of, his mother walks away: trembling with fear he sees his legs, his body with its bright blue dress disappearing from view. What must it be like to be able to pick up the table legs, the carpet, the wastepaper basket, the shiny fireguard with your supersensitive antennae, but not the fixed point in that chaos, yourself?

All right then, she ensures that nothing in this house, nothing, not even a vase of flowers, is moved. The landslides to which he has to resign himself are great enough anyway. The movements of the light and of people, the noises of the wind and the vacuum cleaner, his milk, which changes to rusks, softened bread, mashed bananas: the cutting of his hair drives him to despair for hours, Nellie murmurs his name, exhausted from bawling he lies sleeping in his bed, groaning, grinding his teeth.

However, he does make progress. He is almost three and can sit up and sometimes, with great difficulty, stand up. Seated in a kneeling position beside him she hands him wooden blocks which he examines with his hands and tongue, he has dared to let go of the bears, they lie within reach. She looks at the glow on his face, he is obsessed with the game – grabbing, licking, putting down, grabbing . . . – he intends to continue for all eternity. Time, the measuring of time, means nothing to him. That one thing follows another, has never occurred to him. Why should he show that he is hungry? Cry? Stretch out his hands?

Shortly after he had learned to walk, he also began to talk. One day the mishmash of guttural sounds suddenly resolved itself into two clearly articulated words.

'A quarter,' said Gaby.

Nellie was sitting at the table. Without taking her elbow off the paper she looked up, he was standing in the middle of the room, a delightful toddler, who after again calmly saying 'a quarter' dropped onto his bottom and with his face raised, rocking backwards and forwards, began to stammer the syllables which had nothing to do with the language of his father and mother, Nellie thought she had imagined it.

When she was playing with him in the afternoon, he said, 'Don't do.'

She stared at him, with the ball in her hands.

Without paying the slightest attention to her, staggering from one step to another, he made a beeline for a corner of the room.

'Don't do,' he said and smiled at a cut-glass vase.

From now on it went fast. Within a few weeks he could say all kinds of things. Hello Gaby. Please Gaby. Gaby want to go outside? He imitated her easily. Don't do. Look at me. She became used to his parrot voice. Sometimes, when he sat staring straight ahead, unmoved, she would suddenly hear: 'An etching.' Or: 'Punctual.' 'The operation.' 'Muddy . . .' Does he enjoy it? she wondered. Do the words amuse him or does he take them for granted like he takes everything for granted, figures, forms which simply happen to be in the world?

Summer came. He didn't want to go into the sun, he cried and closed his eyes. In the living room, shielded by the blinds, she watched him covering the distance to the door. She watched him taking steps with difficulty and thought more or less: He started talking because he started walking. That must be why. Walking stimulated his brain. How quickly it is going all of a sudden! He is making up for lost time, walking, talking because of space – which after all cries out for order – he has to call things by their name. Soon I'll start telling him fairy stories, pointing out pictures, reading to him. What luxury! He is walking, he is talking, for all I know he will start flying. Because suddenly that is how I sometimes see it: that words go through the air, across the sea, that they fly back and forth between the centuries. Sometimes I think that words are people's wings.

Like every other family they go on holiday to France that year. It's OK, the consultant at the clinic had said. Even if your child is retarded, you can make something of your family life. They visited old friends in the Cévennes. A farmhouse on a mountainside. Mulberry trees. A wonderful summer, waking to the smell of wild majoram and whitewash, sitting drinking wine outside until late at night and a Gaby on his best behaviour rocking on the swing with Magda. 'Let's try sending him to nursery school,' said the consultant at the beginning of September.

It wasn't a great success. Gaby, a beautiful plump child with nice clothes, once he was dropped off at the nursery, didn't move a step, say a word and hissed like a cat whenever another child came near him. Of course his presence could do no harm. Let's keep trying. After all, he will eventually have to get used to his fellow creatures. For two years Gaby spent his mornings in the corner with the blocks, concentrating on the silence and ignoring every encouragement from outside.

Teasing didn't begin until the school for children with severe learning difficulties. The Down's syndrome children and the strapping backward children were mystified by the boy who said nothing, always sat swaying and was only prepared to let go of one of his grey-white toy bears to draw, and later, to write.

'He refuses to write seven,' said the teacher to his mother.

Nellie took the sheets of paper home and looked at the rows of figures with Gaby. She realized that the seven was putting out its tongue, its active, threatening, teasing tongue.

The move to the day centre turned out to be the right one. Gaby became used to the moment when the taxi came to collect him, 8.05 a.m., to lunch at the formica table: potatoes, endive, mincemeat; and to the moment when the taxi came to take him home, 4.35 p.m. He didn't hiss any more, his crying fits stopped. In the home surrounded by deciduous trees, the young imbeciles did gymnastics, worked wood or sat in a stupor watching television.

They didn't worry at all about the child that spent his hours tapping the radiator. And yet he was a separate case. The staff began to get interested in him when they realized that he drew, read and wrote and one day, during lunch, quoted the manual for visitors without a single mistake.

Nellie appeared at the consulting times. She listened to diagnoses. Imbecile. Schizophrenic. Congenital damage to the brain stem. Sometimes they told her things she already knew. The child understands nothing about its surroundings. Imagine that he comes from another planet, a planet where our space, our time, our sense of the changeability of things do not apply. A chair is only the same chair in the same place. An event only recognizable at a fixed moment in the day. Eyes, ears, nose, mouth, skin – the routes towards the brain provide him with stimuli which he cannot place . . .

He passed his eighth birthday. She sometimes thought he was amazingly shrewd. The problem of shaking hands and kissing visitors he solved by not coming into the living room until they were ready for coffee, offering them a dish of biscuits with perfect manners. His visual games changed in character at that time. Puzzling, looking for hours at maps and cut-out patterns, gave way to a passion for the weather forecast, meteorological maps and everything concerning the moon and the stars. The boy who did not know the difference between 'now' and 'soon' and between 'here' and 'there' and would never learn, started talking about light years.

Chapter Four

Using the small 68mm reflector one can make good observations. On clear nights Gaby can see the moons of Jupiter more clearly than Galileo could in his day, he can see a large number of stars in the Milky Way, the constellation of the Pleiades and can even, without much effort, distinguish the twin stars of Draconis and Geminorum. His observation point is suitable but limited. Gaby refuses to place the instrument anywhere else but on the mat under the north-facing window of his attic room.

When one October evening he grabbed Magda's fist and without a word went up two flights of stairs with her, he did not yet have a telescope, not even a hand-held telescope. While the wine was being opened downstairs and the conversation on the elegance of business transactions was being continued, the two must have looked through the open window at the heavens, which that evening were particularly clear, which became clearer and clearer, dots; even more dots, glowing patches, luminous nebulae, and probably Magda then named aloud the two constellations that everybody always mentions.

'The Great Bear, the Little Bear.'

Gaby must have held his breath for a moment. To his delight he must have recognized something identical with another situation. Shortly afterwards the textbooks, magazines and prospectuses appeared in the house. Nellie liked it. She liked the way her best friend and her son bent over the celestial maps and discussed the signs of the zodiac. When Magda translated the foreign articles and wrote them down neatly in a ring binder, Gaby looked at her hand, at the chubby white woman's hand which drew a procession of letters behind it. Then real friendship enveloped them. Nellie felt that she was quite involved enough when afterwards Gaby, pale, a blob of spit on his chin, came into the kitchen and said,

'The largest optical telescope in the world is the six-hundred-centimetre Zelentshukskaya in the Caucasus.'

Erik bought him a telescope. Out of the desire to understand the instrument properly Gaby sat next to his father at the table and listened and nodded until the text of the directions corresponded to lenses, adjusting rings and fingers. However, he discussed the surface of the moon with Magda.

'That must be the Southern hemisphere,' she said, leaning against the frame of the attic window. She passed him the telescope. 'The silhouettes of the craters are very clear,' he said after a while.

'Yes. How large do you think they are?'

'The smallest craters are about seven kilometres across, do you see that dark patch?'

'The Mare Imbrium.'

A year later a telescope was ordered from the firm of Ganymedes. The beautiful instrument arrived one rainy February afternoon. Erik was allowed to unpack the components from the tissue paper, put them together and try them out. He was also allowed, when it turned out that the tripod that had been supplied with the telescope was completely unstable, to spend a whole weekend making a pillar tripod weighing twenty-five kilos. Gaby waited politely until his father had positioned the construction, carefully, patiently, suppressing a futile enthusiasm, by the attic window – 'And now let's hope the bad weather will clear up, Gaby!' – he waited till his father had left the room before starting the research programme which no one, not even Magda, would be able to understand in detail.

Rings appeared under his eyes. His skin became blotchy. At table he held forth about the interior of the stars. Nellie managed not to fret about his sleepless nights.

Perhaps you should not even try to understand another person fully, she often thought at that time. People are mysteries, simply accept it, when it comes down to it Gaby is even more clearly a mystery than anyone. Do you still remember his parrot period? It began with a book full of colourful illustrations, all the varieties were in it, you gave it to him and within a week he was holding forth about the parrot which has the greatest propensity to talk, an ash-grey bird from Africa. After a while all the utilitarian objects in the house reminded him of the palate bones, the wing shape or the backward-pointing toes of the parrot, in addition he only wanted to wear clothes which corresponded with those of parrot feathers, which was of course not that difficult.

Do you remember that you sometimes looked at the summer sky and thought: Australian cockatoo? Finally Erik brought home a wonderful budgerigar for him. Do you remember the astonishment with which he stood looking at that bird in its cage, at its pecking and pooping, not until evening would he say anything. Parrots fly in all directions, he said, do you remember that you understood what he meant?

Now he is using another code. A summer night, an open window and his eye to a lens which magnifies two hundred times. In themselves not illogical measures. You enter his room, you are not disturbing him at all, without noticing you, without making that concession, he stares indiscriminately at the moon. Contemplating the incomprehensible. You look at his shoes and at his woollen sports jacket. You think, and the thought is very serious: I shall polish his shoes, that jacket must go to the cleaner's.

Sometimes in those days she enjoyed answering his monologues. After a treatise on a supernova explosion when he fell silent, when he began simply waiting for his tea, his cinnamon bisuits, his small syrup wafers – he loved everything sweet – she had the impulse to talk a bit herself, to tell him in a leisurely way, listening with half an ear to the wind which was always whistling somewhere in the house in its high location, something amusing from her childhood, or his childhood, no matter what, something about a sleepwalking incident or a favourite dream. Why shouldn't you enjoy carrying on a one-sided, extremely intimate conversation.

Artificial light. The sound of the bell and a customer who remembers to wipe his feet. Nowhere does she feel more comfortable than there, in her shop, at the bottom of the slope with the decorative lampposts, which leads directly to the sea. Along the broad promenade walk the holiday-makers. In the summer there are many of them, noisy and suntanned, in the winter they battle silently against the wind. With great regularity one of them gives in to the impulse to stroll more closely past the bars and boutiques at the edge of the pavement. Then the shop door is pushed open and Nellie looks up obligingly. She knows the slight embarrassment of her customer, the astonishment that here, less than a hundred metres from the sea, the force of the sun and the salt is wiped out at a stroke, has given way to a silent, manageable world of gold, silver and crystal.

It's for my wife. It's for my mother. Can you think of something for a man? she is asked.

She thinks for a moment and gives an affirmative nod. She always knows. On the glass top of the showcase there appears a case lined with blue velvet.

Since Gaby has been going to the social centre four days a week, Nellie has been the salesperson in her own shop. Her manageress was just planning to set up in business for herself, a part-time girl to fill in had been found immediately, Nellie had made her decision. She bought a couple of expensive suits and had her hair done. Of course Gaby doesn't mind a bit. Only when he has left the house at a quarter past eight – he now travels by himself on the bus – does she get into her car and drive to the shop. Just after nine she drinks some coffee, the security grille has by this time been pulled up, the shop window cleaned with spirit. The first customer rarely appears before ten o'clock.

Doesn't she miss her long, totally silent days? Her accounts, her flowers and the thoughts which occurred to her at the oddest moments in the empty house? . . . Yesterday he reminded me again of an old blind man . . . No, not much has changed. Whether she puts down a clock in her window or opens a case containing antique tie pins and gives not the least impression of worrying about anyone except her hesitant customer, she suddenly thinks of the face with which she has been familiar for an eternity, the cheeks pale, sunken, the eyes duller than ever after a sleepless night, I bet the weather was clear last night, stars, moon, because look how beautiful it is outside . . . Oh dear! How serious he always looks!

Her customer was still undecided. Nellie saw the tension in the woman's face. It was always like that. Those who came in here were enchanted by the idea of buying something beautiful, an object for which they had often saved up for a long time and which must incorporate not only the essence of the loved one but also the good taste and the very best sentiments of the giver. Not a single object which left her shop was the same object as before.

The woman looked from the tie pins to Nellie.

She asked, 'Which one do you like best? With the round stone or the oval one?'

Nellie took the pins off the velvet one by one. She put them on her palm and compared them.

'Personally I would choose the oval one.'

The woman turned her head a little to one side. Then she gave a deep sigh.

'Then I'll take that one.'

'Fine. I'll gift-wrap it nicely for you.'

Nellie laughed, full of sincere understanding.

Chapter Five

There is no point in lying in bed any longer. This day comes, goes, and will be just as disturbing as the previous days. In a few minutes it will be half-past nine. If I don't get up now, I shall have a headache the whole day, shortly, in the front row of the church, I shall do my very best to think of Magda through the black spots floating in front of my eyes, recalling her beautiful blond hair, something I have not been able to do all week, not really, it seems like witchcraft, for the whole of this week Magda has no longer been Magda, but someone to whom something incredible has happened.

She gets out of bed and walks over to the gently waving curtains, she opens them. It is a rainy day. The air which pours into the room makes her shiver, just right, it is time for her body to be shaken up. She moves away from the grey view, stretches, yawns, slips the straps off her shoulders and catches her nightdress with one foot. When she looks in the mirror, she sees that there are bags under her eyes. She thinks that she looks the worse for wear, there is something evasive in her look which does not entirely please her. At the washbasin she scoops up water and splashes it on her face with two hands. My dark blue dress, she thinks a little later. She looks among the clothes in her wardrobe until she finds the mousseline dress, which she hasn't worn for years. The sleeves close round her wrists, the skirt is a little tight, for a moment she feels like on a Sunday in her youth, a little on her best behaviour, a little special, not entirely familiar with herself. I'm going to have breakfast, she thinks, I'll go and see where Erik and Gaby have got to.

Then she raises her head. Outside there is barking. That is Magda's dog, Anatole, his despairing sound is driving me mad. She looks out of the window and sees Erik with the three dogs on the terrace. Have they been for a walk in the dunes? They all look rather dishevelled. I don't mind keeping Anatole here, if necessary for good. But those little brats?

She cannot at first take her eyes off the man and the dogs on the sand-covered terrace. The group emanates a mysterious unanimity. She looks from the claw-like paws and lion-like snouts of the Pekinese to the – hopeless – waiting of the Bouvier and then at her husband. Erik is sitting hunched, the legs of his suit trousers stuffed into boots, on the wall of the balustrade. In amazement she realizes: he really is very upset! And has been since Monday. Now he bends forward a little. He purses his lips and raises his eyebrows. In all the time we have been together, I have seldom seen him so shattered. He looks up, his chin drops, a gull is sailing through the sky. Erik has been completely knocked out since he, of all people, on Monday, was the one to find that dreadful pair: his childhood friend Robert as a crazed murderer and Magda, a woman who if you ask me never meant very much to him, in the most absurd state that a human being can be in, dead.

Probably no one will ever uncover what actually happened. An investigation is in progress. Some facts have meanwhile been established. The drama, the murder, took place late in the evening, when the heat was still excessive and the storm, which had been hanging over the village for hours, was still being delayed somewhere by God knows what.

We, Erik and I, had been to visit them that evening, we must have sat talking with them till about eleven o'clock, outside, in the yard in front of the kitchen. Robert was gloomy and silent, almost surly like he always was recently. He didn't do much except drink, sweat and stare at the row of trees along the Oude Zeestraat, at the chestnut trees which were always blacker and more voluminous in the dark. I too found it very difficult in that oppressive atmosphere, you had the impression that the approaching night was squeezing the oxygen out of the air.

The only one of us who remained herself, cool, lively, apologizing for an empty glass which had been noticed rather late, was Magda. How is Gaby, she asked me, he doesn't like the heat, does he? Yesterday we wrote to the observatory in Pittsburgh, I'm curious to know what will happen. She was wearing a very short dress, her legs shone with sun cream, she had painted her toenails. I remember that her behaviour irritated me, perhaps I was just too tired, too exhausted, in any case I didn't behave very responsively and when Erik got up to leave, I was delighted. Robert did not react to our greeting, except by closing his eyes and putting a virtually finished cigarette-end to his lips. Magda accompanied us to the gate. She bent down to open it, her hair fell over her shoulders, and let us out. The last thing I saw of her was her arm, waving under the lamppost, standing out white against the trees.

It has been established that they remained sitting for a while, there, in the neon light, that a new packet of cigarettes was opened which was found with the smashed glasses in the morning on the muddy terrace. The front door was not locked. The dog was roaming the garden soaking wet. At a certain moment they went upstairs, the light was left on in the corridor and in the bedroom. Then the moments arrived on which everything hinges, the moments each of which, in their succession, may have been arbitrary, incoherent and even a little childish, but which together constituted an inexorable fate. If you ask me, Magda kept her mouth shut to the bitter end.

The strangest thing is the murder weapon. Robert must have gone downstairs at a given moment to retrieve the thing from a box full of junk. It was a Tibetan dagger, perhaps blessed, perhaps cursed, which had once lain on his father's desk as a letter-opener. Neither Robert nor Magda had been taken with the elegant object, long, narrow and wickedly sharp, they had put it away and forgotten it. Magda did not die immediately. She must have tried to escape from the bed. Already badly wounded in the region of her heart and lungs, already deathly pale, she slid onto the ground, amazed at the thick, warm sticky liquid that drenched her petticoat.

In an attempt to turn round she stretched out a little. She coughed. When she began to feel terribly strange and light in the head, she closed her eyes. Slowly but surely everything went silent. From outside, from the street not a single further sound penetrated. Then the storm broke loose. With a pathos in which he himself did not believe, Robert tried to slash his wrists.

Living next to a good-humoured enigma who combs her hair and keeps the house in order: when he comes home she wants to hear about the transactions of Noort & Co. and a little later, at table over the wine, is also very communicative about her own day, she has bought some shoes, she is translating an article about aerodynamics, she has been deeply shocked by a report on the foreign page of the newspaper, she has cried. Slowly the situation becomes unbearable. Her silence begins to exceed his comprehension. To drive him crazy, crazy with fury. He begins to be convinced that if he is unable to break this silence, if he doesn't succeed in tracking down those two vanished years, penetrating them, and fitting them into his view of the world, life will not be worthy of the name of life for him.

That distance ... that coolness, that damned cheek, not coming clean ...!

It must have been around Christmas 1972 when they first heard about the therapy, Gaby was almost nine at the time. The results were astounding. Children who had never looked their mothers in the eyes, laughed at them, felt their lips, imitated their expressions.

Not long afterwards she sat with a hissing, hand-flapping Gaby in a consulting room. Outside it was snowing, inside tropical plants were growing. With a heartbeat which became slower and slower she listened to the psychologist, a woman who had studied the therapy in America where it was considered that a child whose mother had not looked into its eyes in the first few hours after

211

birth – no, new-born children are not blind – and that during that same time had not been stroked by her very calmly and lovingly over its chest, belly, head and back, that such a very young infant could feel rejected by its own kind and withdraw into the world of things.

That same week the treatment commenced: Nellie embraces her child, with great force. She is lying on a mattress in a darkened room, with her blouse open, her shoes off and hugs the boy to her, he doesn't want to be held. Naked except for his underpants, he arches his back, stretches his legs, he wriggles about in the craziest way. She does not give up. Wherever the impulse may come from – she hears the grinding of his teeth, she sees the expression on the child's face, oh, he is afraid – she uses force. In order to be able to restrain his body, which is already strong, she holds his wrists behind his back, the twisting of his arms hurts him. She feels sorry, she doesn't feel a drop less love, but the violence which is in her, in its confused way has always been in her, has recognized the smell of the mattress, the four walls and the fear infallibly as a familiar area.

Don't give in, she had been told. Persist until the child gives in, cuddles up to you and for the first time in its life finds your eyes, you must not give in! Nellie had listened and nodded in agreement. The theory of the icy, inadequate mothers silenced her. Their emotional world is so vulnerable! When you are feeding don't talk to other people, they are frightened of your one-eyed profile, don't look at TV, they see only your full face, with both eyes, as protective. What else could she do except nod without a word and try to make the best of it?

The therapy of forced cherishing is no more cruel than dragging a child from in front of the wheels of a car.

Nellie looked at the psychologist's face which was as calm as a garden pond. She swallowed, fiddled with the rings on her fingers and agreed to the suggestion of imprinting on her son by force the fact that his world was warm, soft and full of maternal cherishing.

It lasted an hour, an hour and a half, her clothes were sticking to her body, Gaby was also wringing wet. Was he giving in? Sometimes she was able to get a hand free, that was important, now, pushing his head back, she could stroke his scalp, whisper to him how sweet, how lovely he was. The rage persisted. The battle remained undecided. They were expected back in the treatment room once every three days. Once, when she had pressed his face against her neck with a roughness which had already become routine, she felt his shoulder muscles relax. His breathing became as light as a bird's. After she had let him go and he lolled meekly against her and finally rolled on his side, she bent over him expectantly. Then she felt like screaming. His face, frozen, with closed eyelids, had the expression of a small Egyptian mummy. This lasted only for a moment. Before she realized he had assumed an attitude which she knew very well: the hands folded together, the knees pulled up. His mouth dropped open. He was asleep.

Chapter Six

She walks from the room to the kitchen. Strange, an hour like this that simply has to be passed in expectation. The funeral will start at half-past ten. All her actions, however unemotional, are defined by that. She makes coffee, waters the plants, sorts the post at her leisure, why not, there is plenty of time, indeed, this hour is almost overflowing with time. Why should she not pay full attention to the pine tree behind the house, the trunk, the ugly lower branches, and in passing remember the grazes on her legs as a girl? Watery, sticky. She looks. On the left Erik is busy combing the dogs. A little further on there is a beach chair. A newspaper flaps against the broom which is almost dead. A patch of blue sky provokes vague, benevolent metaphysical thoughts, does God exist, does eternity exist and if so, where?

In the middle of the room sits Gaby in his black clothes. Would you like some coffee, she asks. Yes. It doesn't worry her in the least that he doesn't feel like talking. When she hands him his mug, he remains staring at the round centre leg of the table, he puts out his hand like a blind man. In order to cope with the exceptional course of this day, the interference with the rhythm, the logic, he has to keep his thoughts together. She stops by him for a moment. What are you thinking? He is sitting slurping with a frown.

At this time he is usually in the workshop. A large hall, with tables, neon lighting. Surrounded by colleagues who like him have a screw loose, he sits at his typewriter and does useful work. Enjoyable work too. Gaby enjoys letting his fingers, long, white, with their tips bent slightly upwards, play over the keys while his eyes take in the facts of a railway timetable or government brochure. He types faultlessly and quickly. It does not interest him in the least that the machine converts everything into braille.

Everything which is presented to his eyes, will later be felt by the hands of a non-sighted person. He likes the sound of typing. Next to him sits an imbecile of Asian origin. Soon it will be twelve o'clock and a trolley with rolls and soup will be wheeled in. He does not mind. It doesn't interest him greatly that the figures, the words, the punctuation from his hands will pass into other hands.

He is not suffering from a psychosis, she has known that for years. He is not in a terrible rage. Those were the days! The accusing finger pointing at the mother has been withdrawn, no one talks any longer about breasts which were so fat that they blocked the nose of the infant, frightened him, causing lifelong panic. Nellie looks at the boy sitting waiting, as always absorbed, as always lost. New insights were much more acceptable. This kind of child has brain damage. It bites its hands, pounds its ears, looks into the fierce sun. This type of child ignores the primordial rules of instinct.

Yes, she thinks, but what a lot he has been taught! He talks, eats, dresses, tells the time, reads, writes, buys a bus ticket, shakes hands and says his name. Sometimes, completely uncomprehendingly, he goes on an errand for me. Pop this into the letterbox at Magda's, I ask, he disappears. But what's wrong? After an eternity he comes back, with the letter still in his hand. She wasn't home, she wouldn't have been able to read it, he looked through at the window for a long time, but no, she wasn't there. His eyes glide indifferently away from me, he discovers a tin-opener, grabs the thing and starts turning the screw. I leave it at that. What can one say about it? In the system of his billions of brain cells there is an aberration which cannot be measured, let alone remedied. All I can say is that I will feed him, warm him, protect him from rain, storm and verbal abuse and as sure as I stand here will make certain that I outlive him.

With the three damp, beautifully combed dogs Erik has come in. While he is pulling off his boots, his face still shows that restrained astonishment, when he looks up she sees that his pupils are as small as pin pricks. 'We should be going,' he says. She nods and turns to the draining board to pour coffee, she lights a cigarette which she keeps in the corner of her mouth as she walks to the conservatory windows at the front of the house. 'Are you coming?' she asks. She feels a vague pity, a vague friendship, she would like to put him at his ease.

Then seated for a while, silently next to each other – Erik drinks with his shoulders hunched – they look at the rainy sky full of birds, at the undulating dune and the scrubby grass on it, at the houses, the water tower, the signpost *To the Beach* and the pattern of half-buried, badly paved roads where quite a few people are walking and cycling and where considerably more cars are driving than they are used to at this hour, at the end of the season, in this village which despite a tourist industry which is more profitable from year to year is still friendly. 'It's going to get busy,' says Nellie.

Yes, it will get busy in a little while. All of us will walk together from the chapel to the church behind her, cherishing our grief, our feelings for her, how nice she was, how good to look at, and with slight astonishment we will put the days out of our minds, completely forget them, when we greeted her with a stiffness bordering on the absurd, served her brusquely in shops and at the most with a supreme effort sometimes stopped for a moment to stroke her dog's head. Soon we will all follow her, metre by metre along the road which each of us can see with his own eyes and not understand in the least, to the fishermen's church which is so beautifully located in the Voorstraat, obliquely facing west, so close to the sea, and between the white walls we will listen to the peal of bells, in which you can still sense the dead bodies, ravaged by salt, seaweed and driftwood, that people are used to mourning here.

'It wasn't a natural death?' Gaby asked recently.

No, I said, and I had to explain to him about the murder. How? With a knife. What kind of knife? A dagger. Who did the

216

dagger belong to? Well, Robert's father actually. How did the father come by it? I don't know, it was a dagger from Tibet. Tibet? And I simply had to look up the country for him, first in the atlas, and then in the encyclopedia. He began by reading the article in the encyclopedia. Afterwards he sat bent over the map until late in the evening.

My cigarette is finished. Erik looks at me, I nod. In a few minutes' time the three of us will walk down the dune. How will Gaby behave, in a little while, in the front row of pews where we are expected? No one can force him to assume an appropriate expression. He knows nothing of our kinds of tears of farewell. Why should he feel remorse? Seated between Erik and myself he will observe the spectacle that greets his eyes with interest. And rocking furiously forwards and backwards, he will picture Magda's stillness, her emphatic separation, there in the darkness under the flowers, and perhaps more sincerely than the closest relative will – in his way – mourn her.

She comes on Saturdays. After talking to Mama, first in the bedroom and then in the kitchen, she says hello, smiling or sometimes serious, my mood improves threefold, Saturday is the day of news and of learning new things. I give her the mail, which makes her bend forward and put her fist to her cheek, wrinkles and eyelashes, smell of soap. She opens a magazine, leafs through it, her sleeve, her flat hands, this page and no other, we sit down at table. Silence and cheerfulness from top to toe. I look alertly, but without a single thought, at the English words, I intertwine my fingers and wait till she has juggled the letters in her head, turned the system round, which happens soon enough, she talks. Without interruption she tells me where and when and gives the names of unique, measurable light sources. Nemesis is a weak dwarf star which penetrates our galaxy every thirty million years. I rock a little from my hips. My tongue pokes through my lips while she writes down everything, everything about physics . . . the gravitional pull of the pulsar is ... the neutron star has ... she writes, I feel pleasure, her hand has its advantages.

Is she a friend? I asked Mama once. Yes. What must I do? Buy flowers for her. I get alarmed, where and when? On Saturdays there is a stall by the lighthouse. I do it. I buy a bouquet, I pay and take a chance and stand in front of her as soon as she comes into our house, her shoes are pitch-black, her feet pure white. She bends down, takes the bouquet, laughs and shows her teeth and keeps on doing that, from then on, every week, bouquet, bending, teeth ... Mama says: you could just pick a branch, a dune rose, a pine cone for her, so I do that. It works, laughter and teeth, she puts the pine cone next to the tea, her hands hunt for cigarettes, matches, then we leaf through the celestial atlas, Aquarius, Orion, today the astronomical sunset begins at 3.13 a.m. and ends at midnight. Dark, a dark substance, no one touches you.

It wasn't a natural death, says Mama, it was with a dagger. What kind of dagger? A dagger from Tibet. I think: Tibet is a European name for a country in Central Asia located on the plateau between the Kwen Lung mountains and the Himalayas. The way of life of the majority of the population is nomadic. Goods transport is entirely by pack animals. Then I think of the map and the freezing summits which are sometimes over 6,500 metres high, the rarefied air, no clouds, no dirt, no light at all – at night – from the earth ... Only the dots ... The rushing blue and white sparks ... The southern sky with the constellations Whale, Swordfish, Flying Fish, Bird of Paradise, Crane, Eagle, Phoenix, Dove, Peacock, Raven ... I feel an urge to laugh.